IN STASIS

Ashley Peters

ISBN: 9798993280233
Library of Congress Control Number: 2025924822
A Novel From The Liber House, LLC
Austin TX

This is a work of fiction. All characters, events, and story components are fictional and any resemblance to reality is pure coincidence.

Content warning: This novel contains in some capacity gaslighting, grief, medical content/trauma, blood, gore, injury, death, anxiety, panic attack, confinement, gun violence, survival, natural and man-made disaster.

<u>Dedication</u>

To all those who must do hard things in challenging times. You are capable of far more than you gives yourself credit for. You're not alone in your fight.

To my loving partner, Danny, for supporting this wild endeavor from the start, theorizing logistics, and reading every version to make this the best version of In Stasis.

To my fur babies (Bently, Fredrik & Bruno) for being the combined inspiration for Janus and for keeping me sane during stressful times. To all the versions of Janus out there that provide solitude for their humans.

<u>Note to the Reader:</u>

Dear Readers,

History is a funny thing, as events deep in the past can seem very present and relevant when stripped of the main players names, locations, etc. In Stasis is influenced by life during decades and centuries long ago. The story you are about to read contains fictional creations that are more deeply connected to 7th century India, 1917 Russia, 1933-1945 Germany, 1947 Taiwan, 1964 China, 1980's America, and 1996 Afghanistan than anything of our current day, excluding one isolated historical event (2016).

So as you're reading the story of Jessi, Janus, and their survival, if any man of orange or tangerine variety enters your mind, know that the villain you are about to meet, (Blake), is conjured from the depths of history and far more suave than any current person you may be thinking about. Though if you recognize repeatable history, what does that say?

Besides, In Stasis is a story about those who live through and survive tyranny, not the tyrants. Thank you for joining my characters, in this gritty tale of endurance that I believe we are all capable of in moments of necessity.

-Ashley Peters

Chapter One
Take a Walk

Now
<u>November 20, 2046:</u>

Moments of solace in the wilderness were always a pleasant reprieve, so perhaps it's no surprise I fled to its safe haven when shit hit the fan and society broke. The trees look different this time even, if they are the same. Before, it was a nice suspension: a respite. A place away from society as an escape into some *other*. Once cosplaying as an outdoorsy camper—now, this *other* is my everything. A sanctuary of elements I am forced to face alone, not including Janus. While walking amongst the crisp fallen leaves, searching for any ripe wild berries, I feel a bit remorseful it took this long to realize.

The silence of nature is deafening, especially when all alone. A cacophony of vacant stillness taking up the maximum space available, and then desiring more. It's almost crushing. A weight on your chest like the hydrostatic pressure pushing against a wet suit in cold waters. It's enveloping, surrounding every crevice; but then you breathe, and time halts as this overwhelm washes away. How foolish it feels that it took the collapse of all we knew to appreciate an interlude in the wilderness.

Simple thoughts that attempt to summarize something so immensely complex, and clearly incredibly misunderstood. Humans say nature is silent—not because it is, but really because we don't understand. How could we, when it's so beyond our way of being?

The freeform chaos in harmony that refuses to stay on the confines of a music sheet. It dances in a symphony of "silence" only audible to those who actually pause to listen. There is no direction, and yet it does not need any map. You do not understand, and attempting to make sense of the chaos causes further evasion. The tighter you grasp, the reward will never be yours to enjoy. Nature is a funny teacher like that. Brutal, delicate, and utterly elusive.

Stop trying to make sense of it all. *Stop!* Experience the so-called vacancy with no expectation and let astonishment wash over. In the throes of uncertain times, with no direction, I ran to the forest line. Filled with fear, this place provides a safe landing space with open arms. Standing now, at the base of a giant tree, wondering more than it states.

Maybe, in nature's simplicity, it expects nothing from you besides your audience and respect. It is exactly what it is, and whether that is enjoyable, beneficial, detrimental, frustrating, or perplexing to you —it really doesn't care.

I've come to appreciate such honesty without any transactional expectations. An honesty coded as authenticity we all claimed to want in the old days, and attempted to replicate. But let's be honest as we introspectively muse—*did we?* Did we really want this, or only when it was beneficial? How many really were -'authentic'- versus how many could simply put on an authentic show for situations that suited them best? Authentically compassionate here, when they are rewarded for their compassion. Authentically unfiltered there, when such speak is praised for its genuine, unrestrained bluntness. Authentically dysfunctional, when it's a key feature in their hero's journey, and a trending selling feature of their personal brand. What of authenticity that had no direct correlation to an outcome, and certainly not a transactional one? Sounds nothing like the authenticity here. A laughable mimic. A cheap dupe.

The wind nips but the sun is warm. I used to always say this was one of my favorite feelings. Even through the chaos, it still is. Those in-between comfortable temperatures dancing between seasons. Just enough to where you're able to exist in both worlds. To be comfortably cozy without sweating or chilled.

The sound of my footfall on the ground leaves, both crisp and soft as I gently tread through, trying not to thud. The pitter-patter of Janus scampering here and there, on the scent of a bit of everything and nothing all at once. Chasing the wind of wild inhabitants since gone. The wind surely doesn't help him.

It bellows deeply as it whips through the forest in its gusts. Almost whooping, like it is scooping sound and air from the valleys to the treetops, as we are intermediately caught in the middle of its push and voice. I watch the leaves as they whip around, and old bark as it shreds from trees. They always settle back, though. No matter how surprising the wind may be, they always return to a calm and stable position.

They say simplicity is the hardest thing to master. We gunk it up. Make it messy, ostentatious, and ugly. Adding more, and more, and more, until it's all too much. You can't even see the beauty beneath the trash. Work harder to enjoy more, but time is robbed, so there's no time to enjoy. New homes added to take in the views, but so many are added the view isn't worth admiring. A self-imploding menu of bad decisions leads us to further spiral when our salvation is exemplified in a space we can't comprehend truly valuing.

Traversing on these new-old trails, I often feel like time stands still. We are moving but the landscape is not. A movie figure walking through a painting. What a haunting image that, admittedly, is slightly egotistical. Of course, the space we share is dynamically active! *Who am I to be privy to the scurrying paths of mice on the earthen floor, or the flight routes of sparrows through the tree line? Why would I know of the daily voyeuristic watchings of a bobcat over the hill?* A living dichotomy catered to each inhabitant as it ebbs and flows, within balance. The idea of stability eluding a society still figuring it out. An erratic route without an inkling of what it needs, even when examples are provided—and now it's gone.

Well, not an erased from-existence-type of gone. *Gone* in the sense that what we once knew is no more, and saddest of all, we could have saved it. Disappeared from familiarity. Vanished from comfort. Faded away into elsewhere. As thoughts like this creep in, I push them down to the deep, dark, damp pit where they now belong. They live there in their rage. Inextinguishable embers refusing to let them pull me under.

In some ways, I long for what may have been. Toxic, like a terrible breakup, reminiscing about the good parts while blocking out the bad. Unable to change what happened, and having no intention to wallow. A painfully refreshing change of pace. Refreshing sounds greedy —boisterous, almost. As if I'm reveling in the fall of society. It's not that —or, at least, it's not supposed to be. I am very aware of the current luck as this existence could be worse. Maybe it's delusional optimism from a past time, but framing our new lives this way makes the medicine less bitter. When hope trickles in that whatever this is will not be forever, then overwhelm follows. Contemplating attempted solutions engulfs any conviction. Instead, it's easier to not think beyond today, or tomorrow, with only the most immediate tasks to tackle. There's an unspoken thanks to this place and its inhabitants for their acceptance. For not crushing us under the brute force of natural events or mauling us for our resources. For allowing us a space to attempt to exist. A pitiful plea. *Thank you.*

I step amongst the trees, almost home, absorbing each isometric moment witnessed in our terrarium. Never identical but always enchanting. Alluring nostalgia creates a haze, numbing sharp memories with nature's hypnotic novocaine.

Chapter Two
Home

Now
<u>December 22, 2046:</u>

We got so fucking lucky. Coincidence couldn't have aligned things better. Almost cliche or comical, but I dare not scrutinize my fortune. The sheer luck of it all! Without the inherited funds from a beloved passed aunt, this wouldn't exist. Building from nothing would have been financially unobtainable, and while I was handy, this was a task that needed more hands than mine alone. The luck of subliminal knowledge buried beneath too many random documentaries, and a crew who were excited for a kooky creation. The luck of ideal geographic placement making it a perfect rental, but an even better refuge.

Who would have thought that vacation house you owned would become your new hideaway home? A once-trendy treehouse fort, harkening to any hipster in distance of Wi-Fi, (which it ironically did not have), has now become an offered sanctuary. No longer only a quaint spot for cute shots. Gone is the opportunity for city dwellers to live an alternate life while simultaneously being surrounded by creature comforts. Called up the ranks to rise to the occasion from glamping to survival—with some adjustments.

Proud of the unexpected transformation into home base. On some level, as dream designs percolated this build, part of me must have internalized a multifaceted quality. A curated place that bathed in the aesthetically pleasing elements, but with practicality hidden in every corner. A real wallflower in this post-democratic society.

Sitting twenty feet above ground level, home is nestled amongst the branches. *Treehouse* is not a term slapped on lightly. If I was marketing this rental as a treehouse, it would be a real-deal-damn treehouse. All grown up, like the kid in me had the keys to the creative kingdom and the funds to finally follow through.

Now, though, this is perhaps an auspicious attribute because of how humans tend to operate. We don't look up. People typically look around where they're walking, at eye level and slightly above, but not twenty feet up. As long as nothing catches their eye, they investigate no further. Clever little treehouse. It's why a 120-pound mountain lion can gracefully sit above the branches as hikers walk along a trail, completely unaware even though the big cat is right there. A heavy pounce and they're done. Fortunate consistencies of human behavior.

No one may be looking twenty feet up, but if there's a spiral staircase wrapping its way around a tree trunk onward and upward, they might. To prevent anyone from noticing, and definitely to deter anyone from nosing their way upwards, the staircase had to go. I still mourn that staircase. Its whimsy was always a favorite feature, and seeing the top few lingering steps, like a mangled limb left uncut, leaves a little part of my heart aching. A necessity that can't be overrun as anthropomorphizing lumber won't help me here.

Instead, the luggage pulley system, with its wooden platform, becomes our personal lift. An eccentric device, once seen as a luxury to avoid hauling luggage up all those stairs, now gets to hoist us up more or less daily. A funny new alternative doing a job it never asked for.

The treehouse: a familiar space, and in many ways, that made the transition easier. There has been so much change, chaos, and stress that my head is spinning, but this is stable ground, even if we sit in the sky. There was already a slight stock of basic items for renters, and it was outfitted as a retreat into nature. A desk with a comfy chair, books, a kitchen with a small potbelly stove, a queen bed with linens, a bathroom with compostable toilet, and even a wrap-around porch with a pair of chairs to peep through the trees. If it wasn't for the state of things, it would almost feel like a vacation. Instead, it's just an escape from reality —or maybe just a door to a different one. Either way, there's the illusion of normal.

A lookout porch with views in every direction. An escape route out the back via a rope ladder to the nearest neighboring tree, and an ATC set up to rappel quickly to the ground, just in case. Maybe the silliest modification was for Janus, and that was in the form of a potty patch on the deck. *Who adds a potty patch for their dog when the world as you know it is ending? Well, me, apparently.* Nice for when we don't want to descend that day. So, yes, it's ridiculous—but there's nothing I wouldn't do for him, so welcome to my ridiculous abode.

It stands on a large plot of land that's all ours, though property lines in these remote areas mean little now. A solid five miles from the nearest neighbor's land. Any housing they had is tucked away if anyone is there. Surrounded by natural running water, valleys, hills, and caves. Traversable if you know the terrain. Challenging enough that if you're following a topographical map, crossing our land would not be your first choice. Limited exploration so far, increasingly expanding on excursions, and making a DIY map along the way.

Caches have been placed across the area. Some buried, some stashed in caves, or cracks, and others elevated in the canopy. Hibernating creatures store away supplies in various locations in the event that one hidey-hole is discovered, so as to not lose the whole stock. So I squirrel away any surplus of precious supplies across the land in a similar manner. We have resources in our treehouse, but these caches offer hidden assistance if necessary.

In the old days, we'd joke I was a chaos gardener and in these days, a similar rogue, natural-style gardening has become the plan. Mixing together all sorts of plants that benefitted one another, but to an untrained eye, it looks like complete chaos. The methodology works well, especially in this new world. Petite little gardens here, and there, and over that way, and up the hill, and so on. They're small, irregular, and random. To anyone casually looking, they'd assume what they saw was wild and natural. Not a designed garden. It lessens the chances a portion of our food supply will be found, and diminishes the chances that anyone will suspect our existence here.

Hiding right in plain sight, like camouflage. Unseen and ever watching. Clever and comfortable, trying to adapt to a changing climate. Home sweet something-hidden-in-the-trees.

Chapter Three
That Night

Then
<u>November 8, 2044:</u>

We've been holed up at the bar called Tipsy's with our usual corner table since dinner. While the burgers and tenders may be basic, their fries are drool-worthy with all the loaded options you could imagine, and they have a surprisingly wide selection on tap. It's not the most glamorous place, or the sexiest, but it has a charm that has become ironic though we found this place well before it was ever on the radar of a "best of" list. We always thought so, but now apparently half the city does too. It's eclectically decorated, with Christmas lights up year-round and a disco armadillo sculpture sporting a tiny cowboy hat behind the bar. Cult classic movies play on both TVs, mounted side by side, often creating a ping-pong effect of viewers' eyes. Well, typically that's the case, anyway. Tonight, only one movie is on (1985 Clue with Tim Curry), while the other screen shows election results as they stream in.

Entranced, glued to the election coverage, though the mania of Clue occasionally tries to pull our focus. Holding our table off to the corner with a view of the whole bar, anxiously munching and sipping. Our home-away-from home corner table, where all big discussions and, often, decisions have taken place in the past. A taut tension ensnares all attendees as Anthony, Dani, Sam, and I sit in wait. Elijah stayed at home, not wanting to get wrapped up in the night. He's like that—casually caring but never in the trenches too deep. Ironically opposite to the my father long since vacant, fallen to the fight. We've been standing in the canals of political theatre for so long our boots filled with bureaucratic mud.

As correspondents talk on the screen about states whose results really aren't all that surprising, I internally scoff that this clown is even up for consideration. But he's suave, and self-righteous, which not everyone hates. By technical definition, he may be qualified, but beyond technicalities I'd say not. I'm hit with distant memory, recalling when Blake came into the political sphere, roughly ten years ago. He had been greasing the wheels before that, but this was when we as a country first heard his name broadly across news outlets.

Anywhere along the way he should have been ejected from the game, but he went on to hold state-level offices. A career made of mostly soundbites versus actual accomplishments. What his base would say are accomplishments, we say are appalling setbacks. A megaphone with actual power to not only spew heinous rhetoric but to take actionable steps toward laws and policies. While wishing there was truth to the thought that he's a dumb puppet, a talking head for more sinister politicians lurking in shadows, deep down I think he believes what he says. I think he wants it, too. Maybe he likes the attention—publicly working out some abandonment daddy issues of a megalomaniac. To the point of qualification, though? I don't even know if all the nation is using the same rubric.

We watch, daring not to blink. Results are popping off, lighting up the map like popcorn, and color is filling in. More color consumes the map, eating away at unclaimed portions, tallying them up. Each addition chips away at the island of hope that holds on. It's not filling in, though, as expected. Thumping in my ears, my chest is tightening with each result. It's filling in with stark contrast to what had been hoped or predicted. I feel my breath become shallow, quick, shuddered resisting this.

This is far too close. *How can the votes be this close?* All the experts wrote off anything like this. Surely it will change as more results come in. Sitting, and watching, and waiting, the delirium unfold.

There's tension as an increasing vice grip wraps around my chest like a Chinese finger trap. Struggling for optimism, it holds on tighter. Watching but not watching, like children sneaking peeks between our fingers of some horror movie. Time passes in a vacuum where hours feel like minutes, and every minute is in slow motion.

Then the unimaginable, undeniable happens. They call it: James Blake will be our next president. They say it's close but I don't care. They say she fought honorably but that's not consoling. They say the people have spoken but this table is undeniably silenced. Not a word leaves our mouth as shock doesn't even begin to cover it. A ringing echo fills my ears as I'm tunneled into the TV's closed captioning.

The floor drops out beneath my feet. A rug is ripped out and I am falling—swallowed, enveloped, consumed. *Is this what dying feels like?* A coldness spreads across my extremities, and thoughts escape my grasp. Numbly overstimulated, shaken in an unfathomable box desperately grasping for some stable shore. I don't even feel the tears quietly falling from my face as my entire existence feels like it is undergoing spaghettification. An incoherent rage lights my body on fire, leaving me to sit here burning to a deadened crisp.

At her loss, we can see Olivia Miller stunned. Gobsmacked as all cameras are on her at their campaign's watch party. Her face says it all. Aghast, empty, heartbroken, and shattered; disrupting the mask she was told to present as a strong woman candidate. Composing herself, she comes to the podium to speak. I'm sure it was poignantly delivered. Perfectly polished, empathetically compassionate, and undeniably human —but I didn't hear it. Her lips moved but no sound came to my ears. I'm underwater in a fishbowl; mwoup, mwoup, mwoup. Until a clink interrupts it all.

[CLINK]

"FUCK YEA!"

Ripped from my lobotomized state, I am back at our table, in our bar, when the view becomes visible. The bar is split, almost mimicking the results. There are revelers, and they are cheering. Clinking and clanking, whooping and hollering their win. Exuberantly making it known this is *"their guy"* to anyone in ear-shot, whether they want to listen or not. Disbelief washes over me at the sight of these infiltrators. *Who are these people and why are you at this bar? My bar. Our bar! We don't share the same social hangouts. How could people like them be here with people like us? How was I so wrong?*

Scanning in this uncertain sea, Tim Curry catches my sight on the screen, frantically running from room to room, playing out different theories and suspicions. Mania meets mania but one seems far safer, even if it would mean being in the same house as a murderer. In an alternate time, I may find the ironic coincidence funny, but now there is no laughter.

Glancing away from the screen, looking over the dimly lit patrons, our eyes meet. A couple sitting at a small booth across the way, and in their faces I see my own strife. Suspended, away from the gleeful eruptions sitting at the bar. Treading water with no-where to go. Absent of understanding how we got here.

They say Blake was notable because he wasn't like other politicians. He was an "every man". For the people: salt of the earth, genuine, unfiltered, and raw. People who didn't follow politics felt Blake understood their disenfranchised lives, even though he came from pedigree and attended Ivy Leagues. Disgruntled with their government, who did not represent or care for them, the faux empathy enticed their hunger. Big, boisterous promises and punching all the right buttons; targeting all the phobias and classic scapegoats. Their fear and heartbreak manipulated for his gains, unknown to his loyalists entranced by the siren song.

Sure, the nation had been divided before, electing other radicals, aligning with highly questionable allies and horrible sweeping policies—but tonight didn't solve any of the problems or pre-existing conditions. This felt palpable in fury, filled with accusations having festered. Ship them out, lock them up, condemn, proselytize, and starve from existence. Them versus us. Grabbing and hoarding and inching your way forward, pushing anyone else back or out.

There was a time of a blindly positive experiment of hope. A rallying cry of unity where, yes, we can make change. It was set on shaky ground, though. Surrounded by eras of milk gone sour, and seeds of discord sewn deep in waiting. We felt it was a turning point. I felt it was a new chapter. We were beyond in a fresh era; but how naively was the underestimated assumption that rooted resentment ever went away that easily.

Sure, just a decade further past, we invaded a nation searching for the assailants who attacked our cities, but our government was looking in completely different countries while many incoherently believed that everyone in that region was in cahoots with the criminals. Sure, before that there was a banking crisis, a recession, a housing bubble, not to mention the school shooting that rocked the country, but that doesn't mean the government isn't looking out for your interests—not just theirs.

Sure, prior to then was a world-wide pandemic vastly ignored for whom it impacted until a little boy fell ill, and then they cared, but that doesn't mean it was ill intentioned. Sure, city planning wasn't designed with all bodies and abilities in mind, but that doesn't mean the government thought those people should just adapt. Sure, companies have record profits while average people scrape by, but that doesn't mean the government can be bought. Sure, the health-care industry has been privatized, and most citizens can't even afford to die, but that doesn't mean there haven't been investments in wellness.

Time compounds, and feelings fester. Emotions grow inside like a cancerous mold. Initially small with cellular transiting over time. Morphing, growing, gnawing away at the fabric of logic. Pulling everyone further, and further away from any guiding star. Lost without direction; a lonely and desperate spectacle of beings for decades upon decades upon decades, until we end up here. It's been a long, winding path to this point—a depraved destination. Suddenly stuck in an oppressive myth as we are sinking down, down, down by the crushing weight of inescapable doom. A gut punch to the core.

Chapter Four
Break of Day

Now
<u>January 3, 2047</u>:

Breathlessly sitting here, the chatter of the world bickering in my ear fades away, and I am left in this moment. This moment that has cast a spell of pausing time for me to only observe. The hourglass laid on its side. Peaking and pushing into my optic orb unable to look away. Entranced and entrenched in this space and time, as any complex thoughts have vacated my body. The rest of the world is swept away.

As I sit here taking everything in, there are moments when it feels like options are so limited, though no one specifically in this moment is limiting those choices. *What else is there to do here and now but sit?* Sitting back into the old wood chair with hard edges, firmly supporting this body that needs to be held as it gazes outwards. A spirited cold breeze bordering on bitter brushes against my cheekbone as if it's trying to be gentle, when in actuality it's a dilution of the harsh environment. Biting, windy nibbles taking their lick. Regardless of bundled layers, the wind can cut through when it wants; weaseling its way between the fibers. Tunneling its way to the center.

Rays are peeking over the next ridge. A slight hint starting to light up the sky, creating that subtle shift in visibility that sneaks up on anyone watching. Mornings start with a darkness deeper than any imaginable onyx, and then it shifts. So subtle it's like a slight-of-hand magic trick. Raven, sable, noir, soot, charcoal, and in a blink the first cracks of dawn transition the world from muted monotones to vibrant colors, awakening at first light only to miss it in a moment with an errant distraction. Janus doesn't care if he misses it, snuggled up in his standard bagel-esque position, nestled by my side under a heavy knitted blanket. Apparently he's seen enough sunrises that they are no longer notable, while I can't help but watch. They don't grow old.

What first appears to be only blindly bright light, blowing out the colors, quickly transforms to a fluctuation of hues in the sky. Colors with no names dance across the horizon, combining pigments society knew but could never fathom merging like this. Nature creating something in minutes humans could only dream of over hours or days. Admiring artists are inspired yet fail to fully grasp.

Baby blue meets hot pink but doesn't become purple and the golden rays sashay through blue air and fluffy clouds. Orange and coral and yellows melting. Yellow and blue merging true to tone under the sunbeams. My favorite is a sandy coral we've called "saral." Janus doesn't disagree with this naming, though the verdict is still out if anyone else would agree.

The wrap-around deck of the treehouse sits above the clouds that have creeped into the valleys between ridges. Humorous that something so wispy and soft—literally free of solid form—can completely hide a massive, dense, permanent structure. Occupying spaces simultaneously, the dainty little nebula vapors win out. They have that power, whether it's disappearing city sky-scrapers or whole mountain ridges. Regardless of how many times I see it, every instance resonates like a first—awestruck. To sit above it all feels other worldly. *It must be a spectacular view on Mount Olympus, but do they sit and watch too?*

While hiking long ago, seeing the sunrise while sitting above the clouds, I felt transcendent. Pitifully small and insignificant as the clouds stretched farther than eyes would take you. In that moment, plugged into the universe, it felt as if the energy that pulsed through every molecular creation and the cosmic timeline existed, but didn't—all at once. A real religious experience if I ever did know one. Or maybe it was the altitude and thin air. That feeling and moment stuck. In times of strife, it could be leaned upon to wash away anything unwanted. Now those moments can be a regular occurrence like a daily dose supply to block out what can't be seen beyond. A beta blocker of sunshine.

This moment is transparently what it is. Free of all else. Serenity without trouble, if for just a moment. Previously under appreciated on outdoor excursions where hints of this tranquility would pale in comparison. This wilderness is now my St. Peter's Basilica, or what the basilica could only ever hope to elicit. Beyond words or feelings ever experienced in the old days. If only this destination was reachable by other routes. Surely this result was tangible without the transitional turmoil, or current uncertainty. It would be better with my friends, but alternately had ever a moment like this been suggested, would they have come? I've been to this treehouse a hundred times but now it feels like I was hardly here. This space operates outside of the reality I was privy to. An aching length it took to get here.

With the sun now fully above the trees, the day begins to rustle. Before long, the low clouds will elevate or disintegrate. Temperatures will become more comfortable, and more animals will make their way through the forest. It will soon be a bustling environment of daily activities. As if on cue, knowing it's time for us to start our day as well, Janus starts to stir with a big stretch. I stand up, shaking out any residual sleep.

I can't resist but say,"Oh, big stretch."

As if he doesn't already know. Heading in, I catch one last glance of today's prescribed regimen.

Chapter Five
Collared

Then
<u>March 3, 2045:</u>

"Can you believe this shit?!"

I shove my phone to Sam, and Dani across the coffee table. Lit up on the screen is the latest decree from Blake and his administration.

<u>FIGHTING COUNTERFEIT NEWS: ALL NEWS REPORTS TO BE VERIFIED BY FACT COMMITTEE</u>

The report went on to detail the upcoming protocols and procedures. In the ever-present fight against counterfeit news, and memes passing as truth, and biased journalism, all reports must be verified by Verification Officers under the newly established Fact Committee, or a local branch Verification Officer. Nothing was to be published (electronically or in print) until approval was met. Failure to comply would result in fines, and repeat offenders would face federal charges leading to potential imprisonment.

My friends take a moment to take it all in, but they do not seem to match the level of frustration I had hoped. My anger seethes out while theirs barely boils.

Dani hands back my phone and says, *"Maybe it'll do some good."*

"What? How could it possibly do any good?"

"I dunno. Maybe there will be less click-bait on social media. Like the ones Sam's dad shares, and nothing seems to work taking them down."

"Do you really think that the Fact Committee is actually going to fact-check? Do you have any idea who is going to be heading up the committee?"

Sam and Dani look at one another with a tilt of their heads, and a somber look of exhaustion. They've been here before. This isn't our first conversation with a similar topic, and assumptions can be made that it won't be our last.

"No, not exactly. I can assume based on who it's coming from, but I'm guessing you do?" Sam retorts with a semi passive-aggressive undertone.

"I'm assuming your assumptions are right if you've been paying attention to what's been going on. It's a trifecta of adulation. Do you really think that the head of the largest social media platform in the world, along with the largest campaign donor to Blake, and the man who profits from everyone with every sales algorithm in his pocket are going to run a committee that's honest, unbiased, and—"

"What did I miss?"

Anthony joins the heated, slightly one-sided conversation, running a bit late, as always. I want to fill him in but before words can explain they take the liberty to catch him up on all the details, connecting the dots of the information before him and the monologue has stumbled into.

"Well, obviously, it's really disheartening, and beyond frustrating. But honestly, I'm not all that surprised. They were already censoring anything that didn't fit their narrative. This is just more overt and official. I'm sorry, Jessi. I can't imagine how infuriating this must be for you."

"I just don't know what things are going to look like for me moving forward. Everything I've worked for could go away. And besides, it's just fucked up. A total overreach."

"Hey, you're not alone. If it does, we're here to help. You know that."

With a nod of acceptance, I acknowledge the appropriate words that feel comforting, even if they don't fix the situation. His demeanor as smooth as an untouched lake, Anthony knows exactly what to say. Even in the face of daily stress and latest potential roadblocks, he takes everything in stride, while internally I'm spiraling twenty steps down a path we're not yet officially on. Even for someone who always handles their shit, he's always ready to catch others who falter. *How does he always handle it all?* Maybe he's next to me in these feelings but just hides it infinitely better. Maybe he can't afford to let it show. Maybe …

[SNAP SNAP]

"Helloooo! Earth to Jessi! You with us?"

"Yea, sorry. My thoughts took a mini vacation for a second."

"Were margaritas and a pool boy involved?" he asks.

A smirky glint radiates, even in this moment. I'm over here diving into doom, and he's cracking jokes. Knowing him, I know he gets it, but the humor isn't cute in the moment. Saying nothing is a valid response, but I provide a—*"pfff"*—of air.

"Okay well, on that note, I'm going to grab a drink. Then we can dive in."

We do what we can with our hands as tied as they are. The newspaper has already restricted the topics acceptable to cover, and now the limitations are only going to become tighter. Radiating dissent at the state of things would be an understatement. To be trapped and tied. Words bound, working within and against their new-found formula while making little to no ground. A treadmill fight of redundancy and "no"s. What's the point of writing when it's all to be redacted or rejected? *I'm getting ahead of myself.*

Anthony returns with an iced latte, pulling out his laptop to go over the latest numbers. These moments provide us with something to pour time and attention into. Something that feels helpful, even if it's small. A desperate measure to take some control in a cyclone, weakly scraping by to do something tangible.

Sitting there, collectively going over the numbers of how many donations have been received both monetarily and physically, becomes a routine by now. Quantities of canned food, bottles of water, clothing, sanitary items, sleeping bags, etc, neatly tallied. Then there's the assessment of the known communities and individuals, along with requests of who needs what. A Santa's wish list for the unhoused. Our sleigh in tow when the government won't pony up. We'll take all of this information and then, this weekend, disperse the items before Monday, when a new work week begins. Collect over the next two weeks and then, on that second Friday, we'll be back at it again. Gather, log, access, disperse, and repeat.

"Oh, I forgot to mention, I've bought some heat blankets."

"Those will come in handy! Thanks, Jessi" Anthony acknowledges with pleasant surprise but he isn't ready for a duffle bag full.

"You bought all these?" Dani questions with bewildered snark.

"Yea, they were on sale!"

"Mmhmm. I'm sure they were on sale. And on the end corner too, right?" Anthony playfully speculates.

"Yup.", We eye one another as he knows I'd dig through the back of any store to find supplies to help dwindle the never-ending list, regardless of the effort.

"We'll use them, but I don't think ... uh, I don't think we'll need that many. Do you think you can hang on to any extra for future weeks?"

"Yea, of course. They'll come into use eventually."

There are others who help, of course. Volunteers. But these days, everyone is stretched so thin, attendance tends to be inconsistent. Given the circumstances, it's understandable. We have to pander to anyone willing to help, even if we don't necessarily agree with all their tenants, like the church down on Second. They love to help, as long as Anthony's boyfriend isn't around. Heaven gates bonus points—helping those less fortunate. Luckily this still tends to be a trending theme, even if compassion has become less favorable. A trait even discouraged by the administration. Statements claiming the unhoused are self-made in their problems, beyond help, or dangerous have met mixed reviews upon receiving ears.

The ragtag stewardship has generated new skills to help at a fraction of the cost, made newly useful. Sewing, knitting, etc.—a hodgepodge of handiwork. Each contributes, and different clubs, organizations, and individuals do too.

Taking a look at the wish list, it feels smaller. Fewer people have signed up and fewer requests coming in. Examining and re-examining the spreadsheet lines, I assume a page is missing or a mistake has been made. *Nope, it's all there.* No hidden sheet or tucked-away list.

"What's up with the short wish list? Aren't there normally more?"

Anthony shrugs. *"I'm not sure. I guess everyone has their needs met. Or they just aren't requesting."*

"They've never had a problem requesting before. It seems like there's less people as a whole. Not just less requests."

"Maybe there are."

His head burrows in. He clearly would rather be sorting the details than dealing with questions, but it's impossible to shake that odd gut feeling.

"Have you heard the rumors about people being rounded up to facilities?"

"What the fuck are you talking about?"

All eyes are staring now as Sam's exacerbated snap summarizes their group-think all at once. Admittedly, it sounds delusional—crazy, even. Something that would have once been spouted from a conspiracy theorist on a satire blog parading as news. It's not, though. A real concern if it's true.

"There are rumors that they are rounding up unhoused people, and instead of shuffling them to a different part of the city, out of the eyes of the tourists or wealthy, they're being sent to a facility. I've heard it's a care facility to get them back on their feet, but I've also heard it's a work or training facility. They're saying it's to provide skills in exchange for work and it's all temporary. But I don't know if I'm buying it. Some sort of work facility with guaranteed labor."

Stunned, Anthony breaks the silence. *"And why would they do that? How would it even be legal?"*

"Well, if public camping is illegal then they could easily pick them up on that charge and then, I dunno, give them a choice. Prison or this rehab-work thing. As for why, I mean, it gets them off the street so tourists will keep coming and the rich won't be bothered. I'm sure someone is profiting somewhere. They could have a work-force,

even if it was temporary, with skills they found useful. A pipeline for their benefit. And it's not like most people would notice. I mean, the only reason I thought of it was because I heard rumors, and looking at the sheets, how could you no—"

"I'm going to stop you right there. You're flirting with sounding like them before Blake was elected. I'm not saying it's not a good theory, but there's no evidence. It's possible. Shit, it's even plausible, but what can we do about it?"

I sit there defeated, sinking quietly in the seat. Even my friends can't take these ramblings at every meeting. Anthony isn't wrong. *What can I do? Run to unhoused encampments and warn them? Advise staying away from programs presented as help? Insist on researching deeper and sifting through claims before extending trust?* Doing what I can but it never feels like enough. An echo reverberating in my ear from the coffee shop collides with internal thoughts. A tired mind and body; my skin sags in exhaustion and my posture slumps. Let's get at it and do it all again. Another week, another task.

Gently placing his hand over mine, his deep complexion in contrast, Anthony looks with intentional eye contact. He knows me, and subsequently the chaos of empathy housed beneath the frantic thoughts. Those soft, warm hands, like a comfort blanket on a depressing, dreary day, provide limited reassurance.

"We're doing all we can. You know that."

"Yea, I know."

I do, but it's hard to hop off the hamster wheel while the weight of The Nation breathes down on us. Simply existing means trudging onward, even if it's in a world that seems to be nothing but tricks and lies. A cog in the machine with no exit ramp.

"Let's get back to it. We have thirteen care pack requests in East. I can take those."

Chapter Six
Proclamations

Then
<u>April — December 2045:</u>

April 2, 2045
    Barricades Mandated Around All Federal Buildings
In light of two unrelated car bombings by foreign terrorists The Nation must protect its civil servants. Both assailants were former military, born citizens believed to have crossed the southern border and to have been radicalized during service abroad.
    April 13, 2045
    National Book Ban: Banning Access to Dangerous Literature
The children of The Nation must be protected in heart and mind from corruption, and pervasive media. Books featuring and celebrating sinister behavior will no longer be published or sold commercially and will be removed from public shelves in libraries, schools, etc. Prohibited media will be determine and listed by the Quality Citizen Office.
    April 24, 2045
    News Reporting Verified Under Rigorous Checklist: Enroll Today
Citizens may become certified in the verification of news reporting from The Nation-sponsored course completed from the convenience of your home. Earn compensation for your civic duty. Report any inaccurate news or bias news creation to your local Verification Officer.
    May 1, 2045
    Training Facilities Open Nationwide
Learn an employable skill at The Nation's training facility. We welcome everyone regardless of housing, citizen, religious, or orientation status to gain knowledge and skills for a better tomorrow. Lodging, food, and classes provided! Sign up for your educational commitment today!
    May 7, 2045

Foreign Social Media Platform Banned

Foreign-owned social media platform CP is banned immediately to protect the privacy, safety, and security of The Nation's citizens from foreign spies. All CP apps should be deleted from any devices. CP will be removed from anywhere you can download apps. Using a VPN is punishable by law. The brightest minds of The Nation will soon supply a suitable replacement.

May 14, 2045

Illegal Foreigners Found and Deported

The Nation's efforts to find and remove illegal foreigners have been overwhelmingly successful. A tedious door-to-door operation has delivered hundreds of thousands of illegals harboring drugs, weapons, and crime-family-related evidence. The Nation has removed these individuals from our land.

May 20, 2045

Fight Illness with Isolation

The herd immunity of The Nation is strong as long as it is not infiltrated by those more susceptible. Individuals who are unwell with any life threatening illness will be provided temporary isolation housing while they recover as to protect themselves, and the rest of The Nation. Contact The Nation Health and Human Services for additional information.

May 27, 2045

Terrorist Cell Defeated Overseas

A great win for The Nation! After a long battle with the local terrorist cell The Nation's soldiers have rendered them obsolete. They were obliterated with the assistance of new drone technology to pin-point and target any hidden assailants.

June 3, 2045

Easier Shopping for Every Citizen

Every citizen of The Nation needs goods, and shopping has been made easier. As paper money in past years has become obsolete, we as a society have relied on card transactions. New biometric technology allows you to connect your funds to biometric indentation in the form of a retinal, or palm scan. No more concerns about lost cards, stolen identity, or dirty plastic!

June 10, 2045

Two Forms of Identification Required for Voting

To protect the security of The Nation and the sanctity of our electoral practices, all citizens will need to present two forms of photo identification to proceed with any voting procedures. Please ensure all details and identifying photos match one another, as well as the citizen presenting them.

June 16, 2045

Meat and Dairy Industries Receive Subsidies from The Nation

Fighting inflation, The Nation has provided subsidies to the meat and dairy industries. Our citizens need strong, healthy bodies, and The Nation will provide! Subsidies will curb costs—however, please inquire with your local Food Authority for supplemental vouchers or educational plans to incorporate consumption more subsidized foods in your diet.

June 20, 2045

The Nation's News Eradicates Biased Private Journalism

Biased private journalism has run rampant as a scourge on society. All news will be consolidated to approved outlets as verified by The Nation's Verification Officers and government offices. No longer will citizens need to question which news is false or truth, as it will all be provided from our Nation.

June 28, 2045

Cleaning Up Our City Streets

New initiatives from The Nation to clean up our streets from the unhoused population have been instilled. Care, resources, and opportunities will be provided to those in need in a more suitable location. Housed citizens will have their city spaces returned to a more beautiful, original state. If you know someone in need of The Nation Care Facilities, reach out today!

August 1, 2045

Leaving the International Climate Agreement

The Nation is exiting the International Climate Agreement. Our great nation contains resources to benefit its citizens by operating in a more efficient and beneficial manner, without the interference of foreign entities built upon pseudo science.

August 8, 2045

Hostile Southern Border Is Closed

After numerous hostile attacks and crossings across our southern border The Nation will take all necessary precautions to protect its citizens. Effective immediately, the southern border will be closed until further notice.

August 12, 2045

Modesty Considered Admissible in Court

The Nation has deemed that the degree of modesty will be admissible in court as evidence of provocation in cases of rape and assault. Guilt will be assigned in percentages, and the degree of modesty upon all parties will be taken into consideration when rendering the verdict.

August 18, 2045

Journalism Degree Offered at The Nation's Academy

Learn to report truth from the prestigious Nation's Academy! Be taught by the best, detect inaccurate news and craft your own stories of real events. Connect to everyday people for a better tomorrow, like the days of yesteryear our grandparents reveled in. Gain an education and perhaps coveted employment at The Nation's News Offices.

September 6, 2045

Christianity Declared National Religion

The Nation did not have an officially recognized religion of the state in years past. As we righteously move into the future as a leading developed nation, we must do so with guidance. Thus, Christianity has been recognized as the official religion of The Nation. All religions are permitted to be practiced, but not within public educational facilities or government buildings.

September 19, 2045

More Roles Opened for Women in the Military

New roles have been opened to accept women in the ranks of The Nation's Military. These roles have been designed specifically with womanly strengths and skills in mind. An opportunity for patriotic women to provide strong morale, full stomachs, and ensure soldiers are well-dressed for combat. Unsuitable roles will become inaccessible.

September 27, 2045

Civil Service Rewards

In efforts to curb the rising cost of goods, citizens may receive coupons, credits, and vouchers to be put toward necessities such as food, electricity, and water as a reward for their civil service and contributing to The Nation's needs. For specific opportunities, and needs of your local community as well as The Nation, please inquire with your local Quality Citizen Office.

October 1, 2045

Banned Book Ownership Illegal

Private ownership of pervasive media will be illegal past December 31, 2045. As The Nation must protect the hearts, minds, and souls of its citizens, it is vital to take the necessary steps to remove anything that may tarnish or jeopardize their well-being. If a citizen currently owns any banned books, they must relinquish them at a Quality Citizen Office deposit center before 2046. This may be done so anonymously. However, if a citizen would like to receive Civil Service Rewards, they must identify themselves. Post-2046 banned media will be seized

October 16, 2045

The Nation Military Assist Local Police

As local police maintain order in their communities, covering everything from low-level crimes to extremist rioters, The Nation's Military has sent soldiers to provide assistance in both presence and tactical training, increasing police effectiveness. Keeping every citizen safe is our duty for a better tomorrow.

October 23, 2045

Gay Marriage No Longer Federally Recognized

Reversing Obergefell v. Hodges, same-sex marriage will no longer be federally recognized. Decisions to permit marriages and their recognition will be returned to the states. Only heterosexual marriages will be recognized on a federal level.

November 5, 2045

Quality Voter Security Measures Reinforced

Reinforced measures to protect the security and sanctity of The Nation's elections have been installed. Voting is a great privilege and honor of the citizens that comes with responsibility. To ensure all citizens are prepared to cast their vote during any election cycle all citizens must attend a 1-hour seminar provided by The Nation and pass the subsequent assessment. The seminar will cover topics of candidates, policies, and civic duty.

November 12, 2045

Ample Enlisting Bonuses

Enlist in The Nation's Military today and do your civic duty! The Nation is looking for eager, healthy citizens to join up to protect and serve The Nation, its interests, and its citizens. Enlisting bonuses for every new recruit!

November 24, 2045

Blake Considers Takeover of Taiwan

In efforts to protect The Nation and interests of The Nation, President Blake considers taking over Taiwan. After detecting excessive enemy ships throughout the Pacific around interests and allies of The Nation, Blake determines it would be in the best interest of The Nation to acquire Taiwan as a defensive outpost.

December 3, 2045

National Rehabilitation Facilities Now Open

The Nation has opened rehabilitation facilities nationwide. Citizens fighting their demons in need of assistance will be greeted with open arms. These facilities are qualified to cure a wide scope of medically recognized disorders, conditions, and diseases as detailed by The Nation Psychiatric Association as well as Health and Human Services. Payment plans available. Civil service rewards accepted.

December 11, 2045

Bonuses for Children

The Nation encourages families to procreate, and populate. A child is a gift and it is a blessing to be raised in this wonderful Nation by proud citizens. The Nation recognizes their service and rewards those married couples who procreate with financial bonuses, credits, and vouchers.

December 17 2045

Assassination Attempt on President Blake

A failed assassination attempt on President Blake's life was thwarted by the brave servicemen sworn to serve and protect our leader. Dave Smithfield, son of Afghani refugees, and a communist extremist with a vast internet footprint of illicit plans, was fatally shot in his apprehension.

December 29, 2045

AI Detects Autoimmune Disease and Aides in Correction

Citizens can now take part in the AI Autoimmune Disease Detection Program. Understanding your genes allows citizens to take preventative care and, in qualified cases, receive gene alterations for optimal health. Inquire with Health and Human Services for opportunities to participate and to learn about options available (Elective procedures not covered by most insurance.)

January 20, 2046

Parades Across The Nation

All across The Nation, parades are being held to celebrate the anniversary of President Blake's inauguration. Every city is proud to hoist pictures of our leader flanking their main street, welcoming the proud citizens and the processional. Hail this Great Nation!

Chapter Seven
Just Gone

Then
<u>February 20, 2046:</u>

"I'm sorry, ma'am. We've done all we can at this time."

"But you've filed a missing person's report for Anthony Kierg, correct? And you have my number?"

"Yes, ma'am. As I said previously, we've filled the report, along with logging your concerns and his description. If anything turns up or there's any news, we'll be sure to contact you."

"Thank you."

"Now, you have a good day, miss. Goodbye."

Click, and a dial tone. He was lying or incompetent or both.

"Filing a missing persons report seems a little excessive, doesn't it?"

With a ferocity that could snap a chicken's neck, I whip my head around, looking Elijah directly in the eyes at this flippant remark. Sitting there his expression a mixture of innocence and smugness. *Is that arrogance smeared across his face?*

"What? No! It's not excessive."

"I'm just saying, it's only been a few days since you last talked. He, and his boyfriend could have gone away on a trip. Besides, it was the weekend after Valentine's Day."

"They didn't go on a trip."
"Yea? How do you know?"
"He would have told me!"

Silence so thick it's deafening. You can hear the kids coming home from school across the street, and cars going too fast down the city-burb road, as we both stare at one another. The oxygen of connection exhales, and gasps.

"Maybe he didn't. Maybe he wanted some time away from everything."
"I doubt that, but it does sound enticing."
"Maybe he needed a break."

Gathering my purse and keys from the table, making my way to the hallway closet. A cold snap has brought an uncharacteristic frigidness to the air. I bundle in my heavy green coat, protected at least from the impending iciness that awaits, if nothing else.

"What are you doing?"
"I'm meeting Sam and Dani at Darlings for coffee."
"Again?"
"Yea, again. What is that supposed to mean?"
"Just that you're never here."
"I am. But when I am, all we do is sit on the couch, and watch stupid shows while the world burns. You don't want to talk about anything!"
"And you only want to make dramatic statements! Make everything into something dire and paranoid."
"No, I just can't sit by while my friend is out there. I have to try and find him, even if I'm the only one looking."
"Not everything's a crusade, Jessi. Sometimes we can just be comfortable."
"Speak for yourself. I'll see you later. They're waiting."

Before he can rebut anymore, I'm stepping through the front door while he stays on my couch. Elijah only wants to hear what he wants to hear. His activist gusto is beginning to fade. A facade slipping off like an ill-tied mask. Maybe it was never tied that securely but he's good at presenting what you want to see. Caring, but only when it's convenient—that makes me loathe him for this complacency. Sam always saw it but I had been naive—hopeful. Anthony's disappearance has made the sleep start to fade.

As soon as loathing creeps in, guilt accompanies it. Nostalgic thoughts cloud current feelings and I tell myself he means well. Maybe I am being dramatic or delusional. Anthony and his boyfriend could be holed up in some nauseatingly iconic boutique bed-and-breakfast without cell service. It's possible. Still not probable, but possible.

An inescapable feeling that something is wrong won't leave. There is something that doesn't sit right, deep down, regardless of how unhinged it may sound. As much as I try to push it down, it won't go away. Not entirely, anyway. It lingers there, and that creates a hesitancy to completely disregard this nagging thought. A queasy, quivering jitter at the pit of my stomach must mean more than possible consequences of questionable leftovers.

Deep in my thoughts, the short walk to Darlings evaporated into an even shorter distance. Uncrowded streets and lucky light cycles and suddenly I'm quickly crossing the threshold into warmth and welcome. Spaces like this make the world seem better than it really is. They make us forget for a moment, as we're surrounded by friendly faces.

"Hey, Lila, I'll just have my usual."
"You got it. Medium SVL."
"Thanks. Hey, would it be cool if I put up one of these on the bulletin boards?"

As I hold up the printed flyer with Anthony's face, details, and my contact information she glances it over. She knows my concerns. She's heard the rumors. With a nod of the head, permission is granted.

"Sure, as long as there's space. If anything is for an event that's passed you can take it down to make room."
"Thanks, Lila. I really appreciate it."

Grabbing my drink, I head over to the bulletin board, dodging a quirky group of theatre kids and what appears to be a book club discussing a hot new book by some rising author that I'm surprised is approved. I see the rallying calls for protests, and marches against the latest proclamations. Outreach organizations for those seeking aid, guidance, and a whole myriad of other services that have popped up under this new presidency. Fortunately, there is enough space after removing out dated flyers of music and social events long past. Maybe someone will recognize him and have information. Maybe the authorities will recognize we're looking, and that we won't stop. Scanning the crowd as I turn around, there in the corner sit Dani and Sam.

"Hey, sorry I'm late. Elijah and I got into it."

"Again?"

"Yea. He was being a bit of an ass, and it went downhill from there."

"Figures."

Sam sits there in silence. This past year has worn on her to the point it's noticeable. The little crow's feet settle in, the circles under her eyes looking a little more purple, but no laugh lines are visible.

"Lila let me put up a flyer. That's something right?"

"A flyer?"

"Yea, I made some extras. I figured you could take some."

A small stack appears from my purse and their eyes clearly widen, seeing what has been done. Ignoring their stares, I hand over the flyers, reserving a few for myself and future posting. They both take one and look it over before matching my gaze again. Maybe it's too much. The rumors though—they linger. Whispers of other places where people go missing, and there's always an excuse. A reason they can't be reached, an explanation for where they went. They just vanish. Plucked from their lives by an invisible hand, but nobody asks anything more.

Gossip of rounding up citizens not congruent with The Nation's "standards," taking them away to be fixed. The stories could seem more plausible in small towns where majority overrides logical rules, but here, in Austin? *How could this happen here?* A diverse city with a wide range of residents celebrating all the wonderfully weird ways that make us special. If it could happen here, then what is happening elsewhere? Thoughts darkly descend, clouding stable rationale. Fending away the worst fears from this current moment that needs my attention now. Urging me to stay present.

"Do you think this will actually do anything?"

"Maybe. It's better than nothing. Someone might know something. And I filed a missing persons report."

"You did what? Why would you do that? You've heard the rumors!"

"Yea, I know. But even if the rumors are true, it's not going to make it worse. It's not like they can disappear him more than they already have. And if it isn't true, it could help."

"It could make things worse."

"I can't just sit around and wait. At least it puts them on notice that we know he's gone."

Sam shakes her head and mutters, but neither of us can make out what she said.

"What?"

"You think they care?" she asks.

"No, probably not, but we have to try. Anthony would do everything for us."

A sullen truth sinks in as the pressure drops before a storm. An undeniably heavy weight we move through in discomfort. Something is wrong. Tangibly felt without proper description to articulate. Each theory slightly different but with an unspoken commonality of the shadowy threats that lurked woven through.

Chapter Eight
Standby

Then
<u>July 6, 2046 :</u>

I'm sitting in my office on the old mustard-yellow sofa that reminds Elijah of bile—but I adore its character, like goldenrod. Delicate amber light accompanies the dry, thick smell of antique books and papers. A mini museum capturing moments deemed worthy of saving for inspiration as I type any articles within boundaries.

Pieces that matter are preferable, but trash articles are more often approved, while moonlighting more sensational stories for shadowy readers remains an option. The ones that would never be accepted at work are submitted anonymously elsewhere. Most going nowhere but to a writer's void.

My cell buzzes, scuttling across my desk, come to life by the call ringing through. Dani's face beneath a pile of purple hair pops up on the screen.

"Hello."

There are no words. Actually, there are many words, but they come out at a rapid fire. A hydrant at full blast with only bits and parts landing in my ears. *Delayed. Help. Wait.* I interrupt a full-blown flustered Dani on the other end:

"Hold on—what happened?"

Sam and Dani had applied for a visa to move abroad two months ago. To leave and never look back. Run away somewhere safer for them. How dreamy that sounded—*maybe I should join them, if I couldn't convince Elijah, which seems like the more likely outcome.*

"They should have been approved by now!"

Dani is distraught and not trying to hide it. They rarely show a state like this.

"It'll be okay. I'm sure they'll be approved any day."

"They should have been approved weeks ago."

"Have you talked to the embassy? Or that immigration guy you hired to help handle the paperwork and transition and stuff?"

"I've tried! The embassy keeps running me in circles. They keep saying there's been an influx of applications and that's caused a delay. They promise to look into it and get back to me but they never do."

"And your guy?"

"Same thing. Except it seems more insulting when I have to remind him which of his clients he's speaking with. I honestly don't know why we hired him."

I've thought the same thing. He's made a lucrative hustle out of a necessity, while doing the bare minimum. That man is about as useful as an appendix.

"I'm sure he will prove to be beneficial in the long run."

"I hope so. I think they're all becoming a bit annoyed with me. I'm tempted to go to the embassy, and just sit and wait."

"Yea, because that won't get you arrested."

It had been a long time, and I've noticed it too. *Has there been such a substantial increase that the offices are overwhelmingly swamped?* The offices have always run slowly, working at their own pace with no regard for anyone's concerns or needs. Oblivious outside the world of their desk, stamps, and papers. Somehow, the offices seem to have become even slower—acting as molasses in cold weather, indifferent to the frantic worries of the applicants.

Maybe it's the other countries. Those receiving the fleeing are no longer as excited to receive as they once were. Perhaps they're becoming overwhelmed as well. Too many needy are knocking at the door. A tapping, rapping has become a pounding that's interrupting their day-to-day activities. Undeniably loud as they struggle to ignore the fact this rush of people may be symptomatic of other systemic problems. Bandage the bleeding, but don't dare look for the wound. Surely it'll all go away if we just tune it out. Limited space, and limited supplies with too many outstretched arms asking.

"The whispers of capacities being reached are making us nervous. What if they close their borders to us?"

"Why would they do that?"

"Why does anyone do anything? I don't know… to hush the people feeling like there are too many of us. To take a less complicated stance. To—"

"I don't think they're going to close their borders. Not anytime soon, at least," I reassuringly remind, partially reassuring myself with the words.

" And what if Blake closes our borders?"

"There haven't been any rumors of that."

"Yet! The southern border is closed, but what if we can't fly?" Dani interjects.

"You're right—yet. We don't know anything will come to that. It'll work out."

"I hope so. It feels like time is slipping away."

A cynical thought, but stripping the fluff from stories leaves us often with the bare bones of truth. *Would a country actually be so intentional in its cold shoulder?* Wouldn't be the first time. Maybe, I'm just a sour journalist who's witnessed too many seedy historical events. Of course, none of this is mentioned to Dani. Surely these thoughts have already been connected, but something about speaking it out loud makes the suspicions more real. Anything to keep the dangerous, intrusive feelings at bay on imaginary shores.

"Don't worry. I'm sure it'll all come together before you know it."

"Let's hope so. We're getting desperate."

We chatter a while longer and I work to keep my thoughts present. Sitting in standby, waiting for what's to come with our hands tied. Unavoidably drifting to what this could mean. But for Dani, I put on the voice of a happy face. I'm sure it will get better. I'm sure it will resolve. I'm sure it will.

Chapter Nine
Friends

Now
<u>February 17, 2047:</u>

I look at the stars tonight and think of them. Wishing I could say I feel them, even though I don't see them like that silly quote says by some unknown author. Something about how friends are like stars; you may not always see them but they're there. Nice thoughts that feel hollow while looking toward dark skies. I feel nothing but a vacancy. Tiny pits once occupied, full of love and joy now empty with the residual film of what once was. A memory that's painful to remember, regardless of the fact that it was itself joyful. Maybe the fact that it was joyful makes it more tainted in pain under the circumstances.

If friends are like stars, there are far too many in this night sky to compare to my social circles of the old days. I would take just a scattering of Ursa Minor. The dipper clearly visible, shining from my desk as I peer between branches. Bright enough to shine beyond any visual obstructions, with no need to step outside and brave the cold for a view. I'm glad to view from a comfortable spot on a squishy seat, with warmth radiating from the potbelly stove, allowing for longer lingering and the ability to stew in my thoughts. As the moonlight brilliantly streams in and I struggle some days to avoid lunacy, I can only look.

The days of being able to do absolutely nothing but sit are in some ways gone—or, perhaps more accurately, they are just different. Do absolutely nothing in moments like this to soak in what's offered as enriching entertainment while subliminally being on constant guard for what may unexpectedly happen. As the next piece of a puzzle goes in from the scattered pile upon the table, it's a faded memory as to whether I ever completed this puzzle in the old days. Opportunities, if the time had only been set aside. Now, my fingers plunk in a familiar piece while the night sky calls my focus.

Before, I could sit, indulge in the silly luxury of complicated drinks surrounded by noise and friends, in no real present danger, while suppressing all the work, drudgery, and looming threats to a corner deep in my mind. A worrisome box in the abandoned storage closet to be dealt with another day. Same but vastly different. Those days of laughter over inside jokes, and catching up on weekend shenanigans. Those moments of shoulders to lean on when everything seemed hopeless, and the support to overcome the inconceivable. These memories flood the mind and escape, streaming down my face as sentiments overflow. A reservoir tapped in longing grief.

I wonder where they are now. *Did Sam and Dani make it out? Is Anthony still missing?* All questions and no answers. My stomach still curdles at the thought that I didn't bring them with me. *Couldn't.* They weren't home to bring. Dwelling on what more could have been done. Should have been done. *An impossible request, demand to exhaust all options—failed.* No update to anything more.

Stars plucked from the sky, once shining brightly, no longer visible. As if a magic eraser wiped their orb from the dark tapestry. The night sky is duller as the galaxy of society has been redacted to far-flung mystery places along with absent friends. I search for their faces in every picture we come across. Any names being read, I listen vehemently. A silence of deep space echoes with nothing for me to hear.

The cold may be outdoors, but there is an icy aching settling in my bones. Creaking and crickety; fragile in their movement. I'm painfully aware of the dull, cavernous sensation spreading inside. Even the hot tea stationed at my lips can do little to help, though the cackle of camaraderie would spread a thaw. If only, but the air is silent beyond ambient noise. There will be no galaxy or Ursa Minor—just my North Star. It will be just me; just us. Janus and I forever and ever, until it all ends.

That's how it has to be, considering the options are unfavorable in various ways. Firstly, how would someone attempt to make friends in this world? Social media apps have been discontinued and replaced by sanctioned versions. Meet-up groups and book clubs aren't exactly prevalent. To no one's surprise, there's not a regularly accessible hot yoga gym nestled in the hillside. Guess we all had more important things to do and forgot to build one.

There were friendly acquaintances who had rental properties somewhat near, but no closer than five miles. I don't know if they made it, as they haven't been seen around. There's the Trading Post with its bar and shopping stalls, but the myriad of characters that pass through would be as good of an attempt as grabbing a lifesaver in a stormy sea from a weak-armed rescuer. *Good luck.*

This is all hypothetical, because logistics aside, beyond meeting a potential friend, there's the factor of trust. It's no longer a matter of trusting them with a secret of breaking that fad diet by sneaking fries. It's secrets that could cost us our lives, our security, or, worst of all, our sanity.

Someone's loyalty to The Nation can never be read accurately. We're all loyal and patriotic from first glance, presenting our best rah-rah-rah. Everyone's fleshy underbelly is guarded by a hard shell. It's entirely possible, in the process of trying to peel away layers, to expose oneself. Then it's all over. Done, and the jig's up! There are those who are not particularly loyal to anyone. Advantageously looking out for themselves. If a beneficial opportunity was presented, there's no guarantee they wouldn't seize it with vigor. In the old days, there were therapists to help with harboring these types of feelings. Now we all dysfunctionally teeter onwards.

Janus and I are safe. Anything else is not worth the risk. We can be an island that lowers a draw-bridge, but only when safe. Content in protected isolation and independence—a shining Polaris. As the fire dwindles, it is getting late, and Janus is ready for me to join him in sleep. The galaxy may be stunningly bright, putting on a show, but while the Ursa Minor makes its presence painfully known, I look to my North Star, feeling satisfied with this moment.

Chapter Ten
Survival

Now
<u>August 3, 2047:</u>

To continue existing, regardless of the surrounding circumstances and events taking place, leading us to here, I'm required to muster more. Dig down and grab on. Clasp the grit buried deep below. It's there, if you look, instilled in every living thing—just don't let go. Diamonds are built under pressure; gemstones encrusted in the soil of cavernous ecosystems, dwelling deep below the earth's surface. Living their own life beyond the obvious sight of any observers, intentional or not.

As I bind the plants that can be dried in thread, to hang them in ventilated spaces for a later day, it's a wonder this boring method has provided extended sustenance. A necessary task to continue undetected. Possibly, a human evolution to survive, but it's not quite as creative as our creature counterparts.

The spicebush swallowtail caterpillar dons a dupe appearance to avoid detection. It creates a clever camouflage during its lifecycle. First predominantly brown with white streaks, resembling bird shit. Later, as they become green, they grow yellow and black rings, appearing as a snake. They even have the ability to puff up to a more formidable shape. The bird is none the wiser, and passes what it thinks couldn't be edible. Look the part. Don't draw attention. Simply fade in the surroundings in neutral colors, neutral style, and appear as one of the vast other things that no one is looking for. Hidden in plain sight so that one could fly right over and would never see its prey residing right below. A tasty score not snatched. *We are boring members of the human mass when co-mingling.*

In South America, the tree ocelot vocally mimics. A cat that contorts its voice to sound like a wounded monkey. An attempt to lure the unsuspecting simian troop in to rescue the injured friend—and then it pounces. It's important to be aware of what is real and what's not. Verify the accuracy so as to not fall prey to a trap. How cunning to partake in the psychological warfare of sounding like another. Talking the talk and blending right in. Deceiving their ears and overriding any logical sense that may alert them otherwise. What a talent to sound like one of them in a manner to nearly get by. *We sound like them, and they can sound like us, but which is real?*

A jackrabbit can run upwards the top speed of a standard moped. It must, to not be caught. Small, with considerably weak defenses, especially compared to those hunting it down. When fight is not an option, the ability to run fast and far must be well-tuned. A resilient cardio, quick on their feet. Weaving and dodging between trees, over hills, and across rivers to evade capture. Never underestimate the benefit of a solid sprint. The defense of fleeing in a fleeting flash. *Keeping up the ability to dart today calls for some variety of workout on the deck—perhaps this afternoon.*

Mice, though, have the best strategy, that is perhaps the one least praised. It's not flashy nor does it don any special name. Understated but incredibly successful. Mice hide right under everyone's noses. They skirt the edges of the scene, preferring to stay in their holes that are perfectly fortified for protection, only darting out when necessary. When they step outside, it's never directly in the open. Under a leaf. Behind a branch. Quietly scurrying from point A to point B in the most reclusive and unassuming way. If they are heard, the predator goes to the ghost of their existence, where the sound emanated. Driving themselves mad with sounds to nowhere and only the most minor of physical evidence. Coexisting unwillingly as they're suspected but unseen, with only whispers of their existence. *We're better off not being known.*

There is the slow change over time to learn to be better. To acquire new strategies, and novel techniques. Drying plants to preserve wasn't always obvious for living undetected in a world full of predators. A learned experience with a lethal bell curve.

It's not like there's a choice, though. Adapt or die; they are always looming. Watching and waiting for the moment there's a slip up.

There can't be, if the choice is to continue. Every day, a new challenge with newfound threats. Every day, an opportunity to be more clever, to be faster, and to create stronger fortification. Beyond any guarantee besides a cyclical means to a never-ending experience.

Do mice hope? I don't think so, besides maybe in the moment. That fearful, panicked moment when hope seems to be lost. That moment when they run home to somewhere safe. Otherwise, mice run their race only focused on one step in front of the other. Tasks to complete day in and out. Full of necessity though teeming in monotony, but they don't mind.

Requirements of running a race you never signed up for. Navigating a maze with no apparent exit. *How did we get here, anyway?* It doesn't really matter. We're all caught on the same wheel. The only difference is that humans hang on to the notion of hope. Whether that is beneficial or not. Hope for a day beyond today. Delusional hope for a break from the monotony. Desperate hope for relief.

Chapter Eleven
Wet Sand

Then
<u>August 30, 2046:</u>

There it is, blazingly flashed across my laptop screen like an obnoxious screaming banner: "REJECTED UNTIL REDACTIONS AMENDED." Being a journalist during this administration is riddled with rejections, redactions, and denials. I should be used to it by now but every rejection stings. It's not a surprise, since it's been almost a year since the proclamations began. If the Verification Officer doesn't automatically reject an article presented, thus killing it on the spot, then it's always returned with redactions. Heavy redactions so thick there's more blacked out than that what remains. A series of back-and-forth to end up with a piece that's merely fluff on its best day or pure propaganda at its worst.

A blanket of frustration and disappointment settles upon my spirit to have my name associated in any way with these articles. As if that's not enough, to boil with the frustration, I know that after all the work and rewrites, each enduring article provides less pay per piece than an academy graduate-to-be. Ever since the degree was offered from The Nation, they receive priority. Even though it's new, and no graduates have completed the full program yet, the students interning receive slightly more pay than I, and graduates will earn significantly more. That is, if we non-academy graduates aren't replaced with new, groomed journalists by then.

This recent redaction-riddled rejection was an article on the wildfires on the western coast, about causes and prevention strategies. Of course, it also mentioned the destruction of natural fire-suppressant landscape and controlled burns in favor of ostentatious and jammed residential housing—even at its skyrocketing prices, built with shoddy materials for profit margins—and that the only solution would be to reforest and refrain the billionaire mindset to a more ecological tune. Yea, that may have all been in there, too. *Oops*. In the first draft, anyway.

As each redaction was returned, the article lost more and more teeth. Dentures on paper of gummy journalism.

With this latest rewrite, it will provide updates about the amount of fire damage that occurred and easy DIY steps every citizen can take to help fight forest fires. Plant fire-resistant shrubs that retain water and are less likely to catch a blaze. Make sure your fire pits are fully extinguished. Don't flick cigarette butts out the window. Clearly, our hacks can fix what has been bestowed. Digestible for the masses, freeing The Nation of any blame that this preventable occurrence could have happened differently. Disgusting rag littered with letters that pays my rent. *Who believes this empty dribble?*

Today, a rewrite for this article is in order, and tomorrow the office beckons us in for our weekly staff meeting. A real "coming together for a better tomorrow" obligatory gathering of journalists to ensure we all feel the camaraderie. A push from the top for a unified compliance and the group-think they've implanted. Engaging each individual's fear that the attendant next to them is more patriotic than they, and their lack of patriotism is surely noticeable to anyone watching. Keep us on our toes, and quietly not sharing complaints. We're all in this together, and if you're not, you'll be found out! I'm sure the motivational posters say something like that.

This is the worst part of my words. Writing, or rather rewriting, this article that needed no changes. I keep hoping that I can slip real reporting into these pieces. Something that the redaction process misses. Hints, nods, and nudges to those looking. A word search within the reading—but even this feels a bit crazy to me. *How can you send a message when you don't know if anyone is looking, and with a code that hasn't even been decided upon?* Speaking different languages all at once equates to a lack of communication regardless of willful efforts.

The dreary day ticks by but finally, by the end, I can hit send and submit. With the ZWOOSH of the departing message, it's good to be done for today. Grateful to have the evening with a glass of wine and Janus while watching a fantastical nostalgic show from when I was little, when everything was simple and good. A distraction to take my mind off of it all.

I sink into the couch, letting it absorb the residual heaviness of the day. Janus scampers up, always ready for a lap to sit upon. The perfect ending to a day that's anything but ideal.

As the sun rises on a new day, light streams in, and Janus is ready to go. I full-body jerk out of bed, having woken up late, a forgotten alarm not set from the previous night. Breakfast will be a protein shake to-go today if I'm going to make it in time. Arriving late will become a spectacle of fury and guilting. Janus is efficient with his morning routine and I quickly dress, giving goodbye noggin kisses, promising my return before heading out the door.

With just five minutes to spare, I scan my biometric for building and office entry before walking through the heavy glass doors to the meeting room on the fifth floor. Everyone has already found seats or they're lined against the back wall, where I join the crowd in standing room only.

"Cutting it close, aren't we?"

"Nah, just on time," I say with a wink.

Sarah smirks. She hates these meetings too, and probably only arrived a minute or two earlier. Before we can say more, the executive editor, Jacob, and the rest of the administrative staff arrives.

"Good morning! What a blessed day to join together. I want to thank each and every one of you for your dedication and service to the truth. Without your diligence, all would be lost ..."

As if we had a choice in any of this. He continues on and on. A longwinded monologue that is only slightly modified from last week's. An abundance of appreciation, gratitude, and praise for the so-called diligent work we all put forth. Poisonous intent laced in the sweetest sugary-coated words as he boisters and gesticulates with animated arms while his oversized red tie swings wildly.

He continues on, then we move to the pledge like back in middle school—a prayer that's "optional" to participate in—and then he transitions to our wins. So many wins. Wins for the silliest of things but praise, praise, praise until we choke. I've never been one much for the celebration of unremarkable events, but this participation-ribbon-equivalent weekly bonanza grates on my nerves. Celebrating the most-liked article as polled by online readers. Congratulating the article with the fewest words for the impact it made in such sparsity. Praising the most surprising article filled with obscure fun facts.

Once we're done winning, Jacob likes us all to mingle. The meeting is officially done, but unofficially, we'll all stick around for another hour or so. You can't really escape earlier without being noticed, and then that will turn into an arduous conversation. I'm playing my roll, deep in banter of pleasantries over shitty coffee and dry donuts, when Jacob approaches, awkwardly awaiting my acknowledgement.

"Jessi! Enjoying the spread?"

Does he get tired of asking the same question every week, as if I could honestly say no? Forced to converse, blatant patronizing is the easiest route. I don't have the energy to fight everything. Mouth full of powdered donut, partially covered in politeness: *"Mmm, yes, so good."*

"I wanted to speak with you about your article. Thank you for submitting with those necessary changes. Much improved."

"Mmm, thank you."

"Moving forward, though, we will be moving you to other topics."

"Excuse me? Why?"

"It'll be a better fit for everyone. More productive with less rewrites. No more wasted time over revisions."

"Okay, then what topics?"

"Celebrity news! Isn't that exciting? You'll be covering all the hot gossip everyone is dying to read. Especially all the ones in the city. Stories just waiting to be scooped up!"

"Um, I think I'd be better suited elsewhere—maybe, to make better use of my skills, since I don't really know much about cele—"

"Shh, shh, shh. You'll be fantastic! This is ideal for your feminine perspective. Even those sharp quips can be put to use!"

Before I can say more, he's moved on to his next victim. I'm left standing there, infuriated and stunned; left smacked squarely between the eyes by the indignant decisions of baseless opinions.

Everyone in the room is vapidly laughing and chatting. All of them acting their role with a mouthy grin, teeth glinting in the light, full of pacifying pleasantries. Sipping my coffee, standing alone, eyes glancing between the couplings. Both amazed and appalled how it seems they can present a successful performance. *Or is it real?* Either way, it's a struggle to replicate.

As time goes by, I count down until we are dismissed. Small talk here and chatter there; nothing sticks as conversations slide off. Thankfully, Sarah has joined our little discussion circle about recent happenings, though her presence is only minimally comforting. She's so damn chipper, and while it's surely all for show, I can't help but find it mildly nauseating to hear. Hysterical to watch, but when the rest eat it up, a gag reflex tries to fight its way forward.

Real conversation trickles in and there's mention of more soldiers and police working together. Their uniforms blur the line of jurisdictions and my attention perks up. Trying to not seem too eager, I amicably agree to each point the speakers have to offer. Just when details are oozing out more fluidly, and a question to pose is at the tip of my tongue, we are called to attention.

"Thank you! Thank you all for today!" Jacob bellows.

Thank you for putting an end to this torture.

"That's all for today. You're free to go home, or if you'd like to stay and mingle more, you certainly can."

I immediately start to step toward the exit when a hand grasps my arm.

"Hey! Want to grab lunch?"

"Sure!"

Not really. Sarah isn't bad, but we're work friends and I'm tired of work today. She's in the good graces of the editors, and sometimes there's the wonder of how good the graces are. Questioning whether she's a resource for them in a capacity beyond her writing. With my recent reassignment of topics, it'd be preferable if that were an option. Maybe she can put in a good word.

We head out to the hippest new cafe that she swears has a lunch worth its weight in gold. She's visibly teeming with excitement, salivating at the thought of what could be devoured upon her future plate. Lunchtime chatter filled with surface conversations. She only knows work me from the office, and I'm content keeping things that way, though she is relentless to try and find deeper details.

"So, what have you been up to? What's new?" she pries.

"Not much, really. How about you?"

"Well, you know Luke and I bought that house."

"Oh, yea, that's right."

"We're going to rip out the whole kitchen!"

"Isn't it new?"

"Yes, technically, but it looks so wild. The colors are almost primal!"

"Oh, I didn't realize. So, what colors are wild, exactly?"

"They're hideous! Reds and oranges with greens and yellows. Looks damn right tribal."

"Oh."

"Can't cook in a place that feels so primitive."

There's no response I can utter without it being insulting. Even coy sarcasm would come out cutting. I'm always happy when there's food involved during cringe conversations so I can shove my face —fewer words escape.

"I could rant forever! I'll spare you, though! Come on, anything exciting in your life?"

I want to say that my friend is still missing, and my other friends are searching how to leave. I could say that Elijah has been distant, filling his schedule with more club meetings than clubs I can recall his membership. Interactions are on auto pilot when conversations turn serious or if they're connected to current events. It's been too long since I've seen my mom, with checkpoints making any travel increasingly slower, dragging out an already long drive. Instead, it's better to offer up meager details.

"Um ... still keeping up with community work, when I can."

"Wow, you're a saint! Living and breathing before me!"

"That might be a bit much."

"No, seriously! Still helping all those who can't figure out how to pull themselves up. Truly a blessing you offer."

"Something like that. And then I've read some new books,

and I'm writing articles, as always."

"Oh yes, congratulations! Celebrity pieces are so desirable! Lucky, lucky."

"Yea, I'm not sure how I feel about it. Seems a little like low-hanging fruit, don't you think? I'd rather be looking into more tangible things, like the rumors of capital cities locking down on top of the curfews they're starting toni—"

"No! Not at all! You'll be so good at it. Besides, it's better than stressing about everything else."

"I'll still be stressing about everything. Just now I won't be able to try to fix it as a journalist. Besides, aren't you concerned the city will lockdown if they feel the curfews aren't enough? No one in or out without approved papers? What will that mean for everyone?"

"Come on, now. Don't be so serious! It won't be so bad. The celebrity pieces, that is. The lockdown stuff—I don't know if it'll all come to that, but if by some crazy chance your rumor has legs, then it must be for our safety. Like the curfews."

"Safety? You really think it's all for our good?"

"Of course! Why else? Don't you?"

She's inquisitively hoping to unearth more about the woman sitting across from her at this table while uncomfortably only crumbs are dispensed, and nothing more. No one should be this curious, especially when all I've seen from her appears compliant, but possibly she's the queen of gossip and misdirection. Snarky under her breath, with quips away from bosses' ears. Relatable bridges that lead to nowhere. Questioning her depth and intention that's all too poised and too perfect to know more. A friendly-foreward bout until the check comes, and we part until another day, when she'll predictably pick up where the conversation left off, always asking.

While my body walks home, I exist mainly in my thoughts. Hating this job and despising that they've made it this way. Something that once held my heart and fury; now, in restricted binds, holding nothing but resentment. Knowing other plausible employment options don't exist at the same pay grade without substantially falling back for a few years, I stay. The requirement to keep writing because food is a necessity, rent is due, and bills will keep coming.

Passing military and police in homogenous uniforms, posted at street intersections stands as a reminder of stories yet to be told, however unlikely to be unearthed in public journalism. An occasional buzz heard high in the sky looking for disturbances, as if the street cameras and armed presence weren't enough. They must be worried people won't respect the first curfew tonight. Convictions tempting to free myself, but obligations hold on tight, pulling down any fleeting thoughts. One foot in front of the other, trudging through wet sand.

Chapter Twelve
Crossroads

Then
<u>October 20, 2046:</u>

There is still no sign of them. Everyone is exhausted, deliriously continuing to look. Turning over rocks that have already been turned over twice. The police are tired of my weekly calls, and have been for quite some time. No novel news. No updates. Anthony has been plucked from society as if he were never a part of it. His existence wiped clean. The authorities are content with his file gathering dust.

At the sound of the phone being placed upon the countertop, Elijah is chomping at the bit to add his thoughts to the one-sided conversation he'd eavesdropped upon. Things have already been tense, and are only growing progressively tenser. The strike of a match would be hazardous in this tinderbox. He can't resist, though.

"Still no news?" he prods.

"No."

"Not surprised. Maybe the weekly calls aren't necessary."

"What do you mean?"

"Just that if there haven't been any updates every week for months now, a weekly call may be unnecessary. It may come off annoying."

"I don't care if it's annoying. It's their job," I retort.

"They're busy. I'm sure they have a lot on their plates."

"Yea, I'm sure. Between rounding up 'deplorables' and sweeping for infractions, I'm sure their plates are overflowing."

"Come on, it's not like that."

"Isn't it? You've seen things changing. You've heard the stories."

"I've heard the rumors. And, I don't know, maybe some of the changes haven't been so bad."

"You've got to be kidding me!"

"Maybe some things are for the better. Homeless people can get jobs now, through their programs."

I can't help but scoff, shoving my hands up. He can't be serious, but there's no smirk anywhere near his face. So quick to dismiss blame.

"Have you seen any of them employed? Anyone actually come out of there with gainful employment?"

"I'm not the one keeping track of it."

"Of course not. They want you to believe their program works! They want you to buy a narrative for reform when you'll never follow up. It's all a lie. They never planned to employ them!"

"That's a bit much! Sounds delusional. Have you lost it?"

"No—you know it's gotten worse! Everything has gotten worse, and it's only going to continue to get worse! Especially after the upcoming inauguration anniversary!"

"Don't be hysterical! You think they're all out to make your life miserable."

"They already have! And they plan to make it worse. You've heard what plans are suspected to come down the pipeline. How could you not care when it's already impacting us, and Dani, and Sam, and Anthony?"

Words clash and conversation descends, spiraling out of control. Voices escalate, and points to be made ricochet off of one another so rapidly that anyone watching would get whiplash. To be viciously fighting in a tornado, flailing, and swinging in conviction. Thoughts spinning, words spewing—things that cannot be unsaid.

Early on in our relationship, I became aware of Elijah's apathy and privilege. Never under the impression that he was as empathetic as I would have liked, but even this was far beneath what could have been expected. Layers of costumes shedding, peeling, flaking, dropping; revealing a core hidden within that I can't unsee. *Has he always been this way? Was he only kind when it was easy?* Caring only to his benefit. Half-hearted advocacy hiding the apathy of his shitty truth.

"They're not all that bad. The cops and military are doing their jobs. Blake is trying to help, even if it's the quiet parts people don't want to say. We can benefit from being on their side."

"Their jobs? How can you defend them?"

My ears no longer completely listening, unable to absorb what this discussion has divulged into, revealing an ugly reality in its wake. Splitting from my functioning brain that has turned off. A subconscious autopilot has taken over still-slinging shots, not to be defeated or stand down. *How can he not care? How can he defend what is happening? How can he be on their side? Their side! Oh, shit.*

My presence is mentally rushed back to the living room in this argument, with Elijah wildly waving his hands, hair flopping, forehead creased, spittle flying. Unhinged, like a wild animal puffing up its chest, looking vicious, leaving onlookers to consider how dangerous it actually is. A jarring sight to see him in this feral state. Words trickle back becoming present. Alarming words that rip me into reality.

"You can't appreciate what they've done! You should be grateful."

Standing there, frozen, absorbing every syllable. Numb from the barrage.

"What? Nothing to say now? Are you just going to stand there?" he badgers onward.

I clear my throat and compose racing thoughts to delicately choose the next words, as the assumed safety here is no longer obvious.

"I am grateful, but that does not mean I cannot be critical. I want the best for everyone at no one's expense."

He seems amused by this. Not necessarily satisfied, but not entirely angered. Chortling, almost. Tempted and desperately clinging to a false memory of identity, I push a bit further: *"You can't possibly be on their side?"*

His face twitches as a nerve is struck. He is with them fully, whether he admits it or not.

"You are lucky to have me. Lucky they haven't done a sweep of this place for suspicious activity or contraband. Would be easy, given your job and all."

He's not feral—he's calculated. Every word intentionally vying for control of the situation. A cat puffing up, daring you to do more.

"What are you saying?"

"What I'm saying is that I'm going to go see Mark, and when I get back, it might be a good idea for all that contraband to be gone."

I can viscerally feel the shift happening under my feet: a tectonic plate of the power structure moving. The antelope becoming painfully aware that a lion is in its enclosure, ready to move. Buying time, accessing what is unfolding, I pitifully ask, *"What do you mean?"*

"You know damn well what I mean! The fuckin' religious books of every flavor! The nude art! The gay flags! Get rid of it—for your own good."

"Are you serious right now? This isn't new."

"I thought it was temporary."

"Temporary?!"

"Yea, I thought, eventually, you'd see things different. I could fix things."

"Nothing needed to be fixed."

"Are you really going to give up what we have for all this?" he asks, questioning our accrued time and implied loyalty.

"What is it that we have?"

"Look, if it's not gone when I get back, I'm calling it in. It's time for this to end, one way or another. Even if I'm not the one to save you, they can."

Standing there, no sound leaves my body in any attempt to protest. Elijah gruffly puts on his black coat and walks outside as the door slams upon existing. A flash of red across the bicep catches my attention but I can't dwell. I'm unable to focus on a fleeting image; a cardinal disappeared into the darkness. Another thought for a different time, separate from this swirling. Janus finally stops grumbling, still standing by my side though it's news to me he ever was.

What just happened? What the fuck just happened? He's on their side! Oh, fuck, what if he instigates a sweep? Makes the call?

A body frozen isn't moving; however, my mind is erratically sprinting, connecting synapses at a ridiculously rapid rate. With a deep exhale, all the loose pieces come together with the focus feature of an automatic camera. Suddenly hyper-aware of standing in my rental unit, a dangerous, belligerent guest having since departed, I look around.

This was my home, but it's now a cage. A trap to ensnare as The Nation falls further. *What now?* It's my rental, not his. I can prohibit him from coming back. End everything. He's angry, and he's different. Those threats keep echoing. *Were they all a bluff said in rage, or is he serious?* If he is, they will swoop in, and I'll be gone too. *He'll make a call.*

As a devastating sadness washes over, the realization deep in my gut—that I can no longer stay at this place—shouts from within. I have to leave. Flee. Run. Somewhere safe and far away. The city will be closed off come tomorrow night's curfew, with lockdown now becoming a sanctioned reality. *Where besides here can we land?*

I'm thrown into motion as my body acts while my mind is still reeling. Checking through the curtains—his car is gone. He said he was going to Mark's and that's outside of downtown. It'll take a bit to get there, maybe thirty minutes. I have at least three hours. He'll have a beer or two, maybe three in his spiteful rant, as they banter.

Not nearly enough time to pack up a life but with no time to waste, I don't wait. Frantically dialing digits, hoping anyone will answer, but the only voices that greet me on the other end of the phone line are the automatic voicemail recordings. No Sam, no Dani, no Mom—no answer to ask if we can come to them. No response to confirm it's safe there. The contemplation of Sarah creeps in, but is just as swiftly washed away. A fanciful option blown away like dust, when it's obvious her complacency would never harbor us. Unsettling feelings of uncertainty make their home in unanswered calls, knowing it's been too long since our last conversations. Their whereabouts as fuzzy as fog, leaving me kicking myself when I need them most.

We have to go. If not to them then somewhere, though, in this moment where is undetermined. The actions remain the same and the scrambling starts. There was always an emergency pack. A go-bag for natural disasters that will do, even though this is not the disaster fathomed. The rental is fortunately tucked away with only alley-way access, and my car is parked closely, as is common with many B units. Loading the emergency bag to the car in this privacy, an appreciation swells for something previously benign. As the pack gets placed on the floor of the passenger seat, hearing the friction between the fabrics squeezing in, the actions of what is happening sinks in with a thunderous reality.

Over the next hour and a half, I make repetitive trips loading up anything in grasp. In and out, in and out—fill every nook. Squeeze it all in. Every ounce of shelf-stable food, clothes, shoes, dog food, a hand crank battery, and more, and more, and more. Packing the car, maximizing the space available, while staying subtle. There will be checkpoints for contraband and refugees. Nothing can raise suspicion or give them reason to prod further. A clever cluster-fuck jammed in that looks boring to anyone peeking. The trunk is full, the floor of the passenger seat is full, and the floor of the back seat is full with blankets on top to cover the items below, while a single duffle bag sits in the back seat. Our life summarized in the contents of the car.

As I look back at the ransacked rental in its disarray, the resemblance of gangly broken bones feel palpable. Awkwardly placed, damaged but reminiscent of a shattered former life. Locking up for the last time, I leave the key under the doormat. No return. Not coming back.

Walking to the car, I put the dog bed in the passenger seat, and gesture for Janus to hop in. Every action comes off obnoxiously obvious. Perhaps paranoia or guilt leaching in, raising questions. Looking around, hyperaware of any curious eyes. No one is looking, or watching but the concern of being monitored is hard to shake.

Time is going by, and I best not push my luck. Driving away, not daring to look back. Fear that some nostalgic feelings will lull us back into a fantasy, clawing at my amygdala. The debate at this point is which roads to take to avoid detection if Elijah sounds the alarm. *When. He'll be back. With others? The locked door will send him into a reactive spiral.*

On the main roads with many other cars bustling by,

creating a cover to blend right in. *There are more eyes.* The remote roads have less peeping people but there are fewer cars. *An unfamiliar traveler could stick out raising attention.* Something in between, if that's possible, would be ideal—whatever that looks like. Stop only when necessary, and be discreet. Getting gas before leaving the city—we'll be able to spread some distance before needing to refuel. It won't be untraceable but hopefully no one will feel motivated to push that far.

Passing by Sam and Dani's house, their lights are off. No one's home. No one to tell or plead. No answers to my questions. A vacant house dismisses my concerns at the curb. Even now, I don't want to leave them. They should know, but I can't stay and wait to tell them. I wish they'd come too, but there's no invitation to extend. *I'm sorry.* Watching the structure fade away in my rear view mirror, a part of me stays behind. Lost in thoughts, the vehicle propels us forward in necessity, refusing to let me drown.

Hours pass in the darkening skies as the sun descends beyond the horizon. Wading through the fog of my brain, I eventually realize how far we've driven. The subliminal going into cruise control though the destination was never consciously confirmed. Familiar signs and landmarks signaling clues. I know where we are and the destination makes sense, even in this fractured evening. Almost twenty hours away, to my vacation rental property. The other me, subconscious me, is not stupid. Elijah has heard of a rental referenced somewhere but in no detail, and he's never been there. We have a long way to go but it's a relatively easy drive if you know the way.

"You doin' good, bubby?"

Janus snores, completely passed out, comfortable in the passenger seat, unconcerned with the ride. With a loose concept of a plan my heart is allowed to slow a beat or two. The regular checkpoints that inevitably no longer seem daunting. We're going camping. Meeting with family, and going camping. There's nothing forbidden about that yet. As jitters stabilize, mental control submits to mental fatigue, and a steadying the hand guides the way toward a future never imagined until today.

Chapter Thirteen
Intuition

Then
<u>October 22, 2046:</u>

Knowing without knowledge. Conviction without clear cause. Something inside stirs from unknown sources for no apparent reason. We've been taught to ignore and push these feelings away. Discredit their value as nothing more than coincidence. Shrug off silly notions, all in our head, that make you feel special. Dispose of useless whispers—*but why, then, do they linger?*

Reduced to a laughable footnote not worth acknowledging, and yet they don't let go. A nagging tug, like a thread too thin to notice with some invisible force pulling on the other end. Hints to look this way for what you must see. Nudges to walk this path, opposed to another, for what awaits. Before you go, make sure to do X, Y, and Z because future you needs past you to take these actions.

Choices full of conviction, and determinate knowledge founded on hunches. Appearing downright delusional to anyone not seeing the same signs. To anyone not privy to the insider secrets, it's laughable. To anyone not aware of invisible forces guiding us for survival, it's lunacy. It's understandable why they wouldn't believe, but right now we can't afford to not.

Actions made defying logic or leaping to connections. Skeptical onlookers don't understand, and even undercut the thought, ready with skepticism and jeers. What pulls me is not for them. In that moment, reassuring voices are audible, if only inside my body. With my whole presence, I am right—undeniably, accurately, critically correct, regardless of the lacking concrete evidence. Let this gut feeling guide on a blind path in the dark as I dutifully follow. Directing away from danger and into safety. Lean in to survive.

It's no different than the deer that smells a change in the

wind, ousting a hunter yet to be seen. Something but nothing is there. A whiff of concern faintly dances through, almost entirely unnoticeable in a moment. *Why am I crazy, but the deer is not?* Listening more closely to what is not said. Heeding the warning, it lives another day. They call it instinct; I call it intuition. We both get to see tomorrow.

Chapter Fourteen
No Trace

Then
<u>October 23, 2046:</u>

Even if I can assume that no one knows of this place or presence that's no guarantee to rely on. Nothing to indicate otherwise to any happenstance onlookers. No red flags for anyone searching. No clues for anyone curious. I was never here. You can leave now.

There's a story about children venturing deep in a forest who leave a trail of little breadcrumbs to mark their way for fear they will get lost. They can follow the carbs on their way out. How stupid is their logic, with no concern that a passing creature would gobble them up. Their fear of getting lost is my fear of being found.

As I pull into the dirt road that leads to the rental, the car only goes halfway up before pulling off the road and tucking in behind a boulder near some fallen trees. There must have been a recent storm, fracturing trunks and toppling branches. We're lucky to have no early snow at this altitude, at this time of year. The ground is hard with no tracks to cover.

Looking at everything in the car, an urge swells to empty it as quickly as possible, before the sun falls behind the next ridge over, but this will be a task in trips. Grabbing the pack, duffle bag, and dog bed, we head toward the treehouse. It is our host, and we are nervous guests. A long moment since we've seen one another but we're so eager for this reconnection. Instead of bringing a casserole, all our hands carry are the remaining worldly possessions in tow.

There she is, waiting for us. Stoically standing amongst the trees, welcoming us with open arms. Omniscient—ready for our arrival. Standing taller, a stronger force, not to be underestimated in the playfulness of her appearance. A reunion of sorts. A funny story we'll laugh about one day. Not today, though. Right now, it's all business, but she reassures us that's alright.

I set the luggage on the wooden platform with its pulley system, and we head up the spiral stairs. With each step, a little pang stabs my heart. I love these stairs. They look like tree branches and vines made something architectural, growing from the sky to the earth. Beautiful where they stand, they are a novelty, and we can't risk anyone becoming intrigued. They'll have to go and it makes my soul ache. *Why must good things not be allowed to last?*

Inside, as feet step through the threshold, we're transported away from all the gnawing haunts left in Austin. Everything looks spotless and in its place, completely unaware of what is happening. A quaint dinner party in the Keys while a Cat 5 hurricane barrels down. It's almost startling at first glance. As my eyes glide over these surroundings, soaking it all in, they ultimately resolve it's a good thing.

Something familiar to numb the pain of this new life. A little less shock is welcomed even if the mundaneness was itself initially disorientating. Janus could care less. He remembers, and it is immediately joyous inside his canine cortex. Rooting around in all the old smells left for another day: today. While he is happily content exploring the crevices of the treehouse, I bring in the luggage after pulling it up and then head back for the rest. It's actually a bit sad when there are so few trips necessary. The car felt so full. Packed to the brim. But the platform only needed three hauls, which probably could have been condensed. It's a big platform. *No, it's a small carload.*

All loaded in, the car sits there, staring back where it was left. In the forest, it looks odd and incongruent. Raising eyebrows when I need them to stay lateral and bored. The boulder obscures it from the main road, even if it's doubtful anyone's eyes can see that far. Paranoia shows, demanding the chance glint of reflection to be blocked. Scanning the surroundings, there's fallen branches nearby. This will work well enough, as long as I can drag and place them in an inconspicuous way. *Clearly, it just so happened to fall that way and conveniently hide a car. Is it obvious? No.* It's a pine with the big, fluffy branches obscuring more space. Awkwardly rotate the dense evergreen into position. Predominantly covered in camouflage, a small sense of relief comes through at the sight of what is hopefully good enough.

The road, however, is still there. It doesn't extend all the way to the treehouse so guests were able to be surrounded in nature without a reminder of the society they left for a little while. The obvious human portion that stands out in its solid shape amongst the trees needs to be unrecognizably splintered. Erratically, I push dirt from the path off of it, and pull dirt from outside on-to it. Scattering debris across to disrupt the linear pathway. Sticks, leaves, etc., erasing the gravel road, leaving only a resemblance of something from a long-gone time. Gazing at the veil separating our space from the outside like a two-way mirror. We're in the watching room while they're in the tank.

Inside with assessment, everything is simultaneously pleasing and horrifying. Our stock is substantial, and the space is secure as well as comforting, but this is it. This is everything. The stark newness in high contrast to a week ago dials into full focus, forming a divide in my mind of my existence. Everything feels marked as before or after these moments. A time stamp for all future references.

The furnishings and fillings of an accidental home. In absorbing the details, a mirror adjacent catches my reflection. It's startling how familiar I still look, and not like a woman who fled hours to disappear here, all off a feeling and a fight. Appearing content, almost satisfied but certainly not unhinged. I look like me. A slow revelation that the previous existence was crumbling, and part of me died there.

Startlingly swift, a jarring thought jumps from my eyes. The danger of being a young woman here, and now. Looking like a young woman who's alone in the woods during a misogynistic revival will only attract bad news. Riffling through various drawers, eventually in the desk I find a pair of craft scissors.

Androgynous and bland is the goal. Basic is best when unique can be dangerous. Slowly starting, the first snip is holds the most resistance. My hair has always been long but this is what the situation calls for. *I can't deny what's required.* With each cut, a sense of emboldened resistance reclaims some power in these fragile moments. Solemnly serious, a little smile creeps in at the ridiculousness of what I am doing. A weight cut, and a cloak donned. Reminiscent of an ambiguous boy band member, smirking in the mirror, reveling a little in accomplishing this silly incognito aesthetic that isn't half bad. I see a stranger I've always known.

Finally, I can sit. After a long journey in the car, sitting all those miles, and yet nothing sounds better than sitting in this moment. Janus is ready for his dinner, and I'm famished for mine. While the kibble vanishes almost as fast as it was dropped in, water in the kettle begins to heat on the wood-burning stove. Just enough for the MRE, and then the log can dwindle down. A cuban-beans-and-rice dish of sorts from a plastic bag never tasted so good. It washes away the guilt of leaving everyone and everything behind. Validates the insanity I know to be sane. It reassures the choices made in prevention for what I'm sure is to come.

While concerns of the possible dominoes that have been tripped won't subside, I remind myself that it no longer matters. Here we are in this cozy refuge. We are fed. We are safe. We are granted a moment of solace, and that is enough. As the sun fully sets, the threads tied to my old life fall away. Drifting into a dreamland, I lay comfortably with Janus, suspended beyond worry for a moment.

Chapter Fifteen
A New Day

Then
<u>November 5, 2046:</u>

Sun glowing through the windows, Janus is already stirring—and, consequently, I am too. His wakeup call is my alarm. With a big stretch on both parts, we step foot onto the chilly floor, getting ready for the new morning routine.

It was maybe a day or two before we realized going up and down the pulley system first thing in the morning for Janus was not ideal, so a makeshift potty patch was an immediate quick fix. Dirt and a layer of soil with grass attached in a large baking pan on the back portion of the deck. Ingenuity for the win, even if a baking pan is sacrificed! A shame of a loss that the spiral stair had to go, but they created a risk not worth taking. All that remains are four or five steps dangling off the front of the deck.

Today, after a breakfast of oatmeal and dog food, we'll spend our day organizing, scavenging, and making plans. Just before we arrived at the treehouse, we stopped at a pet store and purchased four, large dog food bags with long expirations using a gift card. It won't be a forever solution to feed Janus, but it will delay the hurdle of sourcing food, ensuring his diet is balanced and he is full. Eventually alternative options will need to be explored, but for now the bags are sitting on the floor, taking up so much space in the form of a tripping hazard with a need of being stored elsewhere. *Under the sink or on the floor of the closet? Neatly tucked away.*

My food has been organized in the cabinets and along the countertop. Like item by like item, stocked as you'd see on the shelves of a store. Items expiring soonest toward the front and moving backwards, with an accompanying list cataloguing it all. Quantities of each item and, with each use, a pencil mark erased then updated. I can't afford to be caught off guard and losing track. Lots of dried goods, grains, pasta, canned items, a few spices, some snacks, and MREs. Ideally, the MREs would be left for times of real need, coming in clutch as a reliable resource when nothing else would deliver.

It has been a little while since there were renters, so everything is tidy. Formerly, I would approve all vacation rental requests, and after they left, a cleaner in the area would come to reset the space. No requests in weeks prior to my departure. People didn't have the funds to vacation. Everything had been so slow, I had recently put a hold on bookings, debating its future. A loose plan was to come up around Christmas for a little stay, and maybe make some updates or revamp. Maybe even bring Elijah. *Well, part of that came true.*

After breakfast, dishes, and mild organizing inside, it would be beneficial to take stock and access anything of value. If recollection is correct, there's a small ski town not too far from here, maybe ten to twelve miles. Memories conjure images of a place that was tiny and not glamorous. Those visiting elite ski slopes in the range would sometimes pop in but never stayed long. Let's say it wasn't nice enough for their discerning taste. More of a locals-only location. Rumor has it that small isolated towns like it have "regressed" to reinvented trading posts where items have as much value as money and questions aren't asked. I decide to go through our items, searching for something worth exchanging.

Regardless of The Nation, some things never change. Metals and gems always have some value. With no use for the jewelry, and a willingness to part with them all besides a ring from my grandmother, it seems like a waste to keep. Besides, the rest came predominantly from Elijah or myself. As a snake sheds its skin that no longer fits, the jewelry can go.

Looking through clothing items to possibly offload, there's a hesitancy to rid too much, swept up in this purging energy. I peruse through the books on the shelves to see if there are any to part with. A few classics and a couple on alternative medicine. Surprisingly, books still have some secret allure, and that equals worth, so finding a few worth parting with seems advisable. My binder of seeds is not up for consideration, even though I know they're deeply desired. A hold-over of good seeds from past gardens still have value, even to us. While I don't have any cigarettes, there is a bottle of tequila and a bar of chocolate. Both considered a luxury because of their rarity, and their cost can fetch something nice. Everything else is too valuable and necessary to part with.

Gathering the items to bring to the potential trading table, I wrap them up in a cloth to put them in my pack. Cushion prevents them from breaking or creating too much racket. The journey is too far for today. Sometime soon though, when we can set out early and be back before dark. People are still driving, but not in a car that someone may be looking for. It's best for us to walk through the forest, deep in the tree line, beyond the eyesight of anyone on the road, only popping out in the proximity of the small ski town.

I dress in warm clothing as we get ready to step out. A snack of a lunch first, but before long clothes are bundled to be comfortable during the chill. Together we kneel upon the platform and pulley our way to the ground. The goals of this excursion are to find and harvest edible sources, plant some rogue gardens, and get a better understanding of all that's around.

An abundance of wild edible plants exist in the region, though not as neatly labeled as a supermarket. I've brought a small notebook to loosely map where any finds may be in relation to the treehouse. Hoping to avoid the possibility of a delectable score disappearing because of lack of bearings the next time we look. There's watercress by the stream, and blackberries hanging onto the vine. I find some wild onions but only take the stalk, as the bulbs are so tiny they're not worth it. It's better to just let them grow back, as they quickly will. There are acorns that can be milled down. The milled acorn can be used as flour or a thickener in soup and they're full of protein and fiber. Remembering that in a novel I read somewhere, hoping it's true. We continue to search and gather what we can. All those nature walks with Mom as she had spewed out foraging details like a hydrant—now I wish I could recall more than the minimum that stuck. Tidbits of useful details hopefully revealing, more still buried in memories, if the words were actually absorbed.

Fantastic finds are overshadowed due to the season and it feels dire. Summer foraging will have more to offer, but now everything is starting to go dormant. Hibernation that even impacts the plants. Salivating at the thought to one day find asparagus, and mushrooms, and prickly pear, but it's entirely the wrong season. Comparison creates disappointment in what's been found. Foraging isn't easy. Gems hidden deep in the earth's resources are not made obvious, and even when you do find them, that's it. Accept what's offered, regardless if you'd rather a different ingredient. Even if you like this ingredient, you can't take too much. Over harvesting will damage the plant, and that stress could kill it. Stay at thirty percent or less; otherwise, future you will be fucked.

While there are plenty of pantry items, the plan is to keep them as a reserve, not the primary resource, and instead tell myself there is gardening. Some plants may not be native or wild here, but they will grow with the seeds. Potatoes, radish, kale, cabbage, brussels sprouts could work. I don't know if the soil type or pH is ideal but it will have to do. At select locations that seem favorable and discrete, I unleash my rogue gardening. Chaotic and wild with no real structure. A vague round shape roughly between two to three feet across, and irregular in portions; unearthing a few inches of soil to plant a mixture of seeds. Not solely one crop left to stand alone but a myriad vegetable community to thrive and hide together. Re-cover with soil and then a scattering of leaves. Anyone passing by wouldn't notice or would see only green, but not a garden. Looking at the little spot that holds so much hope, knowing there will be critters who take their share, but that is the cost of doing business. I'm not the only one trying to survive.

This is an investment. A bet on tomorrow. Some seeds will begin to sprout within a week, and will be ready for harvest shortly after. Others, like potatoes, will grow all winter long while I wait for their starches. They move along at their own pace, impervious to urging for expedition. A timeline is not contingent upon me left to wait and nervously hope they do deliver. Optimistic that this gamble pays off.

As we're exploring, and Janus is investigating all the good smells, I notice there are several interesting geological features. Natural hidden spots to hide your secrets. Nooks between rock enclaves. Empty knots in a tree trunk. A vacancy willing to contribute. Reminiscent thoughts of an old show we used to watch, where people would pretend to survive together as a community of strangers, and sometimes rewards or advantages would be hidden in spots like this. We used to always point out random spots in nature when we'd see them and think, '*Oh this would be perfect to hide an advantage!*' Never thought a fake reality survival show would contribute to my actual reality. It may be a good idea to create a few caches and stash them in places like this, just in case we need them. No obvious hidden spots in case anyone else also watched the same reality show and thought the same.

    The sun is starting to set, and once it gets behind the ridge-line, darkness will descend quickly. The sky is already showing hues of pink, indicating we should head back. I quietly signal to Janus as we make our way through rustling foliage, and along the way obsessively make meticulous plans, running through theoretical options for another day. There's so much to do for tomorrow, and next week, and next month. Survival may be a lazy concoction of conserving energy, but setting up a foundation to survive is anything but idle.

Chapter Sixteen
Ancients

Then
<u>November 18, 2046:</u>

Almost every night, the sky lights up with star clusters putting on a display. Dancing across the horizon, performing an entrancing exhibition. There's Orion and Andromeda. Taurus the bull is over there, while the bear stands aside. Visible hints of Electra, and her six sisters.

Legends passed on from generation to generation. Stories we repeat that never grow old. Tales that shape our subliminal views and outlook on values and people. A great man was killed by a scorpion but the man's colleagues were so upset they killed the scorpion. To make sure they never fought again—they'd never be seen in the night sky together. Uncompromising, and inimical resolve. *Talk about an inability to move on from a spiteful grudge.*

Then there is the story of a beautiful woman. A daughter of royalty with parents who wouldn't shut up about it. So much so that another woman became insanely jealous, and in begging her father to do something, he sent a sea monster. The sea monster was destroying the coast of the kingdom belonging to the beautiful woman's family, so her father (the king) chained his daughter by the sea as sacrifice to the monster. She was not without hope because a dashing young man stumbled upon her. After making a deal he was able to defeat the sea monster and marry the beautiful woman as part of the bargain. *Women as commodity: a tale as old as time.*

Oh, and there's the one about the tree with golden apples. A powerful man gave his wife a tree that would produce golden apples. Luscious, rare fruit that was all for her. While more than she could ever need or want, it was hers, and no one else's. To make sure that no one stole any of the golden apples, she had the tree privately guarded by two fierce beings. Many were slain during attempts to steal the bounty or redistribute the spoils. *The rich and powerful always hold on tightly to their wealth and stature in lieu of the concept of sharing.*

Don't forget about the king who once made a powerful being very angry. He was almost killed, but the powerful being was convinced to keep him alive. He obliged, and did so by transforming the king into the form of a golden eagle. Better yet, this golden eagle was to be the personal messenger for this powerful being, and so he lived out his life, completing tasks in captivity under his will. *When death isn't an option, enslavement is available when those who control are all-powerful.*

Lastly, perhaps most tragically, there's the story of a gorgeous woman who was a hunting companion to a male friend. While out one day, a different man became smitten with her—absolutely obsessed and determined to have her. Relentless, ignoring her refusals to acknowledge his advances, he stole her away with details a bit blurry only to then transform her into a bear. She had a child, and then was released to the wild while still in bear form. A new freedom wasn't met, though, as she was hunted down as a trophy. Some say it was by her old hunting companion friend, none the wiser. *A common notion of consequences when men can't handle "no" and feel entitled to so much more.*

These stories are watered down and told to children. Diluted and relayed for the right audience. Sanitized to be digested. But the underlying, unsettling message and content still simmer just below the words. You grow up and likely never revisit the stories hiding lessons written in the stars. Gawking at their pretty form, never thinking what's behind that pretty glow. *Who would have thought ancient myths would still be relevant?* They've stayed with me somewhere deep in my cerebellum. Sunk in, morphing the code of my life. Creating a paranoid edge from the start for no apparent reason. Astutely aware of what can lurk in people. Apparently not much has changed in thousands of years.

Chapter Seventeen
A Growing Ebullition

Now
<u>January 20, 2047:</u>

I wonder which would be worse: to have my theories burst as delusional, paranoid ramblings, or for them to have been prophetic truths. Noticing the crumbs mixed with historic precedence, just in time to string together a theory. A prediction that was unbelievable to anyone unwilling or unable to see. Unfathomable to anyone who refused to jump on the cuckoo train, chugging along to what they were sure would be a plummet in the gorge. They were weary to step anywhere near those tracks.

Believe it now? I wish in some ways I could say that to them, but it feels overtly spiteful. Wish they would have listened or simply obliged. *Did everyone think I was crazy? Doubt it now.*

Today is the two-year anniversary of the inauguration of Blake, and the hand-crank radio is on, humming lowly with news. Sitting here, fiddling, waiting for his speech, anxious for what's next. The pressure multiplies with the desire to hear the words fall from his mouth, confirming my suspicions. People can't deny what oozes out, frothing his own lips.

Everything has intensified, and if you weren't watching the slow burn then seemingly, suddenly, all dials have been cranked up. Local city police have become a hybrid military concoction taking the training beyond only lessons to systemic actions. A solid unit for a common cause under a single command. They're no longer exclusively arresting violators they notice, or if an incident was to happen in view. Now there are door-to-door raids, spurred from calls of suspicion or lack of visible patriotism and loyalty. Your presence from daily life to online posts is brought into consideration, and can be enough for The Nation to question a person's ethics, loyalty, and quality. Even the slightest deviance can be enough to justify a warrant. Demands to appear as their ideal mold, and there's no reason to worry, but differences could result in detainment. Incongruence is dangerous. After all, it's all for the safety of The Nation.

The quantity of military woven within the cities grew rapidly once a casual amount had been quietly integrated initially. A few at first, received benignly. Enough to assist but that was all. As the cities and police claimed they were under-manned and under-funded, The Nation was happy to oblige and send more soldiers. Slowly, more and more trickled in. An alarming presence to many, but easily dismissible as additional so-called safety measures accumulated, presenting proportional growth. It was for your safety, and local authorities requested them, anyway. Before long they were roaming neighborhoods with an increasingly present watchful eye. Rumors of unprovoked raids and arrests spread, but most people chalked them up to just that: rumors.

It was bound to grow. In the months since November, they'd descended upon cities like a swam of locust decimation following alongside. One day they appear, and everywhere you look there's yet another armed guard. Overnight, a pest embedded, and these ones bite with guns, batons, and black bags. Overall, a hush seemed to fall over the inhabitants, realizing it may not be wise to be loud. Everyone holding their breath. Fall in line.

The supposed problems never aligned with the agenda. Margins for tolerance shrank, as anything else would mean imposition of deplorable attributes upon saintly ways. Religious relics outside of state-sanctioned Christianity removed, banned media in any forms—LGBTQ+ paraphernalia or association was an affront, and anything critical of The Nation or Blake was "anti" and deemed terroristic. Generally speaking, anything deemed deplorable or dissenting was considered a treacherous threat to The Nation. It all had to go. Actively investigating to purge. Hidden rooms, faux book covers, hidey-holes became more prevalent but were often discovered. Their efforts would surely expand without the confinements.

Violators were to be rehabilitated under the guidance of The Nation. If someone hadn't already been prescribed to attend one of the many facilities The Nation had to offer in assistance of producing quality citizens, then a violation would be a straight-shot ticket. The list of ailments The Nation wishes to cure grows daily. Before long, most stand a better chance of being broken than not. Nasty women made pleasant; all smiley and sweet. Gay thoughts eradicated. A love for all things meat, red-blooded, and masculine reinstated. Whatever your problem—fixed! Any stain on society would be made clean. It's not only through classes and memorization, but also through manual labor in the fields, mines, and factories, ensuring the engine of The Nation could keep churning. Hoping for the day those 'saved' would eventually be released anew, yet oddly there seem to be so few who make it to graduation. They don't like to waste too much time and skim over the missing, as the engines churn onwards.

What started as subtle is now overt. They're saying the quiet parts out loud. Unabashedly transparent with masses cheering them on gleefully, gobbling up lies as warped truths. Never looking behind the curtain.

Sit and wait while nervous taps escape my limbs. Listening to the updates, the ads for this program or that, and the approved music, all of which sounds eerily the same. A creepy, chipper female voice that's almost robotic singing along to peppy vintage sounds, or a deep, husky baritone man crooning to slow acoustics. Silence would be preferred but I don't want to miss anything. Abruptly, after the last tune came to a close, an announcer pops on the air, giddy with patriotic pride, fangirling for our president about to speak.

"Thank you, thank you! It is a great honor to address you all on this marvelous day! Citizens, I see your commitment to restore our nation to the greatness it once was. With you and God, it is possible, and we have set forth upon a path of righteousness to remedy all the wrongs previously ingrained in society. Together we have sought out the stains, and are wiping them clean. Removing the plagues once scourging our communities.

We have a sacred duty. A covenant to the convictions of hope, purity, and unity this sovereign land was founded upon, and is continuing to uphold. It is possible to restore our values: to celebrate traditional marriage in faith, to biologically create a family, to put in a good day's work that is the backbone of our being.

I challenge all citizens to take a daily stock, and ask themselves: 'What more can I do for my nation and fellow man?' Keep vigilant eyes for dissidents. Open ears for those not contributing, not abiding as you are. Sharp wits as armor against those who would tempt you with charms.

The Nation has your interests always at the forefront of policy, and with every step forward, we are unafraid of the best solution for our people. Now, not all will agree with every decision, and that is alright. Not everyone is willing to sacrifice for you. Not everyone is ready to part with evil ways. Not everyone can see the vision for our future!

However, you, our loyal, patriotic citizens, will be granted a heavenly future as the promise is near! I have seen your struggle and strife. No more! We take back our power. We take back what is ours. The dream will be yours! Today we celebrate this great, powerful nation, and tomorrow we fight! Thank you all for your continued support, and God bless The Nation."

While the radio returns to the host gleefully proclaiming his praise for Blake's speech before transitioning to more approved music, I hear nothing but echoes of his words reverberating in my ears. They irritatingly refuse to leave, having made their home, hooked deep in the cochlea. Receptively resounding a haunting transmission I cannot shake. A warning clear as day of the squalls forming in the distance.

Chapter Eighteen
New Adjacent

Now
<u>July 30, 2047</u>:

No day is new, more or less. Each day feels vaguely familiar, with a repetitive agenda loosely carved out. Nothing truly set in stone. We've been here before. No guarantees as for how the day will play out, with unexpected occurrences waiting to make an appearance when least predicted. A boring set of tasks potentially derailed. Every morning dreaming of a boring day full of simple wins and little disruption. Every moment wishing the peace of those seconds could stay. Pause the good and deny acknowledgment of what looms around any unforeseen bend. Let us enjoy the rustle of leaves without concern that the sound came from anything but a bluster.

It's exhausting, always being on edge. My mind and body only ever half-snooze, like a dolphin, always slightly aware just in case. Alerts sounded and guards raised, never to be fully dismissed, even when there is no apparent reason for them to be armed. A constant disruption to the cognitive system has become my daily reckoning. A regular emotional interruption while attempting to come to terms with understanding this existence, while making amends that nothing feels the same.

Even the daily tasks somehow feel different—new but just adjacent. Almost déjà vu as if we're all living in an upside-down world paralleling what was once familiar. Making oatmeal isn't just making oatmeal. It's creating sustenance that's high in calories, that keeps you full, that's nutritious; it can stretch when little is left and is able to be altered so that it doesn't become too redundant. Never did I ever think I would give so much thought to a rather dull, goopy meal that I once disliked. Never did I ever think I would be rationing out meals to ensure there was enough, in case it wasn't possible to obtain more if The Nation tightened its grip or expanded its watch. Small things have become exponentially consequential.

Moments linger during inaction, and I no longer take these for granted. In the old days it was always hard to sit idly as the clock ticked by when schedules weren't filled. Empty time felt like a waste. As if when it wasn't occupied, I wasn't doing enough, achieving enough, being enough. Now doing nothing means enough has been prepared to be able to do nothing. Ironically, as the person who used to never be able to sit still for much of an extended period, I now yearn for spans of time with nothing calling, but the luxury to sit still. Survival in some ways is mundane, and in the moments of mundane nothingness a calmness washes over that feels temporary.

Shaky satisfaction in small, quiet moments, afraid it's going to fall away. Peeling layers, taking with it any shred of good and sanity. Bark flaking away exposing a fragile interior. Walking a high wire between calm and chaos is my daily task. A rambunctious applause from below collectively whispering *"Will she fall or will she make it?"* The ruckus noise I can audibly hear in my mind becomes the radio crackle Janus can ascertain too.

There are announcements and updates that come across the broadcast, which is dutifully listened to at least daily. Some are nothing more than trivial notes, or progressions of events already discussed, but sometimes there's something new. A myriad of headlines spanning from shocking to expected. The wars rage on as Blake attempts to forcibly take Taiwan, which looped in China, which looped in other South Asian countries to the fight. The wars in the Middle East continue per usual, as The Nation always finds business to be involved in over there. The cost of goods has reached exuberant levels regardless of prior political promises. Eggs, milk, and bread have all tripled in expense.

Of course, there are store credits, but no debt is free. A day will come when it's due, and they will retrieve any way necessary if you read the fine print. Patriotism is a full-time commitment, between reporting neighbors for infringements, participating in Quality Citizen activities, and advancing one's life in the pre-approved ways.

Wildfires rage in the southwest as the timber and

tumbleweeds light up like kindling. A scorched earth washed away in thunderous storms. Crops planted annihilated, and hope of planting more gone with the good topsoil that left with the fast-moving floods. Military and police sweeps have increased and gained wide success, cheered on by those not swept up.

A hive of terrorists to The Nation exposed and captured, many of which were former journalists—however; none with a degree from The Nation's Academy. As if this all weren't enough, the crackly voice across the waves mention technological advancements assisting The Nation in matters of national security. They stop just shy of any specifics, leaving me to theorize while not spiraling, to which the crowd roars. I can hear their supportive claps on bated breath.

Daily updates are a necessity. Woodland creatures may surround us but this isn't a fairy tale, and none of them are singing any messages. Gathering information about what is happening beyond the pines is vital, even though the desire to duck my head deep in the sand is alluring. If I know then there are all the factors to dwell upon. Without knowledge then we're left blissfully vulnerable in ignorant ambiguity. Ignoring events doesn't absolve us from their ramifications. Even the thought of possibly being caught off guard creates a nauseous tension swelling inside. Listening and learning adds to the sensation. The perpetual cycle that could theoretically plateau, much like the infinity knot my anxious hands finish tying while bundling herbs.

A dreamy thought that one day this pressure could melt away, leaving behind only the moments without worry. Mundane, boring moments with nothing but time. The fantasy of a world where the radio isn't a harbinger of brewing danger seems to reside only in the far-off thoughts of my mind. A day to wish for but dare not hope. The amused crowd carefully watches, entertained, and places their bets.

Chapter Nineteen
Quest

Now
<u>September 20, 2047:</u>

These mountains and valleys hold secrets nestled in their nooks that can go unnoticed unless someone is really looking. Actively searching out what doesn't want to be found. Janus and I take it upon ourselves to attempt to learn as much as we can about this place. Nothing can be taken for granted or assumed to fall into any neat category existing without consequences.

We set out with our topographic map, compass, and binoculars unearthed from the hiking pack occasionally put to use to gain a better understanding of areas yet to be charted. Neighbors from the old days have shown no sign of existing. I can only hope that we're as unnoticed as they are. It's tempting to go take a peek, and see if there's any sign of them. We weren't even really friends, just friendly as people would be to not seem rude. Now these small conversations in passing seem warmer. *Or were they more superficial?* Nostalgia glasses fog memories; I know how that could end, even if they are home. Rather not stir up anything unpleasant.

Instead we walk to the ridge line for a better viewpoint. Each step gains a slow elevation, trudging forward. Walks like this are not particularly challenging in the moment, but tonight they will have creeped into my bones, aching all at once, ready to rest as the miles rack up. Janus is happy for the change of scenery, with his sensory factory on overdrive; inhaling whiffs of calling cards he's yet to meet while it all looks the same to me. He's content having never met them if only he can frolic in their same world. That's good enough for him, and who am I to say he's wrong?

Between the elevation and summer temperatures dwindling, the soft air feels welcoming, even though it's mid-morning. Warmth upon exposed skin is reminiscent of casual fun days laying in the city park, doing much of nothing besides maybe reading or people watching. The air holds memories. Collective reminders of memories beyond even my own. Change may be lurking on the horizon in a manner of weeks but it's a slow progression. Gently moving forward, coaxing us to take each step with a trusting hand. All the right conditions to make everything feel almost normal. I can almost forget, and be nowhere but on this mountain slowly approaching the summit.

As the finish comes into focus, there is an overlook with a vast viewpoint nestled away from the ledge. An ideal spot to rest for lunch, and start to take notes of what can be seen. Home shows no sign, yet we know that our house is behind us, to the east, on the next mountain over. Southwest of us is where our neighbors house would be nestled in, just cresting to the other side of the ridge. Nothing visible in the distance of former connections. Almost directly north of our mountain, the topography becomes more rugged beyond the valley that separated us. Its elevation swiftly rises, creating a formidable geological wall. The river runs from the north and it splits to go toward the Trading Post, while the other tributary meanders between their mountain and ours. We've been to the river to wash clothes, gather water besides rain, and swim. The deep blue water continues downstream beneath the bridge the road runs upon, onward to other valleys, and eventually out of sight. A moving river appears to flow slowly through the landscape with a surface that looks as solid as pavement.

To the west, mountains continue onward, one after the other, for as far as I can see, until they disappear from view. Layers upon layers, each fading in saturation the farther away they stand, until they appear to become congruent with the the sky. When the fog lingers or clouds roll in, they're all erased. The river and road dipping in and out of sight. Dancing, teasing, tormenting one another, as if showing off who can go where, while the other dare not tread. Out of view, we wonder where they end up or who wins.

In comparison, it's become painfully obvious, my tiny presence in this vastness. Merely a dot on the map. A fleshy mammal sitting on the site of an ancient geological form, looking out to a world that has existed from long before. It's nice not competing. Taking a role happily where placed by nature. It goes on, and on, and on, regardless of my presence. Beyond anything a map can possibly convey as a land teeming with life jumps from any parchment attempting to summarize it. With all to be seen from this point, I still linger in wonder at a place seemingly so indifferent to the crumbling of my life, the country that once was, or other happenings of humanity that do not involve it. It will go on.

Janus has become bored, or tired of a nearby sniffing exploration coming up empty-pawed, and instead has decided to sit by my side. *Is he absorbing it all as well, or fighting off a dozy nap?* The solidness of his dense little body leans into me, and with my hand subconsciously rubbing deep in the wiry fur of his scruff, I decide we can take a moment more.

After some time has passed, we stretched our limbs to initiate the disembark. Instead of returning the ascension route, we'll make a loop down the more gradual mountain slope toward the road. Having never been the most graceful person, somehow the downhills always seem more slippery.

It's a slow, easy walk following the footpath created by local fauna. As we approach the road yet not visible, we can hear the occasional car quickly drive by as its tires zip across the asphalt. Some days it's something heavier, loudly emitting diesel. What can only be assumed to be a large transport truck because a tank would seem ridiculous. Not today, though. Only an occasional passenger vehicle slips by.

Staying within the tree line, I look for any anomalies along the way, fully realizing this may be a fruitless endeavor. Scanning across the space that at first appears benign until I notice a bright red sign stapled on roadside trees. At first one, and then it becomes apparent there's more. So many more—every 400 meters or so, a tree holds a red rectangle. Staying on our side of the road, walking in the direction of home, I command Janus to stay put in the safety of tree coverage.

Quickly slipping, without a car in sight, I grab a flyer, and rapidly return to cover to rejoin. There are footprints near the side of the road in dried mud that are not mine. Possibly someone passing by, but they were here within the last week, after the last set of thunderstorms. I don't linger too long to dig into deeper thoughts as we walk. Submerging further into the forest, we cut across toward home, creating distance between us and the road.

Awareness that there are others, though it's not a novel fact, spurs a spring in my step. Looking to Janus keeping up the pace, I remind him there's no time to dally.

"Come on. Let's get home, Janus."

With a bright red background and The Nation's symbol translucently imposed, solid black letters loudly proclaim active hunting of traitors and enemies to The Nation with rewards offered. An ongoing endeavor in the distance, now on its way here. They're actively hunting with bounties. Always a far-off activity that made it's way via the radio, not in the form of something physical in this tangible space. They were here. Their people were walking around on this land. Uninvited guests making themselves comfortable, and it's open season.

A shot in the silence. A violation in this natural space that has been a safe haven violated by these treacherous outsiders. Concern of their presence existed, especially in more populated places, but this felt like a distant concern that was managed. No longer a vague worry. The directive asking desperate others to turn on people like me. Everyone could be on the hunt.

Our secure home, cleverly tucked away, can't arrive soon enough. With a quickened pace we make our way back to the sanctuary, barring out the alarming notices beyond these walls. Still threatening and brewing in the region, we've retreated to our sheltered enclave to regroup and rest. The five approximate miles, once a great divide, now no longer feel anywhere near enough distance between home and the asphalt. With deep breaths I steady my heart: *one-two-three-four, one-two-three-four, one-two-three-four, one-two-three-four.* Again and again, until the gripping hold in my chest subsides. We'll rest, and listen. Take our time, and soon go to the Trading Post. For now though, Janus is impatiently ready for his dinner, because regardless of what goes on outside, some things never change.

Now
October 9, 2047:

From the day we fled until now our living situation and stock of supplies has changed. Growing and adapting along the way, adding with needs and editing useless items. Taking in all that we have now draws a stark comparison to how scant our belongings once were.

(1) 60 L pack
(1) flashlight with batteries and backup batteries
(1) hand-crank flashlight
(4) rolls of duct tape
(1) bear bell
(1) can of bear spray
(2) bear boxes filled with MREs and dehydrated food (maybe fifty MREs)

Dehydrated food was never really an alluring meal but in necessary moments, it could stimulate a desperate appetite. At the time I had them just in case there was a natural disaster, the grocery stores closed, and my pantry supplies dwindled. Designed for that in-between time after a disaster struck and before aid arrived. Now, they are a safety net with long expiration dates, and protected from the elements in case our supply was to become scarce.

(1) human first-aid kit
(1) dog first-aid kit
Additional first-aid items such as headache relief, hydrogen peroxide, and rubbing alcohol.
(1) tent
(1) sleeping bag rated for 20 degrees below freezing
(1) backcountry mini stove
(4) backcountry mini stove refuel tanks
(1) set of cookware and attachments for mini stove

(2) sets of waterproof matches

(1) flint

(1) lighter

(1) pair of hiking boots

(1) set of dog booties

(40) hand warmers

(5) gallons of water

(3) packs of water treatment tablets

(4) bags of dog kibble

(4) blankets of various weights

Clothing (a random array of what could be grabbed and shoved in a case)

Some clothing proved to be useful, and others proved to be rags. At the time of leaving, for the sake of efficiency, it was an act to gather non-discriminately and decide later on. Winter coat, knit beanie, jeans, thermals, and wicking wear all made the valuable cut. Any fast fashion garments that snuck in were either used as rags or ripped to strips for other minor projects while their fibers remained questionable to burn. Suddenly the flashy colors and bold designs became a repulsive reminder of the happy hours, and gallery nights. Anti-camouflage, looking obnoxious now.

(1) binocular

(2) tubes of sunscreen

(2) bottles of insect repellent

(1) compass

(1) fixed knife

(1) multitool

(1) folding saw

(12) rolls of toilet paper

(3) rolls of paper towels

Dog toys and chews

Surviving isn't just about the necessities, but a balance of what is critical mixed with what makes us human, or rather canine. Some things can't be left, as the thought of leaving them is an abandonment of sorts. While the judgement is almost audible, I couldn't dream even in dire moments of forcing Janus to leave behind a few of his favorite toys. If this makes the transition for him a bit more joyful then the space or time they take is worthwhile.

  (2) tubes of oatmeal
  (1) bag of cornbread mix
  (1) tin canister of olive oil
  (1) jar of coconut oil
  (3) containers of pasta
  (7) cans of beans
  (1) can of pineapple
  (3) bags of dried beans
  (1) bag of flour
  (2) bags of ground coffee
  (1) bag of powder creamer
  (1) box of tea
  (3) bags of nuts (one each: cashew, pistachio, almond)
  (1) container of lentils
  (2) bags of chips
  (16) granola bars
  (4) bananas
  (1) jar of peanut butter
  (1) loaf of bread
  (4) apples
  (2) heads of broccoli
  (1) bag of potatoes
  (4) avocados
  (5) peppers (poblano and red)
  (3) onions

  If only my departure hadn't been in the span between grocery trips I'd have a fuller stock—but it's not like someone plans on this. There's not a perfectly convenient time that can easily line up. Fortunately the pantry was always relatively stocked for those lazy nights when you want to order take-out, but a full pantry eliminates the excuse of nothing to eat. In a rush, I swiftly snatched anything appearing remotely beneficial, while any item that looked as if it could spoil en route was left behind. Some things were most certainly creature comforts but the thought of surviving every morning without coffee or tea at the time seemed like an impossible ask. Maybe not a forever guarantee, but a luxury to temporarily indulge in.

A handful of books from my TBR
Paper notebooks and writing utensils
Knitting needles and a bag of yarn
All the cash from the piggy bank
My good-luck ring with its sun and moonstone
A bandana and hair tie

Negligible items to anyone else, besides maybe the cash, but there was a little bit of me in each of them that granted them passage. Without, part of all the good would be chipped away. Even in the chaos of the evening, unconsciously part of me suspected the world would chip away enough without my assistance. Now, I look fondly upon these old world trinkets. My TBR is now long since completed. The needles open new options for trade and profits. I haven't died yet, or been caught, so maybe that ring really is lucky. Intrinsically beneficial even if only a placebo. Not everything can be stripped down to quantifiable value, and as I scribble in those journals to record my existence out here, the qualitative makes a compelling case.

Chapter Twenty-One
Trading

Now
<u>October 30, 2047</u>:

My pack full arranged with goods worth exchanging, we plan to make it to the Trading Post today. The former mountain town, renamed and rebranded to those who know. With an early breakfast and meals tucked away for the walk, we'll be able to get there in the afternoon. A few visits ago Hank suggested we could sleep the night on the cot in the back room if we took the closing shift. While I'm not one to enjoy the idea of sleeping in the back room of a bar, I'd rather that arrangement instead of hiking close to thirty miles in one day. A long journey split up is more digestible for both of us.

It's a nice day with crisp air that's not yet cold. The task of trekking always feels more daunting if it's wet and cold, when we'd rather be comfortable in something cozy. Having taken this walk so many times, we know the next steps without looking. A familiar, worn path that is meditative with each footfall amongst the crunch of fallen leaves. Lost in my thoughts out here but somehow always find the way. Janus still insists on sniffing every nook and tree en route, even if by this point they're old friends. Scampering here and there with no consistent cadence or direction causes a smile to manifest upon my face. The oblivious joy reminds me of the walks and fun hikes we'd go on when the world was normal. *Normal—what's that like?* A time buried deep in my memories, but he still treats each day with the same jovial curiosity, almost transporting to kinder times.

Nearing the Trading Post, we cautiously start to head toward the road to cross the river on the bridge. Hoping against the chance of anyone seeing us emerge from the forest, piquing any curiosity about the direction of our route. Instead we appear like a magician's grand reveal when the curtain is dropped. Our gaze peering from behind the tree line until the road is void of any vehicles or evidence, and then walk. Quickly on the shoulder, until the bridge crosses the river, and then back to the edge of grass between the trees and pavement, as if it's always been our lane.

The Trading Post used to have a name, and officially still does, but no one for our purposes uses it anymore unless they're in the presence of particular company. I guess it could be telling if someone insisted on always using a former title. It's a simple town with a single stop.

To the left is a bar that has some food which Hank owns. Across the street is a general supply store with picked-over shelves that are never stocked more than halfway. To the right of the general supply store are the stalls for trading, hawkers, and food vendors. The vendors often change and rotate, only showing up when they have something to offer, which is rarely consistent. While the faces may trade out, the goods and options always have a similar assortment. Canned goods, luxury items like alcohol or chocolate, gasoline, weapons, meats, and so on. Instead of big box grocery stores that have all but gone out of business, the concept has been stripped to a simplistic, rugged version supplying the most basic searches. Meats are pickled and dried, no longer wrapped in plastic and styrofoam. Chocolate, if you can afford it, is sold in little slivers the size of a thumbnail.

We have many of the things we could ever dream to need. Our supplies and planning have carried us this far, sparing the need to lean too heavily upon what may or not be available at the stalls. Instead of finished goods, the search is for supplies to create, and items to make life a little easier. Medicine is the prize trophy to seek out today. Even if not an immediate need, it doesn't hurt to have a well-supplied medical kit. With its high cost, we can only afford to acquire a little at a time.

First, though, we need to offload our goods in exchange for paper money. Walking through the crowded halls, we glance into the various stalls to find the vendors who are selling what we have to trade. They'll be happy to purchase what we have, knowing they can turn a profit with a known buyers base. The vendors with pharmaceuticals still want cash and not trades because in the rest of the world, where they get their medicine, paper money is demanded. You can't trade a loaf of bread for penicillin on the black market of the drug store in the city. By selling goods for money and paying for medicine with money, like the old days, they can go on to one day supply us with more. So the cycle goes. After searching and scrounging, we're able to purchase antibiotic ointment, a generic variety QuickClot, and bandages. Thankfully our rosemary bread, few remaining gems, and knitted garments fetched a hefty price for their value.

I put away the medicine deep in my bag, knowing there are always eyes watching. Greedy, desperate, opportunistic onlookers. People act civil overall, but that doesn't mean they won't turn when it's dire for them. Preferring to not fight anyone looking to attempt a quick grab they're stashed.

Next, there are a few more items worth trading, so we walk along the congested space, peering to see who has what. No one bothers Janus as he stays close to me, and many people fear dogs. The military and citizens have trained dogs to be protectors and agents. Consequently, many people fear them and ultimately don't cross us. Even though Janus looks nothing like an intimidating guard dog, we benefit from scary dog privileges as an accidental benefit.

I trade the remaining knit items for eight skeins of yarn and two bags of unspun wool. A rare, semi-regular vendor who always loves our knit goods. Customers will see the ingredients and potential results, but in moments of laziness or lavishness, will purchase the finished goods for a higher rate. We're able to trade the remaining loaf of rosemary bread for flour, and baking soda. Fortunately, we still have vinegar. Always an arduous pain to lug heavy liquids all the way back— not that flour is light by any measure. Finally, I trade spices and herbs for some dried meats. It doesn't get much but Janus is overjoyed. He knows this vendor and exuberantly wags his tail in anticipation. The vendor must be a dog person, or maybe just kind, because he always slips Janus a fleshy bite on the house.

With goods all packed away we head over to Hank's. Walking into the warm bar, I see him heads above others behind the bar, gruffly grinning at a joke someone must have told. He formidably stands there. Everyone knows that if Hank takes a liking to you, then you're not to be messed with. Former special forces, tactically trained, and growing up on a rural, remote farm, he's had a life full of callous lessons, though he never turned unkind. While he looked like someone who could sling back drinks with Blake and his boys, nothing could be further from reality. A bear who looked like one, too, but was talentley passing as the most rugged woodsman around.

The first time we met, I was so nervous, almost physically twitching with anxiety. It must have been visibly obvious because he offered me a drink, and even though I initially passed, he insisted. He sat and talked, almost rambled, until the tension began to ease. Skeptical, but something whispered that he was okay. When he said the drink would calm my nerves and make me blend with the patrons here, I knew we saw one another. He eyed me, and deep down, like recognized like from days we could no longer live. A secret, relatively unspoken, curious truth we could detect. From then on, I knew I wasn't entirely alone in this isolating world and that was comforting if only when I was here.

With a wave, I walk behind the bar to put my pack in the back, and Janus instinctually nestles into the dog bed in the corner. Immediately getting to work, even though it's well before shift—there's never enough to do to extend my gratitude.

"Hey, Hank, how's your day been?"

"Hmph, same old, same old. Good flow of people but some sure are drinkin' their beers a whole lot slower."

He was right. There were lingering people lounging, nursing drinks. Some traits don't die no matter what world it is, but at least they pay and keep to themselves. Beers are beers, and even if they're bad, people are happy to have them. The diner food generating creature comforts doesn't hurt either.

"Hopefully it's a good night."

"Hopefully. We don't need any more foot soldiers in here, scarin' people off."

"Foot soldiers?!" I whisper-shout in shock at those uttered words.

"Yea, a week or two ago. I guess they were comin' through putting up those signs on the road. You saw 'em, right?"

"Of course, I saw them."

"Well, they stopped here. Really killed the vibe. Sittin' here, and gawkin' around. Askin' questions they thought were nothing, but everyone felt were nosey. You could hear a mouse creak a floorboard. So, no one dared speak casually."

"You need to be careful."

"I am careful. This isn't my first rodeo with the likes of them. You need to be careful."

As I'm bringing over a plate of fries to a couple of men sitting in the corner with their watery beers, I look out to the patrons, many of whom are regulars. A little grouping of familiar faces in this cozy hideaway. Standing in both worlds, here we sit. A few new faces stand out in contrast but they seem neutral enough. A woman with sable hair is chatting up Hank but I fail to place her in my memory. The energy appears collectively friendly, making my guard slip a tiny bit. Walking toward the bar, she gets up to leave, allowing the opportunity to catch a better look at her face. Familiar, maybe, but I'm not sure. Without much conversation to make names stick, some faces fade or blur.

"Who was that?"

"A friend. You'd like her, actually."

I can't help but scoff a little at the thought of random women suddenly becoming my friends, let alone mine, at a friend's recommendation. A novelty I haven't experienced in years. *Do people still do that?* A concept ludicrously humorous.

"You would. Well, anyway, she had a tidbit of information ya might want to hear."

An eyebrow raises in skeptic curiosity, as he knows I want to learn more. *How could I not desire the juicy details?*

"Rumor has it they're actively using drones to help the military search in findin' people."

Seeing the color drain from my face, Hank pulls me aside. My skin feels taut, and clammy as I grip to the news. A mind racing, and the rest unable to keep up. The implications buzzing like tiny little stings pricking my skin to alertness all at once.

Hank's eyes are firm but full of comfort. He knows this is

not the place or time to crumble or let any onlooker see a crack. I pull focus with all the intention available to muster as the blood flows back to my extremities and the humming ambient noise dulls. With a subtle nod exchanged, we table this talk to a later, quieter time, for a more private exchange. There's much more to discuss that can't be risked now.

Chapter Twenty-Two
Phantom Presence

Now
<u>October 31, 2047:</u>

Invisible forces fleeting just out of sight. A presence unseen occupying shared spaces. Lingering between planes, skirting the peripheral corners of vision. Dually existing, or rather coexisting between a dichotomy of worlds. One relatively pleasant, and the other laced with potential hazards. The hazards can seep into the pleasant if the pleasant is too flashy, too visible. The pleasant can creep upon the hazardous, but only if they're cautious.

Humans can recognize patterns—pareidolia. A natural skill that can work on a subliminal level. Tricks played, distorting worlds, but it can be revealing as well. Insightful for those hiding behind the veil, connecting little trappings to illuminate that which was unseen. Traits, motives, truths, lies, plots, all to be visible. It can also lead someone astray. Seeing something that was never really there. A convincing mirage down a nonexistent path. Hidden beings can use this to their advantage. Trick the seekers with well-placed hints that they can string together in their own narrative they believe to be true, regardless of its fallacies. It's vital for the hidden to not accidentally leave anything that can actually be connected to their presence, existence or truth pareidolia or not. Sitting in the desk chair as the last fleeing light casts shadows across the space, I review the notes from today's explorations. Checking all that was seen, and unseen.

Living in the shadows, I feel desires of normalcy unfulfilled. A life mourned as consequences of choices made. A shattered vase that will never return. Possibly reassembled, but it would never be quite the same. Little fractures running through, visible and present, ever so slight. A lofty thought would be that they could become a positive feature moving forward. Painted gold, a kintsugi type of life. A lofty daydream for this moment.

At this time feeling more akin to the yūrei, angry and vengeful. Hating all the chipper, happy people thriving or pretending in their lives. They don't need to experience longing, but I want to experience joy. Not just this new joy, but the joy I had. The joy that holds no certainty that it will ever return. Instead we've been left with an adaptive version of life, creating enjoyment where possible, yet it is different. Sometimes, I don't want different.

Like a lost soul feeling like I'm wandering a plane which I'm no longer a part of. Looking at the books I've already read, the solitary games already played; every repetitive touch to the old days is disconnected and different. Everything goes on regardless of my existence. Struggling to find a place in the world that isn't meant for me. A world left behind but still visible. Haunting choices overthinking and second-guessing. Questioning the conviction that landed me in this realm.

We are safe behind this veil, watching and evaluating. Telling myself this is ultimately good. Carefully choosing when to make our presence known, and only in ways that aren't revealing. We don't need hunters seeking more than what's willing to be offered. This new existence is an adjacent life, sitting like a specter for no one else but I. The shadows are my safety.

Chapter Twenty-Three
Interruption

Now
<u>November 1, 2047</u>:

Before departing to head home, Hank always makes sure we're well fed with a dense breakfast, and each time he gives a parting gift. As if tradition, like an older brother making sure to load up his siblings with all the necessary and unnecessary accoutrements before heading off to university. Besides the gossip intel, he gave us a random assortment of useful objects including piano wire, dried meat, and alcohol wipes.

Leaving Hank tugs at my heart; a worrisome longing digging its claws in with each departure, knowing on some level he may not be here when I return. Words never formulated out loud but we both feel it hanging in stagnant air. Sometimes staying feels like an option to consider. There are so many people, though. It would be a state of being constantly on guard, speculating who would turn on us first for a diminutive reward. One last hug and then we begin the trek back, with each step marching against the elevation gain.

The rumor of drones raucously echoes inside my skull. Boiling with frustration and exasperation, I internally wish they would give it a rest. *Just stop, and let us be.* I wish, and part of me pleads, that Blake and his goons will stop and be satisfied so those of us not wanting to be a part of their world can slink in the shadows until the storm passes. Ride the waves and withstand until it's over, if only they would stop. Their hunger is insatiable. Gorging even when their fill should have been met, never knowing or caring when to halt. It's never enough.

We don't even know what they're capable of. All Hank heard was that they were using drones in their search for people, but that's where the knowledge ends. Whether they can record video or sound, if they have infrared detection capabilities, where or how they're communicating is all a mystery. Surveillance capabilities can be assumed but there's also the concern of weapons, which sounds far-fetched but it's not like the technology hasn't been used before. Afghanistan, Pakistan, Yemen, Syria, Somalia, Libya, Russia, Ukraine, Turkey, and Azerbaijan come to mind most recently. It's entirely possible the line wouldn't end across the sea if enemies needed to be rooted out from within. Unfathomable capabilities or willingness to make amends for the greater good.

Concerns of how to prepare, how to combat, how to hide all swirl. Each trumping the other in priority of needy attention. Each with no real solution or answer. Only theories based on rumors, all of which could only be one scary myth. Precautions against a potential nonexistent threat is a necessary waste of energy.

The forest always has eyes watching in the distance, but now I feel exposed. Observed like a specimen from threatening nonconsensual forces. Every crack of a stick or rustle of leaves holds new threats. Friend or foe, we'll never know until it could possibly be too late. Remaining watchfully alert, even if the landscape ushers in no threatening glyphs. The rumor of new threats consumes every thought, accompanying every step on our return.

Almost home, we steadily make our way between the trunks. Nearby is one of the wild gardens and while en route, it wouldn't hurt to check for anything ready to harvest. There should be some root vegetables and greens at maturity. Maybe some onions or maybe, if luck goes our way, some small potatoes have grown enough for early picking. There's always a glimmer of hope for a good harvest.

As we approach the wild garden the dirt is visibly disturbed, and the flora a bit thrashed. Something has been here rooting around, pulling up the ground, and making a mess. Intruders so close within our boundaries. I can feel my heart thumping louder to a roaring, repetitive beat. They're not here but they were. *Where are they?* As the waves of panic come cascading over, my hand inches toward the holster on my hip. All the hair on the back of my neck stands at attention at the startling rustle on my right, while I can see Janus to my left. In a blink I'm over the fallen log lying between the sound and me, with the nine-millimeter pulled. As the air is sucked out of my lungs, the thought of my book closing darts across.

In a breath, trigger not yet pulled, there stares a terrified badger with a mouth full of greens hunkered just beyond the log. His little life hanging in the balance, evaluating what to do next. With a loud sigh, the threat of my conclusion recedes back to its hole. Staring, daring not to blink at the absurdity of this scene that's actually perfectly sane in this situation. Grateful to have saved a bullet. They're expensive, and we weren't able to get any this time around. I'm just thankful we can all walk away unharmed.

Before either of us can concretely decide how to proceed, Janus chooses for us with a gruff and a bark as he charges in, finally catching up to the commotion. The badger needs not to be told twice and is on his way before Janus can even fully be present. Satisfied with his accomplishment, he resumes sniffing the newly unearthed dirt. As the chaos subsides, I look at the mess. Our wild garden looks truly chaotic, but there are still veggies to salvage.

As much as I rue the loss of yield, an animal doing what it must to get by can't be blamed. An existence long before our arrival. He's always lived this way, taking what is needed. What is necessary. Ultimately this was a space belonging to the wildlings before any human stepped foot here. We are the guests, and consequently must share. I've always known and amends have been made to accept this fact, but it still stings. We're no different in the bigger picture. Foraging for what we can find and living with what is offered. With each hurdle, another foot trudges forward. There's no net to catch us if we slip.

Chapter Twenty-Four
Nutritious

Now
<u>December 12, 2047</u>:

Nutritionists used to say that a grown female needed a minimum of sixteen hundred calories a day, but you could gorge yourself to a whopping twenty-four hundred if you were active. *Does this qualify as being active?* I should think so, considering not a single day goes by that there isn't something to be done. A path to walk, a task to fix, or simply the amount of energy anxiety eats up forever, diligently on watch. Regardless of the numerical value of what's ingested, none of it compares to the nutrition craved from a quality meal on a visceral level. Something more than calories.

Food beyond nutrition can transport you, holding on to reminiscent wafts of fonder times. Memories captured in ingredients. Comfort encapsulated in flavors. Some would say that's an unhealthy relationship with food, but I have always thought food should be like a French love affair. It doesn't just get the job done, but it's transcendently fulfilling in every capacity, leaving you wishing there was more. Elijah always hated when I would say that. He thought it was crass, but he was regimented and bland. Maybe he was jealous, ironically, of the French man that never existed to have a love affair with, and he couldn't understand a metaphor for the fact that some people simply love good food.

A chuckle escapes while remembering these casual, idiotic conversations as I peep at the roasted stew simmering. Its aromas fill the room, creating the illusion of a welcoming home in the quaintest of neighborhoods. Warm, thick, luscious, rich, comforting—all the trappings necessary for a hug to melt into. The harvest in these cooling temps has been kind. While the exact recipe always varies based upon what is ready to harvest, there are always root vegetables, herbs, and onions of some type. Today we have carrots, potatoes, mushrooms, onions, canned tomatoes, rosemary, and parsley. A little flour to thicken the liquids as the produce slowly simmers down in the pot. If someone really wanted to, they could add meat, but there's no need. This is amply filling with only what nature offers. It's almost exactly like Mom's recipe. The one she never wrote down but made so often it's essentially part of our DNA.

I remember the last time she made it. After taking some time off from The Journal for a much-needed break, I went to see her in New Mexico. Time away to talk and think in an environment that was familiar. Stable and resounding to steady, unsure legs walking numbly through the motions. That day Mom added rabbit to her stew. She'd chop up chunks and let them splash down, saving over half the creature to preserve for a later day. Like a squirrel, she always stored away little bits here and there, not knowing what would come next at the grocery.

Prices had been exorbitantly raised, especially on items such as meats. No middle-class person could afford steak any more, and even the less-desired, once-economical red meats like ground beef were becoming a luxury. People stuck to ground turkey that somehow seemed drier by the day. Rumors floated of sawdust being added to spread the quantity at stores and restaurants. Someone could purchase a whole bird if they knew how to break it down. Mom resorted to harvesting her own. Good thing she didn't live in an HOA community. In moments of financial strain, it was a relief to not be one to avidly seek out meat, and to save some money when shopping.

As we're catching up on personal life happenings, without fail the conversation turns to the world, and the mutual feeling of it falling in despair. Mom, though, is not spiraling. She is steady like a rock in the river, refusing to flinch in the face of bullies, even if they are on a national level. I recall pleading with her to take it seriously. *Don't shrug these things off.* She should be taking precautions, being alert and aware, just in case things turned south.

With a wave of the hand, she dismissively pushed away those concerns. She had a stew to tend, and none of my words were part of the ingredient list. Confidently walking around the kitchen with a dash of this, and a sprinkle of that. Unwavering in every choice she made.

"Don't you think I know how to handle myself?"

"Yea, Mom, but you gotta be careful. Things have only gotten worse."

"And I've been doing just fine."

She exaggeratedly gestured to the carcass on her counter with newspaper underneath. If it wasn't for the blood, you'd think she was a game show host pointing to what the contestant could win.

"And it's only going to get tougher. It could end up being a whole lot tougher."

"And I've been through tough things before. Do you think that little shit in a suit scares me? HA-Ha-ha!"

Before I can utter another retorting word of concern, there is a strong knock at the door. Mom turned and grabbed a hand-wrapped package from the table, swiftly making her way to the entry. While she clearly was expecting someone, or maybe was just ready to run at the knock with no trepidation, I hung back. The door in view, close enough to react, but just out of grasp in the shadows observing. Unable to see or hear much; spying apparently isn't my strength.

There are pleasantries and giggles as Mom chats with a woman. I can see her rest her hand on Mom's arm with a squeeze, and they lean in for a hug. She gently tucks a dark strand behind her ear to rejoin that perfectly polished, ravenous bun, revealing a radiant smile seemingly untouched by the world. Mom is glowing too, and just like that, I'm enraptured by what is going on.

Mom comes back with an envelope in exchange for the package departed. I fully expect her to divulge everything that just took place, but what a silly thought to assume. Instead, she goes right back to stirring the stew, forcing me to pry.

"So, who was that?"

"Oh, just a friend. You've met her before."

"No, I don't think I have."

"You sure? I thought you had. Either way, I had something for her. Lilly, that is. And she needed to give me a letter."

"Yea, I saw. What was all that about?"

"Oh, I had some orders for her, and she has some more

requests.”

“You guys have a business?”

“Of sorts.”

More questions than answers. Perplexed that it's never as straight-forward as it should be, and since when has anything "of sorts" not been inherently questionable? I can't fathom what she's up to. In reality, I can, but nothing that wouldn't cause worry. Maybe that's why she's being so closed-lipped.

" 'Of sorts?' What does that mean?"

"People need things, and sometimes they can't get them. Let's just say, they're not sold at pharmacies anymore. The herbal alternatives are confusing to the lay person. So they turn to us. I just help them get what they need."

"And what exactly is it they need?"

"Come on, Jessi. It's what you'd expect. Things for miscarriages, pregnancy termination ... Shit, even just things for menstruation pain and menopause."

"And you're getting them illegal pharmaceuticals? Do you realize how risky that is?"

"Psshhh! Don't forget the herbal concoctions. Call me Dr. Do-Good!"

She lets out a pleased cackle, at her self-prescribed nickname, but I stand there staring unamused. Not by what she's doing, but by the way she's inserting herself unnecessarily into dangerous situations. The Nation is watching, and she's giving them reason to look.

"You'll get arrested if you're caught!"

"Good thing I won't get caught," she snarks with a wink.

"It could put you on their radar, and then what, Mom?"

"Then I don't know. But I can't worry about what I can't control. I can, however, do something to help."

"This is you helping?"

"Yes, and if I go down for it, at least I tried. Now, come on, don't be so upset."

She is earnestly, completely unbridled, and genuine in the convictions that these actions will improve her community. Never was one to roll over; to just take it. Pushing back against the oppressive reach of The Nation's hand was second nature to her. I stare at this incredible woman during a mundane moment and see precisely how dangerous she would be perceived by Blake and his boys. She's untamable, and wild. A threat.

"There's nothing wrong with it, besides the fact that it puts you in danger. They're watching, and it's only going to get worse. January will be here before you know it. You've heard the rumors."

"That's just it—they're rumors. Don't get worked up over nothing concrete."

"And if they're not rumors, we're all going to be in trouble. The two-year anniversary will be here before you know it. People keep saying he's going to ramp it up, having crossed some acceptable threshold of time."

"All worries I can't control. I'll still be kickin', regardless of what happens."

"But you can prepare. You can safeguard yourself!"

"I am, in my own way. You don't need to consume yourself. It's not only you going through this."

"… I know that."

"Besides you let that man take up too much space in that precious brain of yours."

She's not wrong. Occupying too much space and tainting all the thoughts he touches. Exacerbated language has been stolen from my tongue with nothing more to say that's not repetition. The desire to convince her to heed these warnings, even if they sound excessive, knots up my stomach. There's so much out of my control, unfortunately, including her. Looking onward, wishing she'd take it seriously. Desperately hoping that for once she'd listen.

"Now, come on, and stop your worrying. Stew's ready, and you know I hate when food gets cold. Hand me the bowls."

Forcing the ceramic dish into my hand, she ladles the luscious meal into each, as if the food has magic properties to wash away all the concerns. Sitting around the small table consuming what's before us, she's not wrong. Soft potatoes in sauce melt away worry. I remember the remainder of the visit was filled with banter, and jokes, and reassurances. She confidently knew exactly what to say with the most flippant, c'est la vie attitude a south-westerner could muster, and I sat there soaking it all in.

Staring at my stew in this little treehouse with Janus begging by my feet, a warmth of comfort wraps its arms around me, as if she's here —even though that was the last time I saw her in person. As chunks of carrots and potatoes slosh, bits of her essence stare back. Her wit, her cunning, her grounded carefree realness, all wrapped in one. Worry creeps in, wondering if she is okay. If she made it out or had a plan. A longing wish to know what may never be confirmed clouds my heart. Living with warm memories sprinkled with melancholy have become a common occurrence, leaving these feelings stirred by the stew to be relatively unsurprising. Reminders of connections regularly rearing up.

Chapter Twenty-Five
Snare

Now
<u>February 1, 2048:</u>

The deep, dark forest is naturally scary, and it seems unwise to swim in the swells of a storm. Humanity follows trends, and people naturally react in primal ways as unseen strings are pulled. Tendencies, traits, influences, and processes are all wired in on a cellular level. Some credit is due to multigenerational lessons passed down, or due to seeing that one dumb, brave townsperson push their luck, only to be squashed.

A part that's been engrained caused by natural influences, but lets not exclude socio cultural aspects. There's a reason humans associate specific colors with food, or health; making it commonly present in marketing. It's not a coincidence that bold, blocky typeface sends intimidating scares down a person's spine, whereas scrolly cursive portrays a nonthreatening, even delicate essence. Decades upon decades of conditioning from society combined in a cocktail of our natural mammalian fight-or-flight survival response, and you have modern-day humanity.

They didn't stop there, for what good is this knowledge without a motive and a goal? Push the right buttons, prod the right spots, tug here, twist there; like a marionette with the right handler, anyone can dance to the tune they desire. Don't worry, though, they say—it's a fun beat! No one will even notice their feet moving almost independently, like magic. Instead they'll think, *"Wow! I'm really doing it! Look at me!"*

Yes, indeed, just look: independent movements that couldn't possibly be tied to the manipulation of half-truths to garner a response for a desired result that was never mentioned. This result was a mutual decision, surely. No coercion or conning in the least. Just don't look at the strings. We had committed to the daily grind for a one-day-promised retirement that barely sustained us as it was, but they said things were tough because of external reasons. Ringing up broccoli after a full shift, waiting to make it home and cook, who were we to question? Stay focused on the dance. Focus on that reward. Eyes ahead.

Look at the treat neatly dangled in sight but marginally out of reach, making the hand grasp outward. So focused on the goodies promised, even blinking is a questionable choice in case it all disappears. Not everyone has your chance, but their lane isn't yours to watch. A distraction from pejorative whiners! Stay focused and dance, and reach, and train those eyes on what was promised. Almost there; it'll be yours soon, they swear. An extra shift here or a long hour there; you don't mind when it's almost yours. There's nothing that could create a distraction. Nothing that could make you peep behind the closed door, scan through the documents, follow the money, or ask any questions. Nothing to make the promise disappear. Nothing to make you look—and that's exactly what they are most grateful for.

Don't worry if the room feels stuffy or the walls get a little closer. Uncomfortably cozy—scratch that! Just cozy. Nothing to be concerned about. Don't mind that sound, as it's most definitely not fibers dragging across the ground. The shouts that nay-sayers will scream (*"It's a ruse!"*) but their tongues are twisted in lies, grabbing at your slice of the prize. They don't want you to win. Their dissent is not your problem. Don't listen; keep focused; stay diligent.

Times may get rough, and that will be a challenge, but with hard work and dedication to the promise of reward, it will all be provided just around the corner. They tell you to hang on. They cheer that you can do this! One more year to go. Slimmer spending for now. It's only an ache; not to worry. It may feel tight while looking onward, and the air may feel thinner. Don't worry; it's all in anticipation. Besides, short breath isn't that bad, and it'll be worth it in the end. Ignore that friction rubbing around your neck. There's nothing to be concerned with now. Keep working, keep trying, keep proselytizing the greatness of The Nation, and remember their promises. This is all for you, they say.

If you're getting tired, that's alright—just don't lose sight. Keep going, and know they value your bootstrap bravado. You can do it! The best interest of the citizens is always at the forefront, so there's no need to worry. Here to help and support as promised. The walls may seem dark, and shadows might be creeping in. A shade descending, or perhaps you're straining. Don't worry. We're here now, and the only thing to do is trust the process. Trust their words. No one wants to lose the prize at this stage in the game.

Looking around in the dark room, you wonder, *"Where's my promised prize? It should be here."* Panic sets in, too late for those who recognize trouble in the eleventh hour with pleas of confusion, contemplating how they got here. You stepped there and stood. Waiting and listening without question. Ignoring every sound, every sign, every instinct; all due to persuasive reassurance and conditioning.

A promise of escape permitted this moment, and any cost up until now was an acceptable fee because none of the distractions directly impacted you. Couldn't warrant risking the loss of your promise. Alternatives appear impossible from the mess that's been landed, but is that true, or is that them? Unless the enjoyment of perpetual darkness while dancing strung up is the dream, then it's time to grab a pair of scissors.

Chapter Twenty-Six
Dangerous Dreams

Now
<u>March 14, 2048:</u>

We're sitting around at Darlings, but the lighting is low—almost dusky. Almost dark and uncharacteristically dingy, hesitantly waiting on the precipice of time. *Waiting for what?* Across from me, the crew is all here. All staring and smiling big wide smiles: Dani, Sam, and Anthony. Their mouths move but I cannot hear a sound, as if my ears are muffled with headphones underwater. Straining to listen, but nothing helps. It's then that I notice that Elijah is standing nearby at the coffee bar, and a man in shadows looms behind him. An unseen man, indistinguishable. Eyes trained on our table.

The room is getting darker as the sun sets, casting shadows from within while the walls fade away. A fog sets in and as I blink, the room is slowly changing. Enormously large tree trunks appear in spaces that were empty moments prior. Inconceivably appearing as I glance back, standing there, declaring they've always been. Not growing or sprouting —appearing from nothingness.

Something isn't right as the tension building is tangible. A tightness grabs me and my whole body begins to sweat. Clammy, but there's no moisture to touch. The whole space feels like it's closing in around me. Claustrophobically hugging without invitation, and that's when I notice no one has moved. Rather, their bodies do not move, but sit there like possessed dolls while their heads follow. Tracking my movements, refusing to break. Unsettling eye contact. They don't blink. Staring in shock at them, I try to speak and shout my concerns but nothing comes out.

I turn towards Elijah, as if he holds knowledge I don't, but nothing is provided. He stares, void of expression. In the moment of his statued silence, there's a quick whooshing sound. The sound the vacuum a bank tube makes when a deposit was rushed off to the teller. An archaic sound from decades past, remembering in vintage movies calling my attention. I look back to the table, but Anthony is gone.

"Anthony! Anthony! Where are you?!" I mouth into the void.

Looking left, searching, there comes a whoosh from the right and Sam is left all alone. Rushing to them with hands outstretched, I fall into the table, grasping forward. Immediately, as our hands touch, a whooshing pulls them back into the darkness as fog disappears in the daylight sun. Ripped back as the invisible strings yank their return. Gone, like their vacant spots were always empty. Eyes sweeping around, noticing Elijah is no longer there. Unsure whether it just happened or was long ago in the chaos.

I am alone and darkness is creeping in. There's a rhythmic tap, tap, tap of hard shoe soles on the wood floors. Systematically approaching without any hesitation. When my eyes raise up they meet two black pits— I'm staring back in the face of Blake. He's moving directly toward me as I clumsily clamor backwards. Tripping over my own feet, shuffling away as fast as possible. He stands over me and begins to crouch down. My heart is beating so loud I'm sure he can hear. Heavy breath descends upon my face, my skin feeling the moist heat, while seeing a sinister smirk curls over the corner of his mouth. Desperately, in these final unwanted moments, I pull away, wincing to not see what comes next.

[BOOM!]

A thunderous sound shakes the ground upon which I lay and reverberates through the forest. A deafening shockwave of mechanical nature. Ears ringing, eyes darting, attempting to stabilize. He is gone but I don't see where. Vanished from sight; however, not reassuring as a residual smell of him lingers. Breath and sound return, leaving me to sit in confusion. Nothing makes sense, but before connecting any conclusions, there's a rustle. Immediately I jump up and back away, as there are several figures evenly spaced facing my direction. Only silhouettes and vague details can be seen, as the room is dark and the candles they hold create a blinding contrast. My instinct unsure and stuck in place while searching for where to flee. Turning to run far away from these unknown figures, I trip and fall, crashing down hard to the floor with an abrasive *thud*.

[GASP]

Launching up in bed, soaked in sweat, my heart beats through my chest. The sudden jolt has awoken him as well, and he stares onward as though I've lost my sanity. As the room comes into focus, there's the reassurance it was just a dream. A gentle reminder of a fictitious story bleeding into reality. Lying back, propped up by a pillow, calming my breath, I center the racing thoughts. *Don't worry; it wasn't real.* Everything feels a little more solid, permanent, in contrast to the semi-present state of dream matter itself. By now Janus has nestled up next to me, no longer shocked, and assumed his duties as comforter. A long breath vacates, purging the last of the dream that was lingering, and with eyelids closed, sitting in this moment, I pause.

After residual jitters have settled, joining the day feels like the only option remaining. Slowly, eyes peel open, letting new light in as dawn is coming through the windows. Taking in the familiar shelter, my feet confidently swing to the floor to shake that unpleasant illusion as a start to the day.

I walk through the room and glance toward the windows in typical routine to see the sunrise. It's a beautiful morning with vibrant hues streaking across, but while watching, a concerning black smudge captures my attention. Northwest of us in the valley, a sooty plume is billowing upward. It's growing and spreading in the sky. A prickle creeps up across the back of my neck. Eyes fully locked, there's no denying that something man-made appears to be rapidly ablaze.

Chapter Twenty-Seven
Explosive

Now

<u>March 15, 2048:</u>

Yesterday, we couldn't stop watching from a distance as the sky turned gray, filled with smoke from whatever was burning. Entranced by the haze. Remaining close to the treehouse, not daring to venture out too far. Staying cautiously observant, on the watch for who or what caused the fire. Fully aware of the blast that transcended dreams, but unsure of any other unfilled details. It'd be foolish to assume anything is accidental, as fires don't start without cause, but at this time none come to mind.

Today, the air still holds a residual smell of torched materials, and a filtering of the forest to muted hues. A dirty rendition until it dissipates. Curiosity dangles in front of us but it's tempting to duck my head beneath the covers. Pretend nothing happened and any concerns will dissipate too. Tantalizing, but curiosity—or concern—wins out. We head off down our mountain hill, in the direction of where the smoke was rising from. Following the lingering plumes visible above and the smells mingling through the trees.

Cautiously approaching together, we make our way down the winding fauna footpath on high alert. Even Janus understands the importance of calculated, wary movements as he stays by my side, not venturing far for any adventures once we're approaching closer. The thickness in the air is suffocating. Something about a violent natural element consuming an unnatural object in an anomalous manner disturbs the space in a way beyond words. The askew quality can be felt when an orchestra comes to an abrupt halt. Immediate silence descends.

What remains of the structure comes into view. Deeply charred lumber hidden between live trees; some of the nearest received a slight crisping but stand overall unaffected. Everything is incinerated from within. A thick layer of black charcoal, coats all the surfaces, making it difficult to distinguish one piece of structure from another. Limited defining differences in color as it all merges together in a single blacked-out mass. What can be assumed to have been furniture sits in sooty lumps, only showing a metal coil protruding beneath the debris. Remains of a fireplace can be seen at the base; however, the chimney has been blown back with bricks scattered along the ground. Remnants propelled to the property's perimeter. A sweet chemical smell still resides, crawling into our nostrils, almost burning.

Standing at the edge of the corpse of someone's former existence, I feel like a few words should be said in its wake, but none leave my mouth. A eulogy unperformed as I gawk. In a snap, a whole life is gone. A single event can erase an entire world. This structure wasn't on our maps. Living out here all alone, completely unnoticed, even with its proximity. Janus dares not go near the remains but stares on from a distance, as do I. Waiting and watching for any signs or clues until it feels permissible to step closer. An appropriate passing of time to intrude.

We came for information, though I don't know much that can be told besides some simple observations that offer no comfort. The blaze was isolated to the building and did not spread. Fortunate; however, this implies it was controlled. This amount of deep char and indistinguishable melted details indicate it was an intense, quick-burning flame. Accelerants could have been a component to ignite, which would explain the blowback and scents. That raises questions of whether it was an accident or intentionally set. A mental fact-sheet the size of an index card with well-presumed details, and no concrete conclusions. The mountains are shared, and dangers can arise in multiple forms.

A lot of work for little information. I scan the debris while deciding whether to attempt to sift, but only if anything is eye-catching. Unlikely in the litter, but optimistically I still look. There may be something of use, and like the crows, we'd be foolish to turn away any shiny gifts. An overwhelming mess to scavenge through as I play a demented version of "I Spy." *Where's the thumbtack? Definitely not beneath the burnt sofa.* Nothing in the center of the structure can be seen, let alone accessed. On the ground we found a few pieces of silverware with scrolly designs on the handle that could be traded. There's a small assortment of garden tools that could be useful. Part of me wants to hoard all I can when there's any inkling it may be practical, but the logical or lazy part of me doesn't want to lug chimney bricks back uphill.

After a while, nothing new is revealed, and we've exhausted what's available. Through a final assessment we've gathered what we can, and the rest will stay. Leaning down to snap shut the final straps on my pack, there's a sound that's not ours. A movement close by. Shuffling of bricks, or stones softly tumbling. Quickly standing up, I try to find the source. In view on the opposite side of the building, a few pieces of brick lay on the ground. *Those weren't there before. Were they?* Grabbing my bag in one frantic swoop, and I gesture to Janus to stay by my side, crouching low. Eyes fixed on everything I can swivel to without moving. Watching and waiting for something to be revealed. Hoping I'm hidden enough with the crumbles between us and the sound's origin. Seconds feel like minutes, and minutes drag.

With a bolt, there is a flurry of a shadow making a run for it, away from us and the structure. Retreating into the forest behind the building. A person in dark clothing sprints behind the trees. Paused momentarily, I stare before my feet dart to follow. Body before mind, reacting instinctually in pursuit. This friend, or foe, is getting away, diving into the dense woods.

They're agile and moving fast while my legs carry me like a slinky, struggling to keep up. Maintaining a sight-line is the minimum as long as trailing is an option. Trekking up the other side of the ravine, holding steady in hope to reach who awaits. The distance grows, and my body can't keep up. I'm slowly slipping behind. As quick as that aspiration arose, it was dashed. They were gone. Disappeared into the wilderness without any sign or trace of where to next. I stop in disappointment of not reaching what was never in range.

With a skeptical look from Janus, questioning my capabilities to reach them, I catch my breath. Winded, my lungs burn and breathing heaves. The ground is dry, with no obvious tracks. Even if I did find them, time would be so delayed, they'd have no reason to admit their location hours earlier. No way to confirm it. Sooty soles would have worn by then. I admit the unlikely chance that would likely produce nothing.

"Let's go home, buddy."

We turn to go in a mildly embarrassing defeat. I remind myself, everything isn't worth the chase. Each plodding footfall, heavily connecting with the path, resists this sentiment. The journey home is a slow uphill but remains uneventful. A simple, quiet walk is welcomed after the chase. The forest feels fuller now. A shared space more cramped, more observed, and more inevitable to interact. Our biodome crowded out in densification, or shrunken, closing in our perceived worlds. Our lack of solitude is confirmed, even upon returning to our sanctuary. Verified worries unable to be dismissed.

Chapter Twenty-Eight
Security

Now
<u>May 20, 2048:</u>
<u>*(Or is it May 21, 2048?):*</u>

Security is a funny thing. Every living thing desires safety and will take measurable steps to ensure they're protected. All creatures will proactively seek security and avoid danger to prolong their well-being. Advantageously advancing the quality of their lives. A mutually-agreed-upon concept that can become distorted when sly lies and fear are worked into the mix. Mountain lions sit high in trees, watching anything approaching, while hares burrow into dens hidden away. Some even work in symbiotic tandem, such as the remora and shark. They have it figured out, for the most part. We do, to a lesser extent. Being more easily manipulated by our own species is unique to us.

On a primordial level, humans have always feared what is hidden in the dark. Apprehensive of what lurks outside, so instead, staying inside is advised. We remain in familiar groups proven to be safe and cohesive to our lives. Scared of faraway places or strange people with odd ways. Told it may be best to avoid those worlds and their inhabitants altogether. Don't risk the familiar in exchange for difference. Staying in a bubble reassures any concern with the security of acquainted lives. It's survival to be secure when a threat presents itself. The problem is when you're unknowingly presented with a false threat. A non-truth, and your primordial lizard brain reacts reflexively.

Concerns for well-being and protections against those who may act first are always a prime motivator. Armor up, defenses activated, attacks prepared. The trifling idea of weapons of mass destruction gains votes of approval for search and seizures, yet when nothing turns up, it was all in the name of security. When terrorists attack, they must be caught, and if that takes us through every neighboring nation, hopping through as a war machine while communities caught in the crossfire pay the price, so be it. Some oil or other valuables may be picked up along the way, and occupiers may overstay their welcome, but it's all in the name of keeping the citizens secure, happy, and safe. Messaging to wash away actions as many nod in congenial approval.

No one complains for their own good. Protection is needed; otherwise, the desperate, depraved outsiders would claw their way to your wealth, your family, your safety, and all that's held dear. You versus them. Jealous and threatening we can't let them destroy the way of life you've struggled so hard to achieve. Collectively you choose, and when pitted with only two choices, the lesser of two evils doesn't look so bad. Tolerable, considering the alternative. All together, you decide. When the persuasive option presented creates the illusion that there is only one viable solution during dire times, then the choice is seemingly already made. Putting your trust in those who say they know best. Why not?

The concessions aren't all that bad. Give up a little here, sacrifice a little there. It's only a bit and the bigger asks, the larger pains, aren't for you anyway. As long as voting masses are comfortable, the plan won't stop. As long as they're not inconvenienced, it's okay. As long as their towns aren't destroyed, their family isn't detained, they aren't interrogated, then the actions taken serve a greater purpose for our security, and that seems fair. Fair is convincing, as long as it's fairer to you. Initially it won't be big things. Little things; chip, chip, chip; eroding at the foundation you proudly stand upon as you make a deal. An agreement for your security. Chip, chip, chip. Crumbles that tumble, but is it noticed?

A deal was made with a fox to guard the henhouse. He promised that no wild creatures would get past his watch, day or night. Nothing would happen to the hens, or chicks, or eggs inside. They'd be safe and sound as he ensured their security. There were big bad animals that lurked around, watching the coop and waiting for an opportunity to get in. He swore that none would get past, and he held up this truth. During his watch, not only did no threatening animal get past the fox's guard, but they didn't even attempt with the sight of his mighty strength and cunning tactics. Everything appeared secure until one day you noticed there were fewer eggs. He said they had gone bad and were taken care of for the good of the rest. It only makes sense, and so things continued but eventually the eggs dwindled more. The fox said they were damaged. The day came when the fox came for more, stating that the hens were conspiring, and the chicks wouldn't fall in order. He proclaimed that something must be done for the good of the coop; otherwise there would be chaos. He will take care of them with your trust. With feathers flying he did what he felt was best for the security of the coop he was entrusted to guard. Before long, there wasn't much left to protect, but the exchange had been met. A sparse coop, and fat fox remained.

All threats eliminated, and the cost was relative: only a few freedoms traded, subject to change at any time of threat. This was the contract you agreed to. Signed, sealed, and delivered; you are secure in their hands. You're safe by their promise. Guarded and guided by their hand. *Don't you feel safe?*

Chapter Twenty-Nine
Routine

Now
<u>End of July, 2048:</u>

Things these days are definitely not normal, but for the sake of sanity I try to make them so. Attempt to have a routine, just like in the old days. Regardless of the hints of crumbling foundations surrounding us, we try to put together some version of normalcy in desperate hope, or denial, that with enough effort, the bad wouldn't be that bad. A tolerable yet annoying rain cloud we could weather. Attend the happy hours, see the movies, fix up things on your house, invest in retirement, eat healthy, shop for groceries, have a hobby, strive for meaningful work, make friends, work out, and so on. Again, and again, with no end, for a future we had been promised. All for the hope amongst an imperfect system to have it all. To rise with enough hard work. Routine kept us feeling like active players in a game we didn't design without becoming lucid. Routine keeps us grounded, and alive.

In retrospect, there were some irregularities. Glitches in our pleasantly numb compliance of day-to-day activities. Researching the best countries to flee to as women's reproductive rights were stripped. Then go shopping for that week's groceries. Considering how to quickly cross the border over happy-hour drinks, in case we really needed to. Debating which format of currency would be the most valuable, and the pros versus cons of various packs. Watching the latest TV series to be streamed, and escape for a moment. Ogling luxury homes on whatever reality show, knowing it will always be out of financial reach. Turning away from unrealistic real estate and turning toward deep dives of kakistocracies elsewhere in history, scouring for relevant warning signs. A struggle of the past to not allow one stream of thought to consume the other. One demands daily survival maintenance, while the other calls for sustenance of existence beyond the rising tide.

The luxury of opting out is eradicated while living in these mountains. No longer a matter of choice. Every day is filled with chores to be tended, preparations to be made, and precautions to be taken. Wake up, have breakfast, and take note of the tasks at hand for the day. Tidy up and survey the stock of supplies. Visit the gardens to resupply and access the land for scavenged resources, as well as hidden threats. Take the haul to the treehouse, then prep, preserve, and dehydrate for a later date yet to come. Check the house for signs of damage. Wear and tear, in need of repair. Listen to the radio every evening when the night air is clear, for updates transmitting from far away. Sitting and scouring on the deck for signs of hidden life. As the day winds down, our bodies are evaluated for signs of anything needing to be addressed before it compounds. A full dinner lets us settle into moments of leisure, sometimes striking up old hobbies like reading or a puzzle, though they're no longer new ten times over. Wrapping up for the day, one last perimeter check from the deck, lock the door, lights out, and good night. Then we repeat.

Wake up and eat breakfast before addressing tasks. Evaluate supplies, then visit the garden, and take note of the surrounding lands. Crops and foraging prepped, preserved, and dehydrated. Finished goods from days past to be put away. Gauge the house, grounds, gardens, and protections for fixes to be made. Scout and listen, grasping to news, holding to hope, avoiding the threats. Scan our bodies, eat, have some normal enjoyments while winding down. Perimeter, locks, lights out, and good night. Then we repeat.

Wake up, breakfast, and tasks, then account for supplies. Off to the garden, and ground before returning to prep, preserve, and dehydrate the haul. Access fixes to be made, and remedy. Radio and watch for anything new. Take care of our bodies, be fulfilled by dinner, and enjoy leisure. Final checks, locks, and good night. Then we repeat.

Wake up, breakfast, tasks, supplies, garden, grounds, prep, preserve, dehydrate, repairs, radio, scout, heal, dinner, hobbies, perimeter, locks, lights out, and good night. Then we repeat.

Again, and again, and again, and again, and again—with no foreseeable end. Every day is a repetitive routine speckled with variation, but almost identical at its core. Every day, week, and month, we repeat. Repeat, repeat, and repeat again. My attempt at time tracking is weak, and slips as days blur together. The very routine that maintains focus and presence can at times be a maddening hamster wheel.

While some days are easier, and others require more, there is no goal of ascension. A next tier doesn't exist, and there's no promise of rest besides what we can grasp each day. Routine without end can become monotony, but life without routine can spiral into an amorphous sludge. Both void of perfection, but abundant in illusion. Every day, the routine keeps us going for tomorrow. Any further projections or planning become a tethered weight in the deep sea. Best to stay present in the day and reset. Each morning a fresh page, probably slated for similar outcomes.

Chapter Thirty
Whispers

Now
<u>October 2, 2048:</u>

An autumn leaf tumbles along the path, creating little crinkle sounds and tugging at anything it bumps into along the way. So fragile, the wrong force could crush it, but the wind carries an echo, reverberating those sounds. A rustle of fallen form, hollering in a hush. They whisper loudly every year, if you listen. It's becoming evident that a hush doesn't reside exclusively in the natural form. Ears open to receiving messages not directly intended for us. Strung together they shout a story, while separately they're nothing more than wispy words departing lips. Every day, we listen and watch. The days of journalism never quite leave as I gather my notebook and pen while dialing the radio on. Information can blur or be forgotten unless actively noted and reviewed. No red string or tin foil necessary to thread connections together, giving the whispers a voice. I'm always listening for anything more.

The Nation is at war across multiple fronts as the radio made an official announcement eight days ago. Self-proclaimed victim as they marked September 24th as the day *"The World Tried to Steal Greatness"* on all official calendars. Greedy aggressors and selfish derelicts clawing to get in. Assumptions could be made that resources would be spread thin, however, that is not what The Nation is presenting. No, they claim more strength than ever, and even though that can't be validated, one thing is loudly evident.

Their grip is growing tighter as they squeeze out any opposition, international or domestic. Soldiers are deployed for land acquisition that Blake has deemed vital to The Nation, all of which is prickling other countries into a stir. Over a century since one superpower has physically taken space from another. An unjustifiable act, simply because of the players on the board.

The borders are desperately in need of defense as The Nation cries that there are foreign assailants launching attacks, along with smuggling operations. The Nation speaks of its success on this front. Boasting the quantity of villains now captive, but the stories never go further than that. Only enough salivating details dripping out, requesting more. No one bothers digging much deeper, as long as we're safe and the defenses stay far away. An active front requiring diligent efforts from The Nation and soldiers to maintain, continuing to carry out Blake's multistep plan for the prosperity of the future.

Internally, there are protests and dust-ups mainly around cities unwilling to give up the ways before Blake. Cities that refuse to submit to the proclamations and hold in defense the foundational documents like bullet-proof shields, assuming that Blake or his men value these unaltered papers. Cities drenched in sin and swill, as proclaimed by The Nation across the radio, urging citizens to turn away, lest they desire to be turned to a pillar of salt. Cast as a leper in today's society that we must collectively extinguish. Their fire, though, shows no sign of retreating with an intensity that would rather burn it all down than bend.

All sides under strain, Blake reassures the citizens to not worry. Do our part with citizen's duties as well as turn in the deplorables, out the terrorists, and wash our hands of their ways. Reminders to always have faith in his plan. He knew these days would come, and affirms a plan known to only him has been put in motion. Times may be stressful, but the flock should worry not, as long as they are on his side. He vows to acquire what is rightfully that of The Nation. He vows to defend the land from violent infiltrators, even if it means erecting a fortified wall. He vows to hunt down any domestic insurrectionist at any cost and eradicate them like vermin. He vows to see this through and not leave the citizens in their times of need. Whispers of extensions to terms are littered in his words to ensure there is no interruption to the well-being of the people supporting The Nation in these uncertain times.

Not exact words but little hints wrapped in concern and protection. A strong hug holding up for support, shielding us from shrapnel in a fight they initiated with a foe we can't see through the smoke. A convenient series of events. Whispers that can't be hushed, dancing just out of clear range. A promise to come later on for our own good.

Blake alone doesn't hold the news circuit. Those working from within to correct the trajectory of history aren't disappearing. In fact, nearly daily, there are mentions of them on the radio or flyers. Slanderous names designed to make us hate them, fear them, distrust them, and avoid them at all costs. Triggering words like *terrorists, insurgents,* and *criminals,* when the word *"radical"* wouldn't do enough. Anything to smudge their existence as one filled with wretchedness. All things to distance ourselves if we care about our well-being.

This exorbitant amount of effort wouldn't be made for something of no concern. The silly, childlike part of me hopped up on too many superhero movies optimistically hopes they are worried. They are sweating and panicking about what could become. The growing effort they put into snuffing it out only breathe a new life into the embers. Maybe my thoughts are juvenile. Hopeful to root for the forbidden fruit, not only because it sounds delicious, but also because The Nation told me it was poison.

There are rustles of their active existence. Not a boogeyman lurking in the shadows as a manufactured nemesis. I've seen the symbol rumored to be theirs. Once on the corner of a flyer for first-aid training at Hank's, on the bulletin board. Hank couldn't confirm anything, but it looked like what was described on the radio. The other was carved into a tree I noticed while walking amongst the mountains. A tall, skinny rectangle with matching vertical lines coming out of the top and bottom. Each vertical line the length of about half the total height of the rectangle, and neither going through. With six simple structured lines jarring against the natural form the only virtual comparison is to a resistor electrical component. *Does a whisper go by a different title when it's written? Is it a sign when you feel like it's been hand delivered?* More likely it is the imagination creating something out of nothing, clinging to an idea.

Listen closely, and those quiet whispers collectively become spoken. A rustle becomes a gust. Lingering on the edges, fleeting on the outskirts, the sense of presence is as tangible as static in the air before a storm. Unable to hold but fully capable to grasp.

Chapter Thirty-One
Submit

Now
<u>November 2048:</u>

    Peeling the tomatoes from the drying rack to put the dehydrated goods on the shelf for a later day, I inspect each one for problems. About half the rack is lost to fuzzy mildew or mold. Maybe there was too much moisture on the tomato, too thick of a slice, not enough air circulation, or too much humidity in the atmosphere. A disgruntled groan from the depth of my belly, the source of this downfall likely to elude determination. Gathering all the remaining goods, I'm grateful for what was untainted.

    Carrying the jars inside to stock in the pantry, I reminisce on the days when finding spoiled food was a milder frustration, something to be returned and reimbursed. Sun-dried tomatoes in their plastic packaging, perfectly preserved and waiting to be used, calling out from store shelving corners. Simple convenience replaced with arduous obligations.

    The days of easy shopping are so long ago. Well, they're long ago because we're here. This treehouse in the mountain forest that we chose. *That I chose.* Janus came along for the ride and didn't protest. We could still have all the supermarkets and ease of before, had I not chosen to flee. Convenience in some capacity could return if I gave up. In moments of frustration, when everything feels like an uphill battle with the crosswinds of a hurricane, the whisper of creature comforts contains a tempting twinge.

    When a thought of the possibility of submission in exchange for superfluous things crosses my mind, however fleeting, a wet blanket of guilt weighs down upon my spirit. Feelings of internal weakness pathetically exposed in moments of strife. Others have held on through worse, and I could be broken for boxed cookies. Cracks to be spackled when things go wrong after a series of challenging days. Sometimes, when nothing feels like it's going right, I wonder if it would be easier to submit and return to the old world once known. *Is it even an option at this point? What path of destruction and debris did I leave behind?* There's no guarantee of the old life existing, the remaining pillars swept to sea. The possibility is alluring, though. Lie down, stop escaping in an enchanted forest, and return to reality.

There are days when I am tired of the routine. Exhausted by the new rat race but required to simply keep playing. Having taken for granted the tasks arbitrarily labeled as easy that were never actually so simple. No one thinks about what's for lunch when there's always some option in your pantry. Maybe it's not desirable, but it's viable. In truly dire moments, you'd go to the local restaurant to fill the famishment. Enjoying meals is an enormous win that's never guaranteed, and when it fails, I couldn't miss my favorite ramen restaurant more. Selfishly, I wish it were possible to order delivery. What I would do for that warm umami when life is dreary.

Some part of me, deep down, envies those who took no time to lock step when commands were issued. They ducked their heads and looked the other way, doing their best to be scant, while others joined in the raucous whooping with a boisterous round of support that would secure a favorable eye. Regardless of the reasons or techniques, jealously knocks. I know it's not what I want, but I fantasize about how easy it must be and how well they must be doing with shut mouths. Maybe I could have been quieter, smarter, compliant, and calm. Blending in below the radar. An option taken away—*given away*—perhaps for the best, but still.

Like a fever dream, The Nation would welcome me into their folds with my promise to divulge all my knowledge, repent for past sins, and relinquish any resistance. Lay down my sword and give up the fight. Pledge my allegiance to The Nation under God, indivisible. Give way to prioritizing their agenda. Yield my interests in favor of The Nation's. They wouldn't need to know that beyond the surface, I remained the same. The presentation of agreeable nature would suffice. Play nice and surely they wouldn't hold a grudge over previous transgressions, all in the name of washing away my sins. They could "save" me.

Sacrifice convictions for a simpler, easier way of being while waiting for things to pass. Duck my head and be meek. Conform to their standard for exemplary citizens. Listen to the proclamations and don't cause a stir. Don't overreact, don't dramatize; simply fall in line and everything will be fine. Be the damsel in need of rescuing so that Blake and his boys can be the big, strong heroes. Give away these freedoms in exchange for provisions. Be provided a life of promises and protections, as long as I don't think too much. Those who did aren't entirely to blame. While it was hard to leave, that doesn't mean for others it was easy to stay. Stay or stay stuck, but either way they're there to endure in contrast to fleeing to exist.

Maybe it was stupid of me to leave. To choose the more challenging path. A path all my own filled with twists and turns; dips, and bumps. A path to cultivate without interference of influence of an authoritarian force. Maybe I never would have made it back there. They would have seen me, unable to hide unseen signals of my truth. Giveaways that would land me locked up. Traits that deemed me "deplorable" in their vision and black-bagged to one of their facilities. Maybe submission for survival would never really be an option, even if in a different time I had wanted it. A person they'd never deem acceptable.

Little occurrences can create a turmoil that causes a spiraling moment to reel back from. Submission would be a choice of convenience, but living a content existence in that alternate life is unimaginable. Struggles all my own without looming constraints.

Chapter Thirty-Two
Living

Now
<u>February 14, 2049:</u>

Day in and day out, he is there without fail. Face smelling, tail wagging, dutifully waiting to be signaled for what is next. Without a care in the world. I envy his bliss, as if the world hasn't crumbled. As if our lives haven't been upended from what once was in contrast to this new structure. No evidence of longing or missing previous normalities. Janus is exuberantly happy for every moment. Purely present, leaving a sting of jealousy as I try to meditate my way into now.

He must realize the days he once lived are not the same as now. He must notice that our walks are filled with a vast density of trees the city streets never had. Similar to those of a camping trip. And while it's rumored dogs don't tell time the same way as humans, surely he understands we've been so-called camping longer than ever before. Looking at that full-toothed grin, I wonder if he thinks this is one big vacation adventure. *Camp Hideaway : Where escapism is forever.* He harbors no desire to exchange the boundless forests, an exotic plethora of new smells, and uninterrupted hours with Mom for anything else. *Could this be his best day with no end, and he's perfectly content to not return?*

Curious and sporadically chasing whatever calls to him. Determined to investigate every new scent, but not disappointed if the source cannot be found, or if a new one is discovered en route to solving the old mystery. No expectation or checklist to complete. Taking each new detail fully as it comes in its newness, and nothing more. A mental note, pleasing to the senses, to be cerebrally catalogued before moving to the next fresh aroma.

As he skirts between trees, and feet pitter-patter through the crunchy foliage, I'm never far from sight. He regularly checks in, stopping by for a scratch or visually verifying my location, never venturing beyond a comfortable distance. A safety confirmation of support for both of our well-beings, even if it is only psychological. Each of us is mutually aware that the other would never leave, but still we verify for assurance.

My stability is rooted in this world, dependent and forcing my presence. A living talisman, grounding me here, unable to be swept away; tethering me to this rooted place regardless of external world events. Without him, there is no doubt I would be lost to the consuming pressure. Carried down-stream in my worries. He probably doesn't realize the power he wields or the weight he holds. If so, then Janus is playing it cool with no evident ego.

He dedicates attention only to that which really matters. Anything going on beyond this space is of no concern. Every morning and night, greeting with kisses, snuggled up closely. Every meal, a delicious delight. Every ball or stick to fetch is the greatest game. Every endearing connection between us is an electrifying joy to light up the day. Simple, uncomplicated joys. Nothing could be better than right now, because nothing else exists or matters.

Humans struggle to be present, creating courses to purchase so mentors can teach devotees how to live in this moment. My mind wanders to current events, endless possibilities, random thoughts, and fears—both rational and irrational alike. Janus needs no mentor or course, having mastered something I struggle to grasp. To not care even enough to glimpse beyond the veil. Nonchalantly carefree, as if nothing has changed or is worth dwelling over. Every day is the best day. Watching him swirl into a snuggled circle at night, I marvel at this ability for tranquility, even if it's second nature.

When the world reminds me of the looming stresses or threats in the distance, Janus is there to bring me back from the edge. Reminding of what is good, regardless of the clouds dotting the horizon. Asking me to stay with him and not look beyond. Encouraging me to not dwell somewhere else. Wanting to enjoy this time. Feeling his thick bristly fur nestle up against my arm, how could I say anything but yes?

Chapter Thirty-Three
Ghost in the Forest

Now
<u>March 22 or 23, 2049</u>:

The fresh produce is running low in the pantry. Not wanting to dip into the dehydrated goods unless absolutely necessary, we'll need to restock from the wild gardens. Seasonally there should be at least something available, even if it's not an ample cornucopia to dream about. Hopefully spring things have sprouted earlier.

The air is crisp like the fruit-and-veggie section of a grocery store after the automatic misters time out. Damp, sharp, cool, and biting, but a bit refreshing. Not sure whether it's uncomfortable or not, those days hovering in spring, unsure what they want to be. The damp chill lingers a bit in the mountains as the misty temperatures cling to the foliage and forest floor. I viscerally cringe at the clammy, wet feeling of dew upon the skin of my hands while reaching between leaves to uproot earthen vegetables. Wiping it off on my pants with each piece of produce pulled. An old habit that will never die, as if it wipes clean the event in time to take the chilly plunge again.

The selection provides, but is redundant and limited. Each wild garden gives a feeble offering for which I am grateful but as we move to the next, we yearn just a little bit more. A little more desperate each time dashed. Taking what we can, knowing that any creature could end up claiming their share, leaving the supplies even more sparse. I understand and appreciate their fight in the same survival game, but refuse to skew my play for theirs. They can take what they can, then turn to the hills as they always have, long before we planted anything.

Moving farther out to the last of the gardens, and I pick things along the way, eager to be done. To go home, sit down, and relax. It's tempting to finish early and I'm content with my collection thus far, but that would be foolish. Almost a jinx laughing in the face of bounty.

Influencers would have said I'm suffering from "scarcity mindset," but it's not like they're grasping at turnips for their next meal. No benevolent gratis guaranteed for later.

The last of the root vegetables in one bag, wild berries in a different one, and a few more wild onions in sight—our rewards are multiplying. As I reach through the cover plants with them in my grasp, Janus emits a low growl with his mohawk cackled. Still crouched, my head lurches up, eyes swiftly trying to find the cause of his warning.

The throbs of my heart pound loud thumps in my ears, as the world lies silent. Absent of motion, everyone holding position. Watching, knowing Janus doesn't growl without reason. Waiting, refusing to give away anything until I'm certain. A standoff, biding time in anticipation of someone cracking. Janus by my side, vigilant.

I slowly draw in breath when, from the corner of my eye, I see a shadow flash between distant trees. Immediately standing, I stare to where it went, but there is no visible sign. Nothing but vacancy of a once co-occupied space. Smoke since vanished. Barely hearing some footfall far in the distance, retreating and getting fainter by the second. Scanning and searching for more, as my frozen limbs hold their ground with only my eyes moving along the horizon. Observing but dumbfounded, knowing it was more than a shadow.

The quandary disturbance now gone, we are left standing there alone. Vulnerable and exposed for all to see, with little shielding our position. Suddenly all forest eyes are observing. Feeling watchful gazes from beyond the light. A sharp nip in the wind descends. A brutal reminder of susceptibility in our fragility. Hastily grabbing our things, we walk toward home. Cueing to Janus that it's time to leave, I urge his proximity with unknown things beyond.

"Come on, Janus. Stay close."

The whole way back, I'm unable to shake the feeling of being watched. Janus doesn't leave my side. Sniffing exploration can wait for another day. Right now our mission is to return safely. Any crack or rustle or snap sends a jump through my body as I jerk my head to look in the source's direction. Yet, there is nothing to be seen. Only a picture-perfect snapshot, with everything in its place. A quaint image, while insidious concerns hide. Something perfect, suddenly unsettling.

Returning to the treehouse, the door is shut and locked with a thudding certainty. Securely within our structure while a lingering essence of today's events hang over. Warily looking out the windows, expecting to see evidence of peering forces. Someone gawking from the trees. Our once-formidable walls reduced to the glass of a one-way mirror. They watch, and I watch, but in the darkness I can see nothing.

Consumed by concern, I step into the cold evening air of residual winter clinging, to remove the barrier of structure from my viewing. Janus stays inside, already curled up and not enticed when the temperature is this chilly. He keeps a watchful eye for a moment, but soon drifts to a dozy dreamland. Standing up to the railing's edge, I strain, looking in every direction. Under an observation tank, my gaze scrutinizes anything in eyesight, convinced they must be out there. They could have followed us. They could know we're here. They could see me right now. Exposed, the thought of our safety comes into question.

As panic surges up inside a volatile sea of stomach acid, I grip the railing, holding to what can tangibly be verified. There is nothing visible in the surrounding landscape. No signs present themselves that anyone is there. No evidence that we are actively being watched or threatened. Janus shows no sign of alarm. We are safe and aware. Pushing down the fear, telling myself as many times as it takes:—*We are safe, and aware.*

My heartbeat stabilizing, though an extrasensory feeling throughout my skin resides. Finally able to breathe a little deeper, I repeat those reassurances, knowing that nothing in this moment will be solved. The watch on a whole will not end, regardless of today's shift coming to a close. A false bubble of protection popped. They were within the space deemed ours on maps I've drawn. Within the region of our gardens, paths plausibly crossing and creating an unanticipated intrusion. A violation of privacy, and ownership, if that still holds any value.

The catalyst behind the reeling feelings threatening to pull me off balance may be rationalized, but it doesn't resolve the very real concern of this identity. I'm unsure if anything can erase the worries of what this implies, but the mint tea from the kettle calms the residual symptoms. A soothing hot liquid stretching out into every crevice of my esophagus on its way to coat the walls of my stomach cavity, melting away tension along the way down. Folk medicine that's perhaps a placebo in these delicate moments, as I'm clinging to what there is.

Janus sleeps, assured the events of the day have passed. Watching his pleasant sleep creates a longing for my own. A REM cycle refresh washing away what I wish would disappear. Lying down into a dream, I wait for the sleepy night to take me, and tomorrow is a new, less taxing day to rebound.

Chapter Thirty-Four
Sacred

Now
<u>Early Summer 2049:</u>

Down in the ravine, slightly northeast of our treehouse, splits a large river cutting through. Shallow pools form by trapped water in nooks, and aquatic plants flourish. Its accessibility is a reminder it'd be advisable to refill the two empty gallon containers with flowing water before the temperatures rise. Water catchment of thunderstorm downpours is plentiful in spring, but with the onset of summer, results become less consistent. That mountain over there may receive a dousing while ours is parched, or vice versa.

It's cool, and jarring to the initial touch that transforms to a refreshing release on this first truly hot day of the season. Janus stares at the fish he can see swimming beneath the surface, as if they are boldly entering his space, while his paws chaotically step in. Nature's aquarium. He watches, amused by the meeting and unsure why they refuse to play.

Berries are hanging over water, watercress rooted in the shallows. Turning over rocks, I feel around for something rougher than the smoothly eroded stones. My hands search for crustaceans. Hurting anything hurts me at my core, so we'll make it swift. The clams and mollusks in these rivers are easy prizes with lots of calories. At least they don't have a face, but some part of me still feels remorse. I say a little "sorry" for my actions and a "thank you" for their sacrifice. A feeling that I must, but past life me would have sternly questioned this sentiment. *She had a grocery store.*

The mollusks sit in the small bucket of water to stay unspoiled. At home we'll cook, and then dehydrate for an obnoxiously long time, or maybe smoke instead. Tough clams are disgustingly chewy, but I hear dysentery is worse. While they sit, I fill the jugs and balance them on top of one another in my pack. Raising a hand, I catch Janus's attention. Palm up, fingers uniformly folding toward my body. He shakes off and comes to shore.

Rarely do we take the exact same route to and from, unless we are in a rush. Every new path is an opportunity to understand this land a little better. Regardless of our expansive exploration, the different options seem endless. My copious notes of various sightings, plants, geological features etc are so thick they could be a field guide if anyone was ever interested. Almost half-way home, still near the river as it runs west, we come across an old church hidden behind a bend.

Sitting on a ledge overlooking the river valleys, a different me in an alternate world would've been so distracted during services by the scenery that lay just behind. Clearly not their goal, but surely a side effect. There's no one to ask, and I never was an active parishioner. Only enough remnants remain to see a partial skeletal structure of the building that once stood.

The floor now gone; or maybe it's hidden, fully covered with vines, grass, and ferns. Forest ground cover pops up between decrepit pews. The vast majority have rotted out and haphazardly lean into the earth. A few defy the years, still standing with different dilapidated colors than they had originated with. Scattered stones of the back sacristy wall present with depleted sections providing a straight-shot view of the river valley behind. Hints of the base of the back windows are all but wiped out. Every last stone holds some trace touched by nature. Moss and mold cling to every incongruent indentation. Vines climbing, overtaking, defying gravity with no directional purpose.

Nature has staked its claim in what humanity decided to erect and then subsequently abandon. With humans out of sight, the wild moved in. *Why shouldn't it, though? This space belonged to them first.* Staring at the peace that resides, nothing strikes an abnormal or anomalous note. As if it was always meant to be this way. We finally stepped out of the way and let the earth do what was better as a whole. Tranquility returned, despite the monstrosities of people.

A melancholy pang hangs on, wishing to not leave this enrapturing space. This place exists, reminiscent of what it feels like for time to stand still. Not in a moment of panic but peace. An enveloping calm, desiring to hold us in reassuring arms. We pull away from this place, as light is fading while the contradictory thoughts of monstrosity, and monsters slink forward.

Humans have long since told lore of the scary things that go bump in the night. Stories of mystical beasts waiting for unsuspecting human victims. Creatures transforming, shape-shifting, deceiving their homosapian neighbors. They are bad, and we are good. Their oddities, a supposed flaw we capitalize upon to cast out and build barricades. Grab the torches, build the walls, sharpen the stakes, and load the bullets, because a fiendish thing is waiting to suck out your blood along some barren southwest desert plateau when you've wandered too far. *How could they ever be good or neutral when the writer of the narrative is always the hero?*

It was never their space. They never defend themselves. Survival was their main priority as creatures, and they stumbled to unfortunately cross paths. That doesn't sound as scary, and a neutral foe doesn't equate to an automatic hero. A complicated narrative won't do, even though we take their land, resources, corral, and crowd away. We threaten, demonize, and scare into hiding—clearly the monster couldn't be us.

The monsters could never be seen in our mirrors, or so the narrative goes. Every story presents the best version of the writer and their allegiances. Dictators never felt they were the villain. Fellers of mass acreage don't consider the ecological damage or creatures' uprooting they're causing. People who spank don't consider the emotional damage, even if bruises don't show. MLM leaders never cast themselves as scam artists ruining lives. Self-written narratives, and those for individual or community self-interest, can never be considered completely accurate. Real monsters wear innocent masks rather well. Incognito in public.

Nature reclaims, and restores. It doesn't lie because it doesn't have the time, or energy, or interest to do so. *What point would a deceitful nature be?* It won't earn more of anything, and its actions aren't intentionally ill-willed, even if the outcome contains unpleasant consequences. *Maybe they'd survive better if they did.* Nearing the end of our journey home, its refreshing to not need to read between the lines.

These wild spaces have nothing to hide from their truth.

Chapter Thirty-Five
Injured

Now
<u>September 29, 2049</u>:

A shrieking scream pierces the air, crying out in bloodcurdling panic and pain. Janus and I stop in our tracks, both stunned into silence. The unsettling disruption undulates in a volume of peaks and valleys, but the tone doesn't change. A primal wail permeates, sounding more and more akin to an animal. My stomach churns, connecting conclusions of the source. In nonverbal tandem, we swiftly move toward the screeching sound, almost running. An urgency to find it as fast as possible, but also the dread to think what I'll see.

The notes grow louder as we approach within the vicinity. Near the tree base, just in sight there, is a thrashing of brown and white fur with intermittent moments of pause, all to the soundtrack of painful squeals. A wild rabbit has been caught by something, fighting chaotically for its freedom.

I slowly approach so as to not intensify its fear. Signaling for Janus to stay back and sit just behind me. Always a good listener, he won't chase, but seeing the rabbit's turmoil has him whimpering in sympathy. Its hind leg is caught in a jaw trap. At least it's newer, and guarded with rubber instead of bare metal. Skin intact and blood not spilled; we have to only hope no limbs are broken. It's claimed to be more humane because the rubber doesn't hurt. I think the rabbit would attest otherwise. Maybe the hunter should be lurched into one to hear his perspective.

Shaking away the far-off thoughts of rabbit vengeance, we make eye contact as I go to hold its torso still. Careful to try and prevent accidental consequential harm. There is nothing but terror swimming in those wide pupils, and a desperate hope to not die right now. Pinning him with one hand, I place my foot on one side of the machine's lever while pressing down with my other hand on the opposite.

The cold metal is manipulated, designed to create intense damage. Holding the victim in place, a lack of blood flow can cause gangrene. Animals have been known to violently break their teeth gnawing at their tether, attempting to escape. Nerve damage never to be fixed. Indiscriminate weapons of torture justified by man. Gravely fighting the trap's strength and pushing against the spring's tension, hoping it's not too late.

The mouth of the trap creaks open slightly, and then a bit more. Finally, enough of a gap forms to where the rabbit flails its leg from the vice and bolts away, past my grip. He doesn't dare wait around to find out if I'm the friend who saved him or the foe who set the trap in the first place. I barely see him beyond a ball of fur zipping away, bounding down the hill; the fleeing feeling resonates. Slowly I release my pressure so the trap can close again with us both out of its dangerous snap.

There is no doubt in my mind that this can't stay here. Whoever set it will be back and will most likely reset. Best to stave the damage from the source. Following the chain along the ground to its spike in the foliage, I reach in amongst the ferns to rip it out in finality.

"AHHH! Fuck!"

A sharp, searing pain pierces my forearm followed by warm liquid spreading. Deep, caged breaths as I cling to my body and shoo Janus from the spot while he's become alert at my cry.

"No! Stay there! Stay!"

A radiating pulsation consumes my flesh as pain turns to anger deciphering what just happened. Leaning over and looking more closely, deep in the forest floor ferns; a barbed wire woven throughout the plants and circling the stake becomes visible upon inspection. A brutal trap for anyone looking to snag their tool. Egotistically throwing punches in a fight they started but no one wanted. *Fuck, I should have checked. So stupid to not look, and now this.* The wire, having torn away into the flesh of my arm, left wide, jagged slices deep enough to leave scars.

Wrapping my arm in scrap fabric, I lay the piece over and awkwardly around as a temporary fix. Debatable whether it's enough to ensure no future bleeding or reopening, but hope holds on tightly. Swift kicks and stomps fueled by frustration, I demolish the barbed wire beneath my boots. Carefully, with gloves, a do-over, gathering the dirty wire and trap into a spare tote bag with its worn-out grocery store logo, for transit somewhere safer. Any plans we had of further outdoor tasks are immediately scrapped with this new problem to remedy.

Every step feels heavy as the bag's weight grows. Humanity's blatant ego over everything harmed more than it could have ever cared. Fitting, considering the state of things. If only more empathetic minds could have contributed more. A dull ache grows in my arm with each swing in step. Sore and stiff, rusting up along the way. Hardened in its singular position, the tension is no longer malleable.

Chucking the trap into the river to sink to the bottom to never be seen again is an attractive option. Maybe unfair to the aquatic residences, but it really wouldn't be gone either. Still a chance some lucky human would discover it, and some unlucky creature would find it later. The sight of it repulses me, knowing its heinous capabilities. An unknown history hidden within. It will stay in the storage bench on our deck. Maybe if I can lock it away, that will make this moment dully fade and erase the damage done. Repress the harm.

Inside, gingerly pulling up my sleeve, the scrap fabric has stiffened into a crusty exoskeleton with sporadic dark spots. Peeling them away, the now-stale dryness tugs at hairs, leaving a concoction of crusted blood and muck. A bowl of water and damp cloth start to make work of removing the layers to reveal jagged incisions underneath. The exact contents of the not-blood material is concerning. Suspicions are definitely not good. Having heard stories of dirty warfare smearing weapons with decaying animal parts or fecal matter for a long-game return on the enemy, fears intensify and I wonder whether it's possible to undo the muddled mess. Meticulous care and attention is given to wipe away every visible streak. Tediously lifting little bits of skin flaps, incase anything snuck its way underneath. With fresh water and fresh towels, I scrub through the pain with soap. Gritting my teeth as the rag wipes across raw wounds.

A final rinse, a pat dry, and—for one last measure—a splash of rubbing alcohol, then a clotting powder with optimism that it's not expired. *Does clotting powder expire?* An injury so tender, my body barely registers the heat searing throughout my forearm . Let it air dry, and let it calm.

With the passing of time, I carefully touch the nearby healthy skin to see if it is dry so my injury can be wrapped in gauze. Hoping it doesn't ooze too much as our stock is limited. Could eventually resort to scrap fabric, but it's not ideal. Some ibuprofen will have to do for now, leveling everything out if it's strong enough. At a future dressing change, I'll plan to use some of the antibiotic lotion. Right now it seems like the necessary boxes have been checked without being overdone, pushing us into other problem areas. Exact memories of wilderness first aid is a smidge foggy.

Drained and feeling like I'm eight again with a badly scraped knee from riding bikes, but Mom, and Dad aren't here to kiss away my boo-boos. The weight of today settles in, but as Janus looks upward with raised eyebrows in anticipation, I know it's not over. He needs to be fed, and I do too. Cleaning up any dishes and discarding of waste items will probably be the most tasks accomplished because all I want to do is recede into the bed.

With a stiff groan, pulling myself up from the chair, I slowly lumber toward the kitchen. Janus prances at my side, having shaken off today's events, happy for what's next. Letting the residual sour feelings dissipate, I know even when the days are dark, he shines bright.

Chapter Thirty-Six
Wandering

Now
<u>October 5, 2049:</u>

Days have passed, and I am barely here. Struggling to stay awake, and present as a cocoon of sleep envelopes everything. Regardless of where I am, it finds me. The desk, the soft chair, the bed are acceptable places to pull me under and let my body fall limp.

My forearm is hot to the touch, and tender. Pinkish puffy skin surrounds the wound locations. Former scabs are now larger, secreting a slight cloudy ooze. More if you were to press on them. If touched, there'd be a searing pain screaming from a place unanimously hurting. To the point of a pseudo-numbness, it would somehow intensify. A white light of suffering courses through as if I've stumbled into too many things and discovered the unpleasant way.

At first it was fine, and under control. The basic pain relievers were doing their best, and everything was proceeding unremarkably. Until two days ago, when the fever crept up and the meds' defenses crumbled, regardless of efforts. Outmatched and overwhelmed, the tenderness began to set in. The swelling started, and scabs began to look funny. Everything only progressed from there, and quickly a cataclysm of compounding symptoms arose. An arms race of which can be worse, each vying for the top.

Roughly 20% of the world's population died in 1918 due to an influenza epidemic that swept the globe. Prolonged high fevers can cause brain damage. It's estimated that approximately 148,000 annually die alone, and remain unclaimed, so their ashes are buried in mass graves in this country.

Aches radiate from every joint, especially whenever there is a shift or movement. Every limb feels like it's breaking. Warmth bubbling up and boiling over. Starting as something that's deniable, but before long, the illusion is broken. Without a doubt, there's a fever. Ibuprofen keeps fighting, but the fever doesn't retreat. It grows warmer by the minute, until it's running hot. Skin pulled tight and lips chapped. Before long, a sweat is perspiring across my skin, creating an uncomfortable dampness. With blankets on it's too warm, but remove them, and it's too cold. Uncomfortable in every position.

Sleep takes me with sweeping hands, and I cannot resist. Hands upon my shoulders holding tight and pulling back into the comforts of the bed as a cloud of darkness descends. Everything fades to sleep, but not rest. A racing mind cycles through versions of reality, and the fantastical. Deep green forests and talking dogs. Gourmet meal of leaves, midnight sun in winter, life in floating bubbles above cities, and it goes on, and on, with any and every random combination generated. Each a surreal potpourri holding me hostage.

Every year in The Nation, there are nearly 7.15 million illnesses that are caused by waterborne pathogens in this developed country. It was last reported there were over 33 pathogens that led to infection and death only a few years ago. Worldwide, 13.7 million people died of infection, though if left untreated, the specific infection of gangrene is almost 100% fatal.

A sudden awakening with no concept of time past. Minutes or hours are indistinguishable, even by the daylight present, unless it crosses over from day to night or night to day. Somehow in my stupor Janus's needs are still being met, though I'm unsure how it's managed. The question of how many meals or drinks have been consumed is still up for debate, but evidence is present in the form of used dishes. When wellness seems to be possible, sitting upright is a task. Almost beginning to plan, and then a wave of exhaustion hits as darkness crashes again. In and out like this for what feels like days, though I couldn't actually say. Stuck in a tumble cycle of waking rest and restless sleep.

Each step unsure, I gingerly clunk forward toward a target that feels far away, like a reward is dangling at the end of the hall. Cumbersome in slow motion, moving through gelatinous air. Unstable while masking troublesome truths of immense overwhelm, and the serious predicament at hand. Slipping into hazardous territory with only a dinghy against a swelling sea storm. A little dot amongst the waves growing, ready to consume without the slightest concern. Insignificant in our fight, clinging on.

Exposure takes 23% of its victims. Almost 80% of injuries here are sprains, and strains, but not typically fatal. A compound tibia fracture certainly could be deadly with the inevitable complications in a place like this. Fatal wilderness injuries take men at a rate of 78%, significantly more than women, though the reasons for this are not disclosed.

Wishing the swirling would stop, I consume as much water as possible. Desperately trying to hydrate and flush simultaneously with each glass chugged. Shoving down fever suppressants, attempting a return to normalcy. With every cleansing of the arm, an anguish is accentuated by the antibiotic lotion smearing across in despair. An ongoing battle continues with minimal glimmers of reprieve. Small moments that not all is lost. Imagine holding onto a rope tethered to tomorrow. Clinging tightly, being pulled through these ailments. Semi-present, passing from this moment to the next, yearning with no promise.

Chapter Thirty-Seven
A Gift

Now
<u>October 6, 2049</u>:

Sunlight fills the room and a soft glow insists on waking us in its rays. The still bed holds me, my body limp and heavy. Turning over is a painful effort that doesn't seem worth it. Instead, it's easier to lay here and occasionally blink the ceiling into view. Dark shutters open and close, lingering in one position before transitioning to the other. Sometimes they stay shut as I listen to the ambient noise of tree branches swaying and Janus sleeping.

There's a *thud* interrupting the fogginess of a semi-awake slumber that must be a pinecone hitting the deck. Remaining still, I feel Janus tense up. Alert before he launches himself from the bed, fervently growling. Rousing from exhaustion, I begin to sluggishly prop myself up on the edge of the bed. Feet planted and groggily staring ahead, I call to him, but he's insistent. Refusing to leave the door, waiting for attendance.

Demanding to be taken seriously, Janus is adamant that attention needs to be directed outward. Begrudgingly, my body trudges toward my shoes and haphazardly feet are inserted before making it to the door. Vision is as stable as when the drinks start kicking in, and my body moves with the certainty of a tranquilizer still partially present. Still, I make my way to the door and look around the deck, but nothing appears out of order. Gazing at the tree line, all the canopy blurs together with all the leaves indistinguishable from the next. He's still persistent, and not yet satisfied.

Working down the pulley, I almost trip to the ground over my own feet, or the platform, or nothing at all, while disembarking. Looking around, I don't want to venture too far for fear of becoming lost. We keep the base of our tree directly to our back for sanity. Circling the trunk, only the trees stare back.

I almost stumble over Janus, who's infatuated with something on the ground. Assuming it's something disgusting, as dogs will be obsessed with, I insist he leaves it. He won't. I bend over with a hand on the trunk to not end up upside down, and there it is. A small package wrapped in brown paper and twine with a black raven feather tucked in. It glistens iridescently with hints of violet and sapphire, with emerald slipping through. A luminescent sheen dancing to life.

Packages don't show up from the earth. Intentionally placed—that knock of a pinecone seems less likely to have been anything botanical. A gift wrapped up and presented to be received. I grab the find to investigate inside. Ascending slowly, each pull of the rope is weighed down by the weight of what remains unknown. A brick of a glamour.

Inside, it sits at the table opposite me, staring in a duel. Maybe looking long enough will reveal something without yet opening. The neatly crisp edges and precisely wrapped twine, mocking in its contrasting absurdity to this world. The feather twirling between my fingers offers no answers, regardless of how long I stare into its onyx depth. Giving into curiosity, the twine unravels with a tug and the wrapping unfolds, revealing a tin box accompanied by a note.

A handwritten note states: *"This is an antibiotic. Specifically, it's doxycycline for the infection in your arm. Take one tablet every twelve hours for the first day, then one tablet once a day until you run out. With water, and food is advised. Please accept, as you don't appear to be doing well and infections can be deadly."*

No name or signature or any other form to identify the sender. Only instructions and a request to not object, along with the wrapping, its container, and the feather. The feather stands there as a random touch, and I'm unable to make sense of its presence. A stranger offers you candy and it'd be dangerous to say yes, but this stranger offers medical salvation and you question every side. Blurry thoughts struggle to make sense of the circumstance. A language spoken you don't speak and are expected to understand.

The golden fleece, promising to take away the pain when it's needed most, seems all too convenient. Warily looking at the tin I debate its value and how to proceed. Offered up on a platter to heal what ails. A fork of choice. Ignore the gift altogether and keep on the path we've been trudging in hopes of a turnaround without too much damage, or demise in the process. Take the pills, and if the instructions are true, then the journey could be easier with a safer guarantee of success.

Skeptically looking at each tablet with their visible abbreviated engraving that I can't look up. My phone is long since dead, and even if it weren't, there's the possible ping to a tower with this geographic location. Regardless of how long I stare at those tiny markings, a pharmaceutical language verifying or disproving anything won't come through. The desperation is palpable. A canine's salivation at a dangling T-bone.

Intuitively my body leans into them, longing to trust the note as truth. A slight restraint holds back from consuming it yet, as the little pill is examined at eye level. *What if they're not doxycycline? What if it's something else? A trap, or poison maybe—but why?* Two sides of thoughts battling back and forth, weighing out reality versus paranoia and the likelihood of the chances of the ridiculous scenarios I've dreamt up. Whiplash while weighing out possibilities back and forth, until the conversation lands in circles.

Only me and that little pill will provide either salvation or death. A stand-off, backed against the wall, I throw it in my mouth followed by gulps of water until the little mystery capsule hits the pit of my stomach. Sitting there doing what it does and I wait. Feeling like a ticking time bomb, not knowing what is to come next. It's strange to be on the precipice of something. To hope for one result, while knowing there's a chance that was never a possible outcome. Putting all your hope in a note from a stranger still seems delusional, even on this dire day. A trust fall if there ever was one, or maybe last actions from a cornered beast that's not so altruistic.

Sitting and resting in the bed. Fading in and out of sleep, waiting for something to happen. As of now, no bad events are ultimately good. No reason to panic when the promise is not yet broken. Thoughts spiral as the day starts to set and dusk creeps in. Eyes growing heavy with our basic needs met; neither of us opposed to turning in early. There's not much else to do in moments like this. A reminder that survival can in fact be a boring waiting game of who is more stubborn: disaster or me. I hate waiting. I never had and still lack patience. Indulging in pondering events is tempting. Speaking theories out loud to my clawing audience, but tonight I can't muster prose more than the obvious.

Instead, I opt out. Lie back and cover up, watching the night envelop the canopy and darkness settle in. With each breath, the senses of healing and harm fight for my wits, with a conclusion yet to be determined. Slipping into sleep, I think of tomorrow and hope the dawn will bring something better.

Chapter Thirty-Eight
Renewed

Now
<u>October 14, 2049:</u>

Legs limber up, as they stretch out this morning beneath the covers. Toes curling and arching with renewed excitement to easily walk without stumbling. Everything appears fresher than before in this new morning light. Effortlessly sitting up from the bed that once pulled, no longer able to hold its grasp. It's casually dismissed and pushed away, unable to fully envelop. Enjoyable sleep isn't all-consuming; trapping the visitor until their release is granted.

A cicada shedding its exoskeleton, vibrantly free. Only a few days prior it was held captive by a hard shell that no longer serves a purpose. I'm grateful to have broken through the tough exterior and leave behind that which bound me to the bed. Delusionally slipping in and out of a waking state, unsure each time if I would wake again.

The medicine took to healing quicker than could have been expected, and soon its validity wasn't under scrutiny. Death by poison is a priority of concern. As it worked its magic, I grew stronger and the symptoms lessened. The pain dulled, the swelling reduced, the oozing stopped, and the fever broke. As the outward signs subsided, internal energy began to rebound. Before long, simple tasks didn't feel like a chore, and waking every morning was less surprising. Soon everything was almost back to normal, with only minor stiffness and some residual scabs. Leftover evidence in their final stages of healing.

Looking at those little scabs and scars, I imagine a mountain ridge now stabilized with tectonic plates slowing down. Small peaks jaggedly remain, while the base dissipates into the rest of the skin, where a valley of scars are displayed. Remnants of battle wounds, bright and grayish white. A forever reminder of the time man almost ended my existence without ever coming into a direct fight. Anything could hold new dangers, never previously given much consideration. Finding out the hard way leaves its marks.

Walking through the treehouse feels fresh like spring, though autumn leaves fall outside. Each step is confidently placed toward the task at hand. Well-worn rustic floors full of character are appreciated under each footfall, without worry of being a tripping hazard, while stumbling around any uneven edge. Meals taste full of flavor though the recipes haven't changed. Janus is back to being spirited, having shaken off the cloak of worry that was without a doubt hanging heavy as he dutifully watched, unable to do anything besides console. Everything could be summarized in the tidy concept of renewing seasons full of rebound.

A journey conveniently compartmentalized into a simple truth that it isn't a lie, but doesn't fully articulate the wild ride it took to get here. About as neat and simple as the tin with its few remaining pills and leftover parchment packaging still loudly sitting on the desk. Uninvited company that isn't the worst guest to have. A presence whose mere existence disturbs the balance of our solitary space. Evidence of others. Their interactions creating more questions than answers.

I reexamine the pills with a side eye every time with every passing walk, as if some clue was missed from before. Turning over the parchment, I scan for anything besides vacant words. The tin is just a tin with nothing extraordinary about it. The feather clearly meant to evoke some thought or feeling, but it's drawing up nothing besides blanks. Staring at the glistening sheen of the raven feather slowly twirling between my fingers, all I see is exactly that. Beautiful and intelligent creatures. Eerily stunning; however, nothing specific comes to mind as relevant to this life or the medicine. Plain items arranged mundanely containing something extraordinary.

One thought won't subside. The concept of being alone here has passed. Retrospectively, it was a silly idea to think we could always exist in a forever season of isolation, but I had been holding on tightly to the delusional warmth of summer rays. If only it was believed hard enough, we could always sit in those days blocking out anything to come. A cherished memory in dreary times, vividly present behind shut eyes. Regardless of my wishes, the leaves fall in a cacophony of truths.

Ignoring their descent won't change the trajectory. Someone was out there next to our safe haven.

A stranger waiting, observing, and holding all the cards in their hands for any future decisions while I had sat in our safe space, completely oblivious to having ever been watched. Drifting thoughts of reflective eyes watching from shadowy distances. A specimen in its enclosure. Feeling alone is one thing, but being alone and feeling like you're not is a whole different energy. Abandoned to wonder all the what-ifs.

Possibilities swirl and try to run away down twenty different paths at once. Perplexed by who the onlookers could be as I stew. The notion of generosity has become scarce in this new world, especially in a terrain that demands everything for your own existence. The idea of sharing is a rarity. Tall tales that would be an idealistic fantasy of what could be. A utopia that holds no water under The Nation's fist. They didn't only share random resources. Medicine, particularly antibiotics, are hard to come by and highly valued. *Who in their right mind would share that with a random stranger?* Nothing makes sense as a riddle mocks my questioning.

Fighting back cynicism, the fleeting thought arises of someone seeing my state and understanding what was likely to come next, experienced enough to move hearts. *Can hearts still melt here?* Hard to believe. The action itself still feels transactional. A debt now owed with no idea who I'm expected to repay.

There's no solution right now, no matter how many times I ransack the facts. Too many variables and unknowns to dwell on. It was what it was and that can't be undone; I've grown to accept moments will pass where actions are limited. Wasting time wondering will be all-consuming if allowed. Not to neglect entirely, though, as a new watch of vigilance will be renewed. This time mixed with curiosity, not exclusively fear. There's something out there. Someone has been watching.

It is a new day with fresh opportunities stepping out of the cold winter of illness. Each small task is significant, but not in the burdensome way. No, in a way that understands the impact of each individual action. *How lucky am I to be able to take part in them?* More than wounds healed in my hibernation, providing a pause even in the mundane and monotonous moments. For had I not woken, these moments would be nothing but a far-off memory, and I'd be longing to do the things I had once complained about, never accessible again. Grateful for the boring tasks and simple trappings of the treehouse. Looking out, the leaves radiate a little more vibrantly and every tousle of my hand through Janus's fur feels more comforting.

My struggle to put the pieces together of everything that's happened, what caused them to be, and what is next wages on in my head. I try to be here without drifting off. Resisting fading away to moments that are beyond this one. This is all I have. Nothing is guaranteed or owed. Always needing to make my own way. Excel to standards I never set, but the weight of this thought sits heavier. Tomorrow is yet to be determined, but today I'll sit here on the deck with Janus and enjoy the view.

Chapter Thirty-Nine
Buzz Buzz

Now
<u>November 4, 2049</u>:

The harvest from today's gathering has been washed and is inside, all at various stages of preservation. Everything always ends up dried, pickled, dehydrated, or used, regardless of how they originated. It's pertinent to select often and, if they cannot be stored, to use them quickly. Always a bit of a race to gather before they're gone, and to use before they're bad. If we don't harvest them, a wild neighbor will. Every morsel is a special treat, requiring a lot of work to obtain. Every delicious bite is an exhausting acquisition. Finally, enough months have passed to where we have fewer mistakes and spoils. Less catastrophic errors leave stomachs fuller more consistently.

Sitting on the deck, while the produce takes its course inside, this moment is a welcomed break. I let the deck chair support spent limbs, eager for a pause of relaxation. Sun rays brightly speckle the deck, creating warm patches. One crosses over my feet and partially up my legs with flickering cozy spots across my torso and face. A tractor beam of warmth has captured any desire for movement elsewhere. Emanating enough heat to eliminate the nip in the air at the sign of winter approaching in a few weeks. The last remaining leaves dangle, crusty brown and extra crispy. Vibrant oranges now a muted sienna, but still beautiful.

The forest is quiet, with residents calm as the horizon nonchalantly cuts across the view. Soft clouds dot the sky full of radiant light. An airy, nonliving entity exuding a glowing energy, fluffily plopping across. Birds glide in and out while an occasional large one swoops in dramatic fashion. How lucky and freeing to transport effortlessly to anywhere at all. Avian friends always bring out forlorn feelings. They are so fragile in their fierceness, and can be unnecessarily violent to one another. A painful reminder of cruelty too relatable.

Catching my attention in the distance, a large black bird is hanging out, hovering here, and there between sweeps. There must be something deceased in its view as it circles in fixation. I watch as it remains anchored. An unsettling feeling, like some new predator in the evolutionary chain has arrived on scene. A chill deepens in the breeze as I tighten my crossed arms and snuggle Janus closer. Before long, sitting outside will warrant a lap blanket, even in the afternoon sun. The black bird has migrated closer, sweeping across the sky in smooth, linear horizontal patterns. Each path is calculated as it scans the ground. Disconcerting in its mechanical movements, my eyes have since become fixated by the quizzical flight path. It looks big and bulky but glides without effort. Perhaps a vulture of some sort, but it's hard to make out much of a shape beyond the torso.

As I watch and wonder, Janus becomes intrigued as well. He sees it too, and the hair on his haunches bristles up. He emits a low grumble here and there while the hairs on my arm prickle up one by one, knowing he'd never give a shit about a bird, let alone growl in its direction. *What does he see?* Just as the picture starts to form, gathering that something about this whole sighting is off, I hear it. A low, consistent hum of a motorized engine as if a little fan is working overtime.

And just like that it's identity comes into focus. All the strange pieces fitting together into one clear form. The drone is still far away, but close enough to hear, and it's closing the space between. Quickly insisting Janus disembarks my lap as I stand, gathering our items.

"Come on, buddy, let's go."

Heading inside, the latch of the lock gives a resounding *thud*, creating a barrier. Going around window by window, I draw down the shades. The shades I once thought so stupid, because who would ever be peeping in at canopy level? Their presence all due to a friend's passing comment that not everyone enjoys rising with beams of light on their face. With each zip of the cord as they come down, I'm glad that friend wasn't a morning person.

The stove is almost out, but not entirely, and as it gently produces small puffs of smoke out the exterior wall vent, beyond the back deck, it's apparent that options are limited. Fully extinguishing with water would only send big plumes everywhere in the most indiscreet way. I'd be unable to stop it, and clogging it would bring the fumes inside. Instead, I separate the remaining fiery bits, hoping they cool down and extinguish faster. An attempted mitigation with the wish it will go away unnoticed.

Without definitive knowledge of their capabilities, I can only assume and theorize. Left breathless by a spiraling mind running out of control. Recalling anything ever heard. A messy concoction of news, pop culture, and questionable theoretical claims of rumors trickling through Hank. *Heat-seeking technology already exists, but is it the variety that can see through buildings, or do the structures provide a block? If it can view into our space, would it be better to stay near the stove so we could hide as one big, confusing hot mass, or would the oddity of it create more suspicion?*

One could assume at a minimum there are recording capabilities on board, and not only live transmission. The recordings or live transmission could be audio, visual, or some combination. There is the nagging concern of weaponry in tow, as well. The Nation had most certainly used such devices before, on foreign land, years ago. As time has passed and society has changed, it wouldn't be much of a leap to question whether the politicians or citizens of The Nation could justify use of that class of arms here. Lines of limitation have become increasingly fuzzy, and everything has an explanation to be offered.

While the thoughts won't stop running, we sit and wait, doing absolutely nothing. Attempting to stay as still and quiet as possible, I'm worried a loud exhale will be the warning flare signaling our position. Breath held to a near silence while all the ambient, unavoidable noise is amplified in my ears. The remains smolder in their reduction. Wind blowing through the trees sound like stormy gusts. Each breath might as well be Ujjayi with how it reverberates. Janus lies by my side on the bed, his weight leaning into me, watching and listening. From deep inside I will him to find sleep, or boredom, or both. To not have any reason to raise the alarm, with a series of unfortunate barks.

As muffled and muted the walls may be, the *buzz buzz* of the drone drifts around outside. Not seeing it and only hearing the predator rove elongates time in this frozen position. Each time the sound fades, a bit of hope reassures us that we can relax, until the mechanical noise returns to interrupt any microscopic peace. This cat-and-mouse of noise continues, while we wait. Time passes in a suspended animation, and the concept of its passage is all but a blur. We could have been sitting here for minutes, or hours, but lack the ability to guess. Each thump of my heart is a success, having made it a moment longer in hiding. Every thump of my heart introspectively contemplates how many more are left.

The buzz at one point is louder than before, and we both tense up, sitting in wait. I grab Janus to my side, afraid he'll dash to our defense, while my other hand hovers to cover a bark before it can fully escape. The sound feels so close, I imagine it's within touching range from the deck, but with shades drawn there's no way to confirm. Instead, the haunting Doppler of the drone loiters like a banshee roaming. Convinced we've been spotted, I fight back tears, thinking of what the demise could look like. Soldiers all in black rappelling from nowhere to seize the deplorable. A missile launched straight into our kitchen. Someone thousands of miles away watching the live feed and calling out commands as they observe.

As I fight to shove these thoughts back into the box of my pit and pull myself together, the sound softens. Its paths continue within audible range for a while longer, before they dissipate. Desperately cling to the hope that we've remained unnoticed or unremarkable. Maybe the canopy was thick enough to obscure the visibility of our lodging as the machine cruised through. Perhaps it looked abandoned and void of interesting concerns. Hopefully it didn't even register our existence.

Eventually, the sound reduces and finally drifts away to other paths. An echoing silence deepens as the residual hum lingers in our ears long after it has fully passed. The love-hate child of tinnitus and PTSD makes its home deep in the inner ear for the time being, until this too begins to normalize. Waiting until we're sure any movement won't be our flaw, and finally, when enough time has passed, our legs are stretched to stand.

Dusk is falling and the room grows darker. Nature intentionally closes the chapter that mentally I wasn't finished reading. With the evening tasks at hand, each an attempt to shake off the hangover of metal beasts waiting, I'm still on edge. The shades stay drawn and dinner is quick. Nature may have turned the page, but I stay astutely aware until the heaviness of sleep wipes away the day.

Chapter Forty
Ears Open

Now
<u>November 5, 2049</u>:

The low hum resonates like phantom limbs I swear are there, still twitching in their sleep under the blankets. Regardless of the visual evidence that the drone has definitely exited the scene, its presence has left an aftertaste still residing in my senses. It's still out there, and no one can convince me otherwise. The absence is surely only temporary, biding its time to lull us into complacency. The moment I lay my head down to rest, it'll be back.

Watching the horizon with hawk-eyed vigilance, I wait for a metaphorical mouse to pop out. Peering into the binocular from every view-point of the deck, scrutinizing far off scenery. Analyzing each vignette. Nothing here, nada there, absent at every turn of any sign for our visitor. Searching for hidden clues in this high-stakes version of the childhood game "I Spy." I pick apart each detail and obscurity in harrowing lengths, attempting to reassure my inconsolable thoughts. A cup of tea in a tornado, trying to hold down the fort doing its best to not be blown away, while soothing someone's nerves.

There is nothing to be seen for endless miles besides countless trees, mountains, scattered clouds, and the remaining leaves clinging to the forest canopy. It's peacefully mundane in these calm moments where everything appears to be excruciatingly standard, relatively speaking. Had it not been for the drone, I could sit back and enjoy the calm before us. No sign of any disturbance hours ago. Yesterday's events make my heart take in the view, waiting for a shoe to drop. Anticipating all this to be washed away in one fell swoop of a spy plane reappearing, or perhaps even something worse. I'm consumed with the concern it's all temporary. The good and present joys are prevented from fully soaking in. Instead, they sit on the surface of my soul as oil on water in suspension. Not fully integrated, leaving much to be desired as distractions hold my focus.

Stepping inside through the threshold of one creaky wood floor to another, the soft warmth's greeting pitifully attempts to reassure that everything will be alright. Temporarily leaving outside the unknown. Guaranteed paranoia to check back later in exchange for this relatively safe space, ready to welcome us. The radio sitting at the desk allows us to listen without abandoning our watch. With Janus comfortable in a dog bed by my feet, all snuggled up, I turn the plastic dial and navigate static.

Scanning from one station to the next, I grasp at anything that will come in. Each station could mention something of what The Nation would deem as the successes of their drones. With open ears, I wait, and listen, fending off impatience when nothing comes through of particular use. Fore-finger lightly taps the wooden desk-top, anticipating news of similar sightings that will be spoken at any moment. The longer I wait and the more the tapping increases, it becomes evident this station is conversing nowhere near the topic, so I switch.

The next station is more or less the same, and once again I switch. Again, and again, hopping from one channel to the next, each proving as useful as the last. Cycling through the limited options that break through the static, hoping someone will provide any tiny detail to validate our experience. They don't provide the slightest acknowledgment. A child dismissed by adults that the boogeyman is nothing more than scary dreams. As each renders nada, the voices on the other end of the wavelength acquire mocking tones dispersing trivial topics. No updates of substance, and any mention of drones is unheard of. *How could they not know something?* At this point it feels intentional —the utter lack of discussion on their part. As I claw to know, they dangle their whispers in my ear.

The drone wasn't a minor, random event of some hillside hobbyist, but the longer I listen to the radio people speak, the realization sinks in that this is exactly what they'd rather we believe. A fluke event from a citizen is far more digestible than government-sanctioned surveillance and reconnaissance. If it's such an easy-to-swallow bite-sized bit of truth, then why do I feel like I'm choking as the words cling to the inner walls of my throat?

You'd think they gloat at the successes their new tactic has achieved, but maybe there's more to come from up their sleeves. Maybe even this isn't something citizens of The Nation are ready to accept. A possible shred of disdain that Blake and his boys would rather sweep under the rug. Only celebrating when domestic terrorists and deplorables have been captured, while of course omitting the procedures that took place. Only wins reach the news desk. Pondering on the people who used to be called friends and coworkers; I wonder where on the spectrum they'd weigh in on tactics like this. It's never really a line but more of a sliding scale, and it's not hard to theorize what old connections would say was out of their acceptable range of action.

With the charging panel propped in a full sun spot coming through the window, the radio is allowed to ramble on a bit longer. Their chatter is irritating, but the chance of missing news makes their superficial banter tolerable. While waiting on a chance occurrence, I wonder if Hank may know more than just rumors. The best information always accidentally ends up in his keeping from those passing by, and from any connections. Being well-liked and trusted makes him easy to talk to. The low profile he keeps makes strangers spill their stories as if he's pouring a truth serum, not beer. It's possible he knows something more than this electronic box.

Looking through our supplies, it wouldn't be a bad time to make a trip, anyway. There's enough to trade, and some items we could afford to acquire. If the lure of information wasn't enough, the prospect of goods sweetens the value of a long trek. While it's too late to depart now, the passing thought has become a full-fledged plan for tomorrow morning. With the radio still jabbering in the background, I start to gather the items to possibly sell or trade, and stash them away in the pack. Item by item, until satisfied this will gain a worthwhile value with the vendors. Grabbing the notepad, I jot down a few items to be searching for, and on the second page any thoughts or questions about the drones that have been weighing.

Cumulatively, today, nothing has happened to cause any change of feelings or thoughts toward the drone event besides creating a plan. The anxiety of its existence still jitters inside, but my hand no longer shakes with some optimistic thread to hold onto. What a difference an uneventful day and a loose idea of forward momentum can make. No new details, but exponentially more possibilities that have subdued the raging storm waves filled with fear. A little less tension cutting off circulation as the thought of a chance to acquire answers, however small, circulates in my psyche. Sitting back, while I know the watch isn't over but the heaviness has lightened by a smidge. Muscles melt as the security of a plan settles in, comforting the exhausted stress that has burdened this body of mine.

Chapter Forty-One
Fallen

Now
<u>November 6, 2049</u>:

Tomorrow isn't guaranteed, even for oligarchs, and tyrants. I keep telling myself that while sitting here with storms thrashing outside. As strong as their vice grip may be, water slips though even the tiniest of cracks. Slowly escaping away, lowering the total bucket of success that remains. Drops accumulate little by little, forming a wave capable of washing away their sandcastle. As a drop, though, you can't imagine the waves. Especially when you can see no drops, but moisture is tangible in the air. Maybe a storm is coming, or maybe it'll miss us all, leaving drought behind.

Kings who claim god status struggle to comprehend the thought of demise. Arrogant confidence in divinity weighs in on their matters as if this was any deity's will. Laughable but flawed. However, when the people know the self-proclaimed chosen leader upon the throne is indeed not immortal, the first chip is made. They need only wait for the crumble, as the cracks spread. The more apt question is, who will swing the first sledgehammer? The bigger problem is convincing others to see the cracks instead of willfully denying the scale of disarray.

As a journalist, my living thrived on knowing what everyone else was doing. What was happening around the globe in far-flung places by seemingly powerful people, almost always men. To keep a pulse on the actions, and movements behind the faces of leadership fed my article submissions before suppression. Long before lengthy redactions and tied hands, these insights and snappy through lines were praised. *How long ago was the applause loud and support never-ending?* A dull echo of a distant memory. Now I sit here with strung-together theories and memories of historical events, trying to place some standing of where we are in the mix.

Watching rise and fall from afar is wildly different when it's all from the comfort of a well-worn office chair. Racking my memory for anything significant while trudging through our seemingly never-ending real-time regime. While details may slip, and their pertinence on day-to-day life is distant, I'm commiserating on a global scale with those who have also experienced this non-unique existence. All those little drops connected vastly in a global sea, riding the same tide that's traversed the world. Taking its turn here and there, creating chaos where it washes over. Dispensing havoc on all its inhabitants, besides those newly deeming themselves superior. Remembering I'm not the first drop, and likely won't be the last, as if this would be comforting. Instead, it feels like I'm drowning.

Long ago, a dynasty became obsessed with alchemy, which everyone thought was a cute little hobby, or maybe even something holy. They didn't mind until they did, and that was when the people suffered. Neglected, starved, and ignored until tensions broke. The people proclaimed that the side quest was no longer acceptable, and his power was stripped.

Leaders guided by faith subjected minority religions to different standards. Higher taxes, fewer opportunities, more restrictions; not to mention day-to-day acceptable harassment. It wasn't long before the minority group grew fed up and anger boiled over. There are questions as to whether the biases ever truly dissolved, or if they've seeped into the minds of later generations. At least those biases were no longer legal with government backing. Biases would have to be off the books now.

Maybe don't mix religion and politics, as it seems to be a common thread looking back on historical events. Along the sunny coasts of the Med, they certainly didn't stand for it. Some cocky family of a political ruling majority decided to dip their toes into the religious sphere. *Fine*, the people said, *as long as that individual keeps their interests there*. Easy guess what didn't happen. The moment the worlds began to mingle, there was an outcry. Their tyranny didn't even have legs.

Hateful fingers point at vilified scapegoats, harkening the political party under one of the most well-known, arguably the most heinous political leaders to take power. They gave a little wink and nod of approval to others, daring to wickedly spread their wings, as different mimicking societies popped off across the globe during the time. Its ramifications are still felt most prominently today. However, as confidently brazen as they may have been, it all came to a collapse when eventually nobler parties got involved. A heavy emphasis on *eventually*. It was only when one's own safety was threatened and denial was no longer an option that the fight really gained traction. Ironic, considering the circular nature of teacher and student.

Some regimes transform, and perhaps that's more frightening, drawing up the question of whether or not they've truly gone away. Setting the stage for one dysfunctional leader after the next to take their crack, all promising they have the answer. Whether a citizen is thinking of one dictator or another or the so-claimed democratically elected leader who most recently appointed their heir. Each taking their turn, while the people continue living lives more or less the same. A cyclical ruling standard, that has yet to be demolished. Actions Blake has even praised while, of course, not acknowledging any of the stains on the rag of their truth.

Whether it be a little red book, an iron fist, or a faux people's revolutionary—they all have their hook. Narcissism does that. Deeply desiring to be remembered and cemented in history, they have to put on a show. Neglected fools throwing tantrums to create a simulation of praise and love around self-decided righteousness or brilliance. A farce absorbed by too many desperate for salvation, in the form of sweet words. Nauseously sweet, which should be alarming of what poison is hidden, but it's easier to not ask questions, and swallow. So many did. It's time to pump some stomachs.

All those untouchable regimes didn't last in their flaws. I repeat this to myself as a reminder that when the end doesn't come tomorrow, or the next day there are many more ahead. They all fell in the face of their best attempts otherwise. Statues toppled, people rose up, military forces intervened, arrests, and executions took place. Their reigns came to an end. What came next remained unknown in the moment, but that status quo couldn't last, regardless of lacking clarity of the future. A leap of blind faith off a dark cliff, because they couldn't stand it any longer. A step into nothing, as it was better than the ledge they stood upon.

Our people's voices are so quiet, you'll have to listen closely to the whispers escaping these borders. Objectively comparing their history to ours, the alignment is clear, but I hold back from adding The Nation to this mental list. Without a doubt the evidence is there, but it stings to say, even if I'm the only one to hear. Admitting your uncle is a racist is easier to understand internally, but saying it out loud to a third party makes it real. Seeing The Nation lumped in with that lot makes the reality somehow more dismal. Some rebuttal exists even against commonly accepted established tyrannies. They'd surely dismiss these claims if they couldn't condemn some of the categorically worst to be documented.

Heart pounding in my chest at the irrefutable reality of thoughts that surely cannot be alone. Possibly delusional hopes that there are others behind my voice, and one day there can be a chorus. Isolation eliminates any possible internal threat attempting to fortify. They look inward while detached citizens exist, surviving out of sight. The irony of realizing our voices in a vacuum cannot stand forever; residing in fear does not escape me. Sitting in the back room of Hank's bar on my sleeping cot, instead of being surrounded by some version of society.

Inside, something long since dormant, stirs. Desires to be brave previously pushed into quiet submission. An anger only as aggressive as cinnamon, when I need cayenne. We need a whole bushel of the hottest peppers simmering for hours in the same pot, to turn the tides on this system. An order-up yet to be received while I sit and stew, biding for the right time. Delaying until it feels tangible. Hiding, because conveniently it's safe, or maybe it's selfish.

The cot is becoming increasingly uncomfortable, and the noise from jukebox sashaying in my heart begins to grow tired of looking for hope when some opportunities feel like luck, and others are boldly forged through alliances. Neither particularly common, with less to show. *When will the fear to cross the line leave, and I can confidently march to demand change?* It's not today, or tomorrow, and I can almost definitively promise it's not the next day either. Sitting, wondering if I'm cowardly, or smart. *Craven or patient?*

Tonight, though, I will join Hank for a glass after wiping down the bar. It's not a revolution, or challenging much of anything, but his steady confidence creates the illusion that everything isn't that dismal. That everything will be alright, if for only a moment. The elixir to change perspective, though if only a short time, is welcomed. Nothing may physically change but much can be discussed.

Chapter Forty-Two
Selenite

Now
<u>November 8, 2049</u>:

Staying at Hanks for a couple of days while a heavy rain front moved through has been a surprisingly pleasant experience. It's nice to talk to someone who talks back and doesn't demand belly scratches as an answer. While groups of unknown people typically make me twitchy, the bar is a beguiling place away from those worries. As if because Hank had gained my trust, relatively speaking, then by proxy anyone who enters this space must not be too dubious. Of course, that doesn't completely erase the world of distrust, but believing a morsel of it to be accurate lets my shoulders slope in moments the guard isn't fully up. Just enough to let me pass as not paranoid.

Unfortunately, there wasn't much to be learned about the drones besides what was already suspected or known. It had been documented that The Nation is using drones in areas of our borders that have been deemed hostile due to domestic terrorists, anarchists, and general violent crime. Reports have been released confirming the use of video and audio surveillance, as well as thermal imaging. They all state recordings are sent back to their base. A delay does occur, but the exact time lag is conveniently omitted. As pockets of deplorables need to be managed and mitigated, from The Nation's perspective, there have been reports of more extensive sweeps inland. Patrols in the sky throughout the country, actively seeking any signs of non-compliance. While all of this could be expected or assumed, having some confirmation beyond my own thoughts proves to be affirming for my sanity. Reports have sprinkled enough to satisfy the onlookers without revealing any juicy chunks.

The sighting still raises concern for Hank as he validates my own, worried about more prevalence and aggression. There have been more militia men traipsing through with their posters, and questions. The military has intensified its efforts to push forward Blake's policies, and at this point almost everyone knows someone who has gone missing. Anthony's story is no longer unique. There are a million Anthonys, and a million Jessis, none more special than us. Yet The Nation has no shortage of workers, even in a flatlining trade economy. There are always workers to dig ditches, work the factories, and harvest the fields. Yet still the people face mass price jumps, unsatisfactory housing, and overall struggles through daily life. *How?* A perplexing conundrum of likely imbalance with no answers.

As I'm packing the last of my bag with the goods we obtained, and some extra bread that's gone stale from the bar, Hank saunters over, patiently waiting for a pause in my movements.

"Did ya put up that wire I gave you before?"

"Yea, I did. Put it in a few different spots near the house, and near some of the gardens. Made sure it was high enough to not hurt the animals."

"Always thinkin' about the wildlings."

A smirk crawls across Hank's face, clearly visible even below his trimmed but thick beard in amusement by my empathy. His bulky hands almost daintily holds a spool and a bag.

"Well, I wanna make sure you're safe. In case ya need more— and the bells, you can hang in places. In case someone runs into the wires. It'll let ya know someone's out there without havin' to sit around and wonder."

"Thanks, Hank."

Graciously taking the gifts and placing them in the pack so they're not jingling the whole way home, I'll be sure to place them on our walk back in convenient locations. Maybe add more wire, or at least check what's already up to make sure nothing has broken.

"Do ya need any medicine? I have some extra."

"No, that's alright. Keep it."

"Ya sure? It's an antibiotic."

"Yea, I'll be fine."

"Fine, fine. Well, at least take this."

He thrusts an unlabeled bottle of booze in my direction. I look it over, wondering what this batch contains. His boozy finds always vary, but they're surprisingly not half bad, and no one is blind yet.

"What is it?"

"A berry wine of some sort, I think."

"You think?"

"Yea, it's good. You'll like it."

With the bottle descending in my pack, I look up to see a woman with raven hair, exclaiming her praise for the mystery elixir.

"Ooooh, Hank, is that the berry wine you were raving about?!"

She smiles wide and leans over the bar to give Hank an awkward shoulder hug, wildly unobstructed in her movements. She continues on in her husky voice, akin to an aged merlot. Measured but not missing a moment.

"Hey there!"

Her hand stretches out to shake mine, assertively assuming I'm open to greeting her hand, and while the world is different, some old manners don't die. She takes my hand and firmly squeezes with her bony, talon-like fingers. A little faux smile squeaks out across my face, because it'd be uncomfortable if it didn't.

"Y'all met before, right?"

"Noooo, I don't think we have."

"Oh, I'm Lucy. And tell me, you are?"

"Jessi."

If only I could lie, but Hank would absolutely correct my fib in the presence of this woman he clearly knows—even trusts. Watching her chat with Hank, she looks familiar; however, I can't place from where. He'd chalk it up to too many faces or claim kindred spirits, but an uncertainty hangs.

"Are you sure I haven't seen you before?"

"I don't think so. I'm good with people, and I always remember any friend of Hank's," Lucy says with a soft smile between sips of her bottle.

"Hmm maybe you just have one of those faces."

"Maybe."

With a shrug of a shoulder, she's off to the next thought without a blink. Unfazed and steady, on to what's next without concern.

"And who's this?"

Her hands are in the scruff of Janus's neck floof, and he doesn't seem to mind. He withholds affection in general, unless the space and person feels welcoming. Maybe this place, or Hank, or my presence, are enough of a vouch for her. His demeanor toward her should be reassuring, but instead, looking at those endearing eyes, it brings scrutiny of whether he's losing his touch. Maybe he's more open to trade pets from not-terrible new people in exchange for perceived trust when he sees so few humans. Well, at least he doesn't hate her.

"Oh, that's Janus. He's always been by my side."

"What a lucky duo. Well, you'll love the wine. What else is Hank sending you off with here?"

She knows he sends me off with special trappings after a visit?

"Oh, just some bells, and wire, and bread."

"Someone had been snoopin' around her place," Hank interjects.

"Hank, I wouldn't say snooping …"

"They set a trap, and ya wound up hurt. And there was that drone."

"Oh, damn, you are a lucky one then."

I shoot him a quick look, insinuating those lips of his need to tighten up, even if he does trust her. I do my best to shake it off and present an unflustered front. None of those words are untrue or overly specific. Calm the inner guard, reminding them he's not stupid. Stop the alarm bells when there's no alarm yet.

"Yea, you could say that," I respond neutrally.

"Well, I'm sure you're lucky and smart. Otherwise you wouldn't be here."

"Sure, we're just doing our own thing. Keeping busy day by day," I say dismissing her compliments, or attempts to soften my edges.

"Now, I'm not sure if you care much, but I don't think it hurts to have all the luck we can muster. As many powers as possible watching out for us."

"Yea, I mean, that doesn't sound like a bad thing."

"Then take this. Could help, or could do absolutely nothing. But it won't hurt."

Lucy's hand pulls away from the bar-top she'd just plunked palm-side down to reveal a small, rectangular stone. Whitish and translucent, not much thicker in diameter than a pencil. Leaning in to get a better look before picking it up, I don't know how to react. The rigid edges between my fingers are rough, but not sharp as the milky color glistens.

"It's selenite."

Skeptically, I can feel my eyebrows involuntarily rise. Looking over my fingers from the stone in her direction, I fully expect she must have more to offer than just a one-word name.

"I know, who subscribes to woo -woo stuff anymore? But like I said, it can't hurt. An abundance of luck favors those bestowed with fortunes."

"I guess it can't hurt."

"Cleanses and amplifies, or so they used to say. It's a good thing to have around, just in case it's not all a bunch of snake oil."

Too many contrarian thoughts to count pop up, ready to be blurted out in objection, but before any interjection of further suspicion is spoken, Hank is quick to offer his thoughts. Always one to jump in with his two cents, especially in peacekeeping manners, and even more especially between parties of mutual investment.

"Just take it, Jessi. I know ya can find a spot for it in there."

"I like to think of it as a good luck charm. A talisman to the good left in the world, and the remaining good in people."

"See, ya need all the luck you can get. Don't ya want some good?"

"Sure, assuming it's there," my mouth skeptically expresses.

"It is," Lucy says with the utmost certainty.

Reluctantly, the stone is put in my pocket; I know that no matter the cynical feelings, it's not worth the fight with a woman I just met. Best to take it with us in good faith, and any judgement of the metaphysical mumbo jumbo just spouted can resume privately at another time. The little gem securely sits between the fabric layers, nestling into its new home, or maybe I'm anthropomorphizing again. Either way, Lucy can see I'm not lying.

"Thanks, Lucy. I'm sure it won't hurt."

Sharing our time right before we take off is not how I'd ideally imagined. I don't want to leave like this, never knowing exactly when I'll be back, but Lucy doesn't appear to be making moves of departure anytime soon. Janus and I relinquish the fact that this time with Hank will have to be co-opted; any feelings of skepticism or even frustration are shoved down deep where feelings go to hide. Instead sharing these goodbyes will have to do. Swearing to myself the moment isn't tainted, and putting on a Kumbaya face while still genuinely enjoying his company, is possible. Possible—but I don't like it just the same.

He's making a trio of sandwiches, carving the crusty hearth bread. All the fixins' to fill us up and pass as a typical meal we would have easily recognized from before. With each bite, the world that awaits stands further away, held back by nostalgic food. No complaints here, knowing these moments are rare. Eagerly accepting any normalcy when it's presented. The talk has shifted to casual conversation of seasoning herbs, smoking techniques, and the secret to making the bread rise like a real baker. All things I never used to think too deeply on. The words exchanged aren't necessarily deep, but they do take up more of my time than I ever could have predicted in comparison to previously shopping the spice aisle for the pre-mixes.

With a full belly and fuller pack, we rise to leave for the long walk ahead. Hank gives Janus a pat and wraps his arms around my entire body in a big bear hug. Looking at Lucy, she clearly wants to give a little hug with that approachable smize, while I most certainly don't. I think she can sense the hesitation because she doesn't force her will without my consent. Begrudgingly, the results land somewhere in a compromise. Instead, there's a clunky half-hug of a single arm and a lean-in. The A-frame affection of acquaintances or friends by proximity.

"Keep those luck charms close."

"Will do."

Nodding my head as if it holds a Stetson in an agreeable thanks and departure, we make our way to the door. We walk through the threshold into the streets with people just starting to stir. No one sets up shop before noon, as vendors assume no one will have made it to town that early from any reasonable distance. Apparently they have collectively decided the locals can wait. Each step away from society, back to our retreat, is filled with bated breath for the moment to disappear in thin air when no one's looking. Throughout the streets, a biting gloom hangs in the air from the previous cold front, and perhaps something else is sinking in. More flyers from The Nation are plastered about, and stern-looking people watch the market and those walking. Far less spontaneity or whimsy, even if it was sparse before. Almost a ghost town, but with inhabitants still present. A living dead establishment walking through the motions.

Gone and into the woods we go. Vanish behind the veil, into a familiarity of the trees and unmarked natural footpaths. A space dismissed by onlookers, or avoided due to visibly formidable terrain, and yet it's in those features we feel most secure. No one would dare venture. Every moment deeper allows my mind to shift from the dangers of watchers to mulling over our conversations. Analyzing and dissecting even when nothing necessarily needs a further look. No stone unturned, wrapped in suspicion, results in rotating rocks far more than necessary. Fortunately, we have time to give them all an ample once-over as we journey home.

Chapter Forty-Three
Thanks

Now
<u>November 25, 2049</u>:

Roasted vegetables with hints of caramelization and char next to a version of mashed potatoes almost feels decadent. The spread is small, and nothing in comparison to what Mom used to make for Thanksgiving, but it'll have to do. Had there been the same quantity and variety available, such an abundance would be wasteful on only us. It was wasteful then too, but people generally turned a blind eye in the name of festivities. Mom would savor every scrap for days, or send leftovers away, but who knows what happened to them after they left her home. We were all tired of the same flavors by the third day past. All my seasonings resemble an analogous family of spices, because that's all there is here.

The familiar smells of those moments in a distant memory circulate my nostrils. Days of preparation for hours of consumption, some enjoyment mixed with ample tension always looming for one reason or another. It was tradition, and in the name of keeping the same status quo, even the impatient tolerated things they'd normally not entertain any of the other 364 days of the year. All in the name of family and friends, camaraderie, and companionship. A noble table filled with good will, and thanks. A table of performance. Quite frankly, a charade of fallacies wrapped in a bow.

I fucking resented Thanksgiving. It held promises of raw, authentic humanity gathered around in thankful community, but never delivered. It always fell short—hollow imitations at best. The idea: a lie we all reached for, instead of accepting the cracks and dings of our relationships. My high hopes dashed year after year that maybe this time it would be the Norman Rockwell painting I had fantasized about, as all the family was reunited from their own lives. An undercutting remark, slipped with the side of sprouts passed family-style. Innocent questions laced with judgment asked between bottles of wine. All smiles and shiny whites bared. A pleasant disposition masking an argument ready to ignite at the wrong match-striking sentence.

The whole day walking a minefield, wishing it was like the painting that didn't exist beyond the frame. I envied the idea that anyone had the vision we strove for, and deep down subscribed to the notion they must be lying too. Everyone collectively pretending to be pleasantly perfect was easier to accept than the fact that it may actually exist. All while deflecting baiting remarks of the pompous distant relative inserting their self-imposed importance into the conversation.

Janus and I don't need to worry about anyone detonating in the facade of debate. It's simple and plain, but that's peaceful too. The lack of pomp and circumstance is a reprieve in contrast, knowing that no one is going to ruin the event. A nice meal with kind thoughts, enjoyed in a quiet space in the forest, would have been just as satisfying all those years ago. In another time, big money would have been spent on an idyllic memory in the making of a moment like this. People could live out their rugged roughing-it dreams for a week as if this somehow made them feel closer to ancient pioneers, or one another, or the environment. If it did, I'll never know, but I wonder how many took the feeling with them or left it behind on that trip.

With each bite, comfort melts in my mouth, a reassuring texture of this moment where all is good. No one is arguing, fighting, contradicting, or stressing over the superfluous. Seemingly perfect in many ways. Looking to Janus as he begs, I wish words would leave his mouth. He never upholds his end of the conversation and I long for the dinner-time chatter that always had surrounded moments like this, even if they were contentious. Reluctantly contemplating how that arrogant relative would create a lively debate; my mind reasons with itself that he could be tolerable in short bursts to break up the conversational stagnation. In reality, there's a solid chance it'd be regrettable within minutes, but considering the thought can't be disproven in this moment, my self-admiration is riding high today.

If only an invite could be sent over to friends. Remind them that everything is taken care of, but if they wanted to bring a side or a bottle, it'd be a welcomed addition. Daydreaming about which dish or vintage would accompany their arrival. Surely Anthony would have brought his hash brown casserole that oozed with the goodness of a warm hug and could suffocate any troublesome thoughts. Sam and Dani would likely bring their usual—a dry red and queso with chips. A meal in itself at the end of a tiresome day would sit in its own pride, next to the stuffing, but would undoubtedly be finished first. Mushy breadcrumbs were no competition regardless of seasoning. There would be banter and laughter and smiles all around, filling this small space to its brim.

Instead, there is only the ambient noise of wind rustling, a fire cracking, my mouthful bites, and finally Janus settling into a lying position to be more comfortable while not giving up the food watch for snacks. The vacancy makes the daydream richer and my heart ache deeper. An event that never happened, I remember annually haunting this day. It never seemed imaginable to hate the holiday more, but this concoction of memories and non-memories drives the knife deeper. I hate the lies of what it was, and I hate the memories that never existed, and I hate myself for enjoying this peace while missing what could never come together. There's no winning as the twisted emotions contort.

There were foolish thoughts of visiting Hank. Dropping our forlorn presence like a wet rag at his bar, in hopes of some resemblance of a joyful holiday. While an old crusty diner bar, with whomever the winds blew in sitting around the stool tops, wasn't exactly the idyllic painting of my childhood longing, it wasn't a disaster. To be fair, this wasn't either, but that version at least wasn't alone. Instead, we stay right here in our home, pushing away the thought as we're being mindful of the increasing risks.

There's been an uptick in the number of random check-ups from the military and militia men popping in. Asking too many questions has become a more common occurrence at the Trading Post. While Hank insists that short answers with no reason to pry won't spur them to stick around or worse, I hesitate to extend such confidence. Not wanting to give them any reasons to become curious about me, I have began making my visits based upon necessity instead of contentment. Sorry, Hank, if you're eating solo, but it's too high of a price to possibly pay for good conversation.

Scooping up the last of the greens from my plate, I savor every last piece as the reality in all its complex facades weighs upon us. The air may be thick in the absence of voices, but it is also filled with the peace of this present experience. A thought interrupts the spoiled wallowing reminding me to not be greedy. It could be worse, or did toxic positivity somehow slip its way in here too? *Just enjoy the meal, relish the moment, and take a pause.* My overthinking mind demanded to reluctantly halt when it's told that it can't fix everything, especially when there's nothing for it to fix.

Family to argue with on a day of fallacies is a distant past. The friends aren't coming. I'm not with Hank. It's only this moment with Janus and a nice meal in peace—nothing more. Reluctantly, I admit this is enough to be thankful for, even if in some ways a longing remains for it to be a little different. Wishes aren't just granted, so I try to take in this moment with all its fractures as a light snow flurry begins to descend outside, dusting the ground and trees, ushering in a changing of seasons.

Chapter Forty-Four
Intruders

Now
<u>December 12th or 13th , 2049:</u>

A deep chill settles into the forest, as thick as a layer of frozen fog in an arctic bay harbor town. Damp and frigid lingering in the bones. Surprisingly early, especially considering meteorologists would have made note that winter had yet to officially arrive, according to the calendars. Nature, though, doesn't listen to any measure of days confined by small squares you peel off as time ticks by. It comes and goes, progressing by its own determined whims. Bringing what feels appropriate according to only the cosmos itself.

Regardless of how hot the temperature of the tea is, it struggles to retain its warmth if I take too long to drink it. I hold my hands against the radiant heat of the ceramic cup, a reminder that this isn't fall anymore, and warming my core these mornings means slurping a bit faster. As the days grow shorter and the temperature drops we move slower, and our outdoor activities start later. Lazy mornings are still a relevant indulgence. Instead of long walks in the forest exploring every distant nook, our trips become more efficient and selectively sparse, venturing out when needed while avoiding bad-weather excursions if possible. Complete dodging of cold weather is regrettably unavoidable, but neither of us want to linger.

With breakfast done, I enjoy the remaining drops of tea while staring out into the barren trees. The deciduous have dropped their leaves, though the conifers stand boldly in the landscape with snow encrusting their topside layers. Looking like powdered-sugared-covered desserts, my sweet tooth hints that we should find time on our next trip to the Trading Post to look for a rewarding treat. Even a nugget of candied ginger would satisfy the craving, and besides, after all this time, a luxury morsel could be rationalized as deserved.

In the midst of salivating thoughts, there's a jingle-jangle noise in the distance. Loud enough to hear, Janus and I sit there, staring at each other, perplexed. Reminiscent of the chime of bells, the sound strikes me as strangely foreign. Clearly not of the land, we're alert to potential threats, but if the dings of metal bells sound threatening, we're at an almost comical state. Something akin to a kid's toy doesn't exactly strike fear, but it does cause confusion. A juxtaposition—and that is the scarier part. Assuming it is bells, what would those be doing out here besides someone walking with a bear bell? However, it lacked any rhythmic cadence. I don't hear them anymore. Once, loudly jarring, and done. A clamor interrupting our meditative morning.

As abruptly as the sound of bells cut through, it hits. I recognize the sound and know where the noise came from. The bells Hank gave us must have rung out in our wild garden to the east. Something large tripped them to make the loud clatter, undeniably heard all this way. Standing quickly, I go to the windows in a rush. Look in that direction for any sign of the culprit. I peer into a still landscape for any notion of who is out there, but no one announces themselves. If they are injured, I assume we'd hear them. If they escaped, maybe we could see them running. They could wander anywhere, but if they came this way and saw the treehouse, would they avoid it entirely or seek out help? We wait and watch for any news of what took place. Time passes, and we've been peering for what feels like an hour or longer. Still nothing, though obviously something happened out of sight. Bells don't ring for no reason.

Tense breaths hold the moment hostage as I know the answer isn't coming, but we need to know. It's decided—we'll take the walk and see for ourselves, even though the concern of meeting a threat head-on keeps me here moments longer. With both the gun and knife at each hip, I lace my boots and put on a heavy coat. With the uncertainty of where someone may be, it feels foolish to leave Janus, but I insist he stays close by. This isn't time for exploration.

The forest is silent. A gasp frozen in time. An unshaken snow-globe waiting for the inevitable upheaval. Untouched serenity that we're slinking through as quietly as possible filled with static tension. Each step in unmarked snow creaks beneath my rubber soles, announcing every foot fall. In the quiet it sounds louder, and I hope no one hears. Clinging to the thought that it's only loud by comparison. We are moving dots, traversing across a still map toward an unsure destination.

As the garden location draws closer, I scan the horizon on heightened watch, searching, but in mere moments the culmination of what took place shouts into the forest. Pristine snow stained a deep scarlet. A harsh contrast demanding our entire focus. Copious red has seeped deeply and my mind is swimming, struggling not to drown in assumptions flooding forward. No sounds escape as we're frozen from a distance, absorbing the scene staring back aggressively, refusing to shrink itself. A standoff, and no one blinks. I can't look away, captured in a trance, pulling me near. Demanding to be seen, there's no point in resisting. No choice but to listen.

Cautiously approaching, it becomes apparent there is no longer a threat—besides the piano wire, which did as designed, though never expected. We needed defense. Built-in protections for peace of mind, but now they're all too legitimate. This reality was always held as a distant thought. The results were never real until now. A scene fully sketched with the clamor of bells. Frozen in a swell of conflicting emotions drown out everything else, and my body numbly doesn't move. The nerve endings quit, and I can feel my legs more motionless than the landscape. His body is inert as he's lying there with a gaping slash across his throat, and other wounds across his extremities. With a crashing force of the gravity of this prospect, I'm pulled to my knees in its undertow.

Seeing my first dead body outside of movies, breakfast leaves me as quickly as life departed his. While I'm heaving in the snow, Janus is confused. Trying to be my comfort like a good boy trained on simpler tasks, but this is beyond his scope of experience. Even he knows this is serious. He refuses to leave my side while simply watching; I regain composure, wiping my face of any remnants. Running the coat sleeve across my mouth, the air bites across exposed lips along with the leftover moisture from who knows what. A disgusting mess grappling to not unravel. The dead man still lies there, judging my lack of composure, as if I should have known.

Completely average and generic in physical appearance, a pang of guilt winces as this person presenting rather unremarkably was likely of some value to someone. Regardless of what sports bars I'm sure he patronaged or how devoted to family values or comfortable he may have been in whatever society had become—none of those things mattered now. An entire life of personality and convictions reduced to his rag-doll body, lying in a self-made puddle. Wearing all black, besides the red insignia of The Nation on the outer bicep of his sleeve, he is otherwise inconspicuous.

There's nothing to provide an identification by name, but as a man sliding between shadows, thriving in the unseen, this isn't particularly surprising. A name wouldn't change much besides make him more real. Even in the death of one of Blake's boys, there's the question of who exactly he was. Not that it mattered beyond the fact that he was human, and that complicates things. Maybe I should be glad he's nothing more than a body and blank identity. Lacking anything official, it's unlikely he's military, but with the blazoned red insignia, he's blatantly on their side in some shadier supportive role.

"Why did you have to come here?"

You know why.

Traipsing through the forest, he must have had a reason, even if only to search as a stray dog snooping around, convinced the mountains weren't vacant. Hunting a scent on a hunch, he must be a militia man looking for bountiful opportunities in the form of turning in dissidents and deplorables. Staring beyond this place, through the trees, watching for others. Scouring for symptoms, they are here. Rarely do militia men ever travel fully alone. They'll venture off to scout and return to share their findings. It could be hours or days of solo excursions. Sometimes they'll be gone for weeks on long missions. Either way, before long, they will reconvene.

It's almost to be expected that someone will likely be looking before long. If we're lucky, it'll be a few days before anyone starts a search. Looking down at the lump of his remains that have now become a problem, I consider which of the unenjoyable options to pursue. Leaving him for the beasts would be ideal, but there may not be enough time for them to take him. *They can take care of him—if they find him.*

What if they don't? What if they scatter the parts into a confetti of bones? Humans will see that something violent happened, as throats don't bleed out all on their own.

There are trees and branches that could cover, but I'd have to saw them down. *Hide him away!* Across the nearby vicinity no fallen pines appear to be present, and a leafless limb isn't much help. Pile them to cover up. *A pile of sticks in the middle of snow won't look odd at all! No, they see it, then him, then the treehouse, then ...* He can't stay here. His pack will soon be sniffing around too.

Never did I ever imagine needing to move a body. My brain hops from one pop-culture reference to another, attempting to muster up any form of a plan, struggling to assemble some actionable steps. Frozen ground eliminates burial. Carnivores don't guarantee a timely removal. Snow will be tainted. Hoisting him into a tree to decompose feels like an unnecessary risk, if i'ts even possible.

The river isn't too far. It can take him away, and no one will know exactly where he came from. The water will distort identifiable features, and maybe, if we're lucky, the creatures will assist the process. We can go down the mountain-side to the river and make it back in time for a late lunch, though my stomach churns at the thought of any semblance of normal daily activities.

Squatting behind his shoulders, I reach my arms under his and around his chest, ready to lift the core of his weight. Awkwardly, trying to keep his face away from mine. Trying to not make eye contact with the gaping wound that refuses to blink shut. Hoisting up, I strain to move —laboring under each step, almost stumbling. Fighting against transfer, with the lifeless density of his weight compared to the strength of my small frame. This will be slow, if possible. As he resists I release my grip, allowing the torso to fall onto the frozen ground beneath with a solid *thud*.

Evaluating the larger mess now made, I pause, painfully aware this isn't working. A failed plan from a half-baked idea. The blood now smeared by his dragging limbs is a grotesque paintbrush across the snow's blank canvas. The pathetic distance made is laughable, knowing the destination point. I reconsider the wild things waiting, knowing it's not optimal. As I'm contemplating the choices left while glaring at the body that's betraying my intentions when I remember a story heard as a teen. My friend's dad was forced to dress an elk in the remote wilderness, or otherwise sacrifice his kill.

I look to Janus with an exacerbated breath, and he knows it's going to be a long day. With shoulders slumped in heavy sickening, I gesture for him to follow me back to the treehouse.

"Come on, bud. We gotta grab the saw."

Now
<u>December 13, 2049</u>:

Yesterday was a nightmare matching ones concocted by mixing medication and alcohol; however neither were involved. I slept in a comatose state trying not to think, and fortunately physical exhaustion held this form in a heavy muck. A sludge of sleep cradled my weakness in a suffocatingly supportive type of way. We didn't turn in until well past dark, and now rise mid-day still drained.

I could never have moved a man near twice my size in one go, but piece by piece only a couple overloaded trips were necessary. Having realized in the failed attempt to move him intact, we came back to the treehouse for the saw, ax, and knife, not really knowing what would be most useful. Assuming that surely one of these three could get the job done, in one form of hacking or another. Tools and a tarp for transportation.

Looking at his body lying there, I'm unsure where to start, trying to recall buried knowledge. What happened in movies, or shows wasn't that helpful. They all glossed over the body bits once the killing part was done, or it was conveniently addressed with a wood chipper, or pigs, or trash bags sank to the bottom of the ocean—but none of those options were here. I remember random references to field amputees but am unable to place whether it was during a war in history book, or a survival guide, or a movie about a guy stranded in the southwest. The source itself didn't matter, but the method proved useful.

As in dressing an animal post-hunt, or breaking down a chicken in the kitchen, the easiest way to carve a large mass into something smaller is to separate at the weak points. I look at him, imagining the location of joints' connections and where something sharp can be wedged to separate the bones and tendons from one another. Our natural weak points of build-a-block people are easier to cut through than the bone itself. Built in disassembly mechanics.

Pulling back his coat sleeves, I feel where the rotator cuff meets the top of the humerus, the round ball safely sitting in its home. The smallest of separation can be felt at the connection point, where the knife tip starts to push inward. Hesitating at the action that feels foreign in my hands, the skin slowly breaks, and muscles resist as the body already begins to stiffen. Fighting to dig deeper, I blindly navigate between one dense object and a different denser object. The cutting isn't clean and everything is becoming a mess. Gnarled meat filleted with a nail file would look smoother. I am no hunter, and have never dressed a being, but fortunately there's no prize for aesthetics.

Finally the arm detaches and the torso oozes thick tarry liquid, cumulating on the ground beneath it. One limb on the tarp, and three more to go. The legs prove more challenging, tightly blocking access to the joint. I muddle the muscles ripping away, but exhaust myself before the lugging begins. Resorting to the saw, while digging through I look away, avoiding any cardinal spray. Repulsed in an already disturbing series of actions, I continue the saw's rocking motion, cringing with the grating sound of every stroke rubbing up against the femur ball joint. Finally it lets go, and the mass of thigh along with the accompanying legs are heaved over with the other cuts.

A lump of a body laying there looks almost inhuman, or maybe it's only because I've never seen a person look this way. Helpless, though he's been beyond assistance for a while, his corpse appears more desperate than before. I stare at this man and remain bewildered how the series of events led to this. Hands stained in his blood, dirty in brutality. Arguably necessary, but a forlorn haze hangs.

"I'm sorry."

I can't stand to look at that face staring back. His blank gaze is filled with pleading anger and hatred; it mocks my misery. The gash is already there, begging to be completed, and in my frustrations, obliging was easy. The ax made quick work of the remaining connective tissue in a few swift chops. Releasing resentment of everything this militia man stood for with each downward swing.

The severed pieces on the tarp, I pull the rope through the

grommet tightly, using its leverage to drag it like a not-so-merry sleigh. Over the mountain, through the ups and downs of uneven terrain, we traverse, pushing our pace, dreaming of being done. Each stick and rock creates roadblocks to navigate, already challenging landscape masked by snow. It's clunky and awkward, but every intentional step moves us closer to the river waiting a bit farther in the distance.

Finally, the gurgling of flowing water becomes audible, and its proximity more anticipatory. Each step lands quicker to shred the weight of this burden. Approaching the riverbank, the water is ready to wash our heads clean and take away what is left in its guard. A harbinger of secrets swearing to never tell; promising to take care of what we can no longer bear. Looking from the edge for anyone watching. Fully aware of what they'd see: my hands slowly moving to remove him piece by piece. Each limb lowered into the water and pushed far out, catching the current. I watch it traverse downstream, bobbing like a log until the water rounds the bend—and with that, he's out of sight. Seeing his arm disappear from view reassures my worries this can be done. *I did it.* Took care of the problem, and no one needs to know beyond nature's audience, but they'll keep my secret.

With each appendage, the heaviness weighs a little less. The current takes with it the pressure to fix an irreversible problem, and calms my anxiety inside from outwardly twitching. His vacant eyes watch us until the water takes him under, casting one last lingering glance. Almost done, with only the torso remaining, we return to the garden and swiftly make our way back. The sun is starting to set as we're approaching, though we're greeted by a foul smell and the buzz of bugs.

Insects don't waste any time initiating a whole diner party to feast. Fine, but their celebrations must be moved elsewhere. With nothing to drag, I push and roll the largest portion of fleshy remains on the tarp. Struggling to not slip, he finally flops into position, ready for a swim. The walk is slower with each hill undeniably steeper, and every rock or log an obstacle definitively larger, while I am undoubtedly tireder. His torso clings to the shore and a stick becomes an extra limb, as I avoid submerging into freezing water. A twisted gondolier rod, allowing him to be guided to deeper, faster waters, until he joins the flow.

Exhaustion envelopes my crumpled body, as the last of my energy leaves with his departure.

Drained, we begin our return through darkness under moonlight, as the sun has long since set. Snow glistens, illuminating the path guiding us home. Wishing to collapse into bed, the bloodstained ground laughs at this notion. Its wetness is oozing, or maybe that's just melted snow. The edges of snow and slush tarnished with deep reds and pinks. At first, some weak kicks spray fresh snow like sawdust to clean up a mess, only to turn pink upon landing. More, and more, lighter but still there. The ground is now all disturbed, and I can no longer see what is or isn't the problem source. It's all a mess of bouncing light and shadows; moist divots and fluffy peaks creating confusion.

Desperate hope pleads for our return home, for sleep, while walking back. Numb to events, the treehouse reveals itself and we disappear within. It welcomes our tired, worn bodies to disrobe the layers of the day's turmoils. Each movement automated out of necessity, refusing to return to what happened. The bed could have been stone and our sleep would have still been sound.

Now, today, the hours have passed well into the afternoon and new snow is pouring down. Flurries of flakes coat another layer as we all sit and watch. A hibernation of feelings buried beneath something new. I look to the window but the garden is out of sight. As the layers accumulate, each new flake clings to the feasibility that a weather front will bury all my problems. Hide them away to never be seen. End this event for other concerns, and this could be a closed story. With weather dumping its precipitation, and all other mental circuits shutting down, the task of checking the ground is tabled until tomorrow. Let nature work, and then we'll reevaluate.

Chapter Forty-Six
Stained

December 14, 2049:

Wading through calf-deep snowdrifts, everything is painted new. The fresh precipitation leaves all the forest newfound, as if this is its first day. Visually wiping away the memories of any transgressions, burying them deep below into nonexistence. Almost complete erasure, if it wasn't for that spot.

We reach the place where that militia man once lay, and a dark burgundy spot stares back. It's smaller than what had once been. Absorbed by the earth, or buried by the snow. Reduced, but that stain lingers as a tarnished reminder. An obvious banner to any onlooker.

At first, burying it deeper feels like a logical option. Impulsively suppress the problem under more and more of nature's magic eraser. Surely under enough layers it will go away, as the shovel scoops new snow upon the mound. At first, there is only white. An unmarked layer hiding the past, appearing innocent and ordinary. A blanket of unremarkable snow, blasé in every way to anyone who may look. Standing there, staring at the ground, knowing what secrets lay beneath, convinced it's obvious. As if on cue, a little spot penetrates the crisp crystalline surface. Only a small dot at first that then spreads. The stain grows, eating away the whiteness of pure snow. Capturing flakes it engorges its circumference. Stopping shy of the initial size, but still substantially obvious, refusing to stay buried.

A mocking puddle on the surface, resembling snow cone syrup that has been poured in one isolated location. Marring what could've been fine. It would have been fine, had the repressed details not pushed through. Had they been dealt with previously I could be home now, and not dealing with this reappearance. Passed time bleeding into the present, carrying over baggage never addressed.

Some problems require removal. Cut them out so that they can't contaminate their surroundings. A mass is discovered and then removed to protect the healthy cells from being contaminated by carcinomas. Taking great care to have clean margins; otherwise, the fear of their return will loom. Buying time, growing, and waiting to resurge. A body already primed, with weakened points targeted. An avoidable revival, vengeance becoming present. If only they had dealt with it properly from the beginning.

I plunge the shovel into the snow deeply to carve and scoop out any tainted flakes. The wet stained mass perches upon the metal's face, hoisted away from anything it could taint. Walking away into distant trees, one foot in front of the other, marching nowhere specific. Unsure of the destination but knowing a suitable location will reveal itself. A trace of necessity mixed with paranoid panic; my feet carry the way when I cannot think clearly. I'm resigned to this course of action that needs to be successful, as no other options come to mind, and with that a grim swell shutters through.

Far away from where we started, a rocky pass appears with stones jutting higher in the snow. Their pocket holes are still dark, previously sheltered from any falling precipitation. The many crevices curl in and out, offering a wide variety of nooks in different shapes and sizes, with the vast majority providing some degree of camouflage. Sections lacking white cover will be suitable to accept the contents carried here. Dropping the snow heap onto a few uncovered spots, I proceed to smoosh it into the soil. Crimson isn't as stark next to brown, so with the flat side, they're muddled together. My priority to keep it away from any pristine white, fearful a drop of bright cherry colors will jump out. Stopping after this initial load, I evaluate whether the space has absorbed any visible sign of transgressions. They're there, but no one could see them. A character flaw that won't show up even to a trained eye, leaving heaps of unspoken problems unnoticed.

Returning to the hole, a slight bit of red along the edge where it once touched still signals for attention in this pale snowscape. Minuscule, but given the circumstances, the volume of its shouts in a monotone landscape is shattering. Carefully gathering those remaining contaminated lumps, separating them from the rest, I make one more trip to dispose of this event. This time taking the top layer of soiled dirt, fully removing the source of what feels like a never-ending problem. Hoping to put it all to rest.

I collapse the hole with disrupted surrounding snowcaps as a final disguise. *Clearly a series of animals must have trampled through, and it most certainly wasn't the spot of a slain man.* A magic eraser may have wiped the stain, but residue resided heavily upon my mind. A soggy blanket sags around my shoulders, sealing in a damp fog of whiplash. I stand there numbly before dragging my limbs to walk home. Sand-bags wanting to drag me back are pulled along. Ignoring their criticisms, I make my way. I fall into the couch, devoid of anything to hold me upright. The weight of the past few days is compounding, taking its toll and calling a halt right in this moment.

Restless leg syndrome of the mind takes hold, and as much as I crave sleep, it is challenging to rest. Thoughts run furiously in my head and heart, occasionally tripping over one another as too many collide. Almost catatonic from the recoil, we lay there in wait. Wishing away the day for a better tomorrow. Each spent breath is a countdown to when sleep will take over, waiting just out of reach. Hours pass in this suspension until finally something gives way for a temporary relief tonight.

Chapter Forty-Seven

Distant

Now

<u>December 25, 2049:</u>

Vacant is the sound of a scream in a void. Expelled with no echo and no witness, disappearing without validation. Sitting here with nothing but time and thoughts, I am transported absolutely nowhere. The thing, though, is time stands still, and my thoughts have run to repetitive spirals. Mundane observations, while interesting in the moment, offer little comfort over days and weeks, when the observations become less novel.

Prickly spines of the conifer pines stick out from their branches, like a botanical electrocution sprung up in all directions, sprawling away from rough bark. Stark green with deep hues, apparent in contrast to the bright white that has encapsulated our mountain. Little clumps of frozen snow wedged between piney leaves and the branch create the question of which form is supportive to the shape, as they are codependently merged like a puzzle. A strong wind may cast off a spray of flakes, or knock down a chunk entirely, but the vast majority holds its place, regardless of the sway in the gust.

A clean and empty mind only active in the daily tasks, and in companion time with Janus. He enjoys the nothingness of these days, when events are not exciting and simple pleasures are easily obtained. There's no thirst for new activities or faces. Everything to him is content, though I crave a face other than mine or his. A friendly or familiar entity would be a welcome variance from the same-old same-old, day in and day out.

A chance to do something different. An opportunity to do something better. A wish to have something more, because over time this repetition has become numbing, leaving a hole in my pit, longing for expanded depth. Janus's companionship is not to be blamed, but I wonder if he senses my restlessness. Silly, maybe, to worry if a dog thinks he's blamed for an emptiness he cannot fill, but it does nag.

Over a thousand days existing only as a dynamic duo is taxing when so many of the days feel like duplicates, and those that don't are often drenched in dangers. Days fraught in their own disadvantages I'd rather not trade for. Looking back at the days past is nothing compared to the thoughts of how many wait ahead. A never-ending, ever-growing calendar with no definitive termination consumes my calm, creating a heavy tension in my chest. An insurmountable possibility of the worst sends me down a long, lonely hall, away from everything. Strapped to a chair in dim lighting, with only the soft foot-fall far away, like whispers of a source I cannot see. Expectations to exist indefinitely in desolation.

The radio has been spotty, with reception intermittent, as it sometimes does. It's been frustratingly obstinate as it's undeterminable whether it's the gear, or the signal, or the weather, or if they are doing something to interfere. Unreliable connection to the outside always flares up feelings of paranoia. If only I knew why, then maybe it could be fixed, but it is yet another thing beyond control. Only hopes and wishes for any voices crackling through. Clear connections become increasingly appreciated. A rope tethering us to safety, and sanity of something beyond this mountain is fragile, but I hold on tightly with all my grasp. Every news update, every silly song, every chatty commentator, regardless of whether the content was of interest or any real value. Those words are a tie to somewhere else.

Today, there is nothing but static. The voices have been nearly silent for almost ten days, though there was a severely crackled man croaking here and there, occasionally popping in. Nothing since almost a week ago, even though each day we listen. With the heavy snow drifts from this latest round, it's the only voice I can hope to hear besides my own. Even if there was a reason to go to the Trading Post, the route is treacherously covered. A fool's choice daring to trudge through. Instead, we stay right here, above it all—venturing to the ground only when necessary, and even then it's very near to this spot.

Snow comes every winter, and is to be expected, but snowstorms can put a halt to movement and activities. Everything settles into a more dormant outlook. The dips in valleys filled and drop-offs hidden; walking anywhere becomes a guessing game of *'will-I, won't-I plummet and twist something badly or break'*. Any step is slow, as the deep drift acts like swampy waters holding you back with a resistance that settles in wetly. If all the accidents waiting to happen and pure discomfort weren't enough, there's disorientation. Landmarks hidden in the terrain begin to look eerily similar, and suddenly you're down one slope when you intended the other. A compass, though useful, won't always be the savior from a longer harder journey or getting lost entirely. In time the snow will blow away, melt, and compress to a more reasonable amount to venture through. For now, though, we stay put, watch, and wait from our nest.

Looking out upon the landscape below, all we see in any direction are snow and trees. Occasionally an animal may quietly traverse through, unaware it's being watched, and it almost feels like a private cinema to view. These happenings are quick and rare, but looking beyond the deck, a hopeful moment can break up the monotony. Instead of the tasks of the day, it can be brightened with the silver lining of *"We saw a deer."* Something you may say to a friend after a weekend trip in the mountains as a highlight of your adventures.

Heaps already piled high and more flakes are falling down, adding to the accumulation. It falls like we're in a snow globe, far away from the rest of the existence. Surrounded by only our own a space that once was vast, but has seemingly shrunk, and the distance between here and there has widened. Shaken up with only the tree-line views, the same puzzles and books, and Janus to provide entertainment and comfort. Snow swirling in a ceaseless descent. New feelings that aren't really new, just repackaged from the old world and remedied in the same old ways.

Slurping my soup, there's a weak reassurance by sustenance confident in its ability to heal all wounds. In face of its confidence, I question if it can warm the cold hole below my ribs. Each bite is a little better, being thrown into the void. A welcomed distraction, if only for a moment. *Gazing forward, how many distractions, for how many moments, must continuously be filled to continue on?* Better to not think of the thousand future steps, but instead look only to the next footfall. It's easier to swallow that way. When you notice the foot has hit the ground, you're onto the next. *One, then two, then three, and four.*

Chapter Forty-Eight
Dogmatic

Now
<u>January 20,2050:</u>

It would be like any other day if it weren't for the damn anniversary that no one will let us forget. Every year they seem to get louder, more joyful, more obnoxious about it, and yet here I am, still listening to the radio. What awaits is obvious, lacking changes or delightful surprises. Of course, there's not an ounce of static today, which would somehow be an excuse to turn it all off, but I don't. With the voices clearly coming through, it's impossible to resist listening like a rubbernecker, judging the hideous conversations I'm eavesdropping on.

Every year it's more or less the same progression of the day. The morning starts with memories of the past years and their so-called accomplishments, as well as what they call their triumphant rise to power. They fawn over Blake as a pseudo demigod who saved The Nation. Eyes involuntarily roll at their gushy banter that's littered in lies and absolutely disconnected from reality. The reality for some, while others revel in the success of The Nation's latest endeavors. Their nostalgic memories of a rewritten past are curated today. A photo album filled with illustrations instead of images.

Memories are followed by patriotic tunes, then speeches, and then there's always a faux-historic recount of the party filled with stats, along with future plans sans supportive documentation. Blake always speaks midday with a fervent delivery, filled with brimstone, and slogans. *Easy for the masses to repeat on patriotic cue.* There's more patronage, songs, and a nighttime prayer. We only lasted until prayer once. The second year, as soon as we heard it come on the radio, click went the reception with the button pressed by my index finger. Now, we only listen until Blake is done speaking, as if there will be a hidden clue. Hope of inspiration, or some sorted news that we'd rather not miss. Regardless of past shortcomings, this could be the year. Dare not miss it, just in case. Highly unlikely, but in case a cocky mouth runs wild … Something could slip, and I'll be listening.

Listening, it's almost always men—and occasionally one or two women used as disarming props to prove these syndicates aren't all that bad. Cooing to listeners, they must be safe, if a woman would eagerly join these cohorts and sing the same praises. I hear their high-pitched empty words, bantering on the echoes with no independent thought. It's perplexing to wonder how many are aware of their marionette roles that sit upon the men's knees. I can almost see the dummy wood through the radio. Surely, I'm not the only one aware of the performance being put on. *Someone must see it too, right?* It is a wonder how they ended up there. A mystery whether they really believe, or if they're just along for the convenient ride regardless of the driver.

Their history is full of events that seem to have skipped the news and textbooks. Villains that have been painted to be extra evil, and moments in time cast with new perpetrators. An internal war had been raging, that which only they were privy to, and ever valiantly at its forefront, they save us each, day by day. Every year the little voices speaking through the radio remind us how close we all were to damnation—living in a deplorable, spiraling existence—and that Blake, with his supporters, rescued us. We should be grateful for this new world delivered upon our fortunes. Of course, they can't skip the warnings, either. Danger still lurks, threatening to undermine all the glory that's been gained as the jealous, wicked blights on society remain in existence. Demands to report enemies within, as it is our duty; and today is a reminder of our part to the greater picture. They're looking, and no matter the year, that never seems to stop. An enemy always lurking, which may be one thing we agree upon, even if the shadowy figure varies.

Trumpets cue a choir is about to start. Damn trumpets announcing their arrival, as they enter their self-made arena to be venerated, right on par with their branding.

"The Nation is our sacred land,
Fulfilling all that's good and right.

They can never get enough of these lyrics. Countless repetition with various verses, some of which feel new. Having never memorized this anthem, it's difficult to definitively say. Each year it feels longer, with more fight and more divinity. *Maybe I'm not remembering right.* With the instruments only playing the same few sheets on repeat, it'd be easy to get lost. Almost hypnotic, beckoning a melodic trance to any on the other side of the transmissions. If it wasn't so loud, the tune is close to becoming to white noise, but the trumpets and percussions don't allow for that.

Eventually the music trails off, and someone announces that in mere moments Blake will be there too. As if he's not already waiting in the chair next to the announcer, reveling in the buildup. How lucky we are to be joined by his presence, or so the man says. With a dramatic *click,* Blake's voice comes on and commands the space.

It's funny how he manages to have stage presence when there's no curtain to be drawn. Full of pride and pomp, he goes on as father of The Nation. As if all its shining moments were somehow to be credited to him. Hearing his voice revitalizes a loathing on a molecular level, but I can't avoid listening with bated breath. I hate hanging onto every word. Deeply despising the power he holds, even over me, though I know I won't turn the radio off until he's finished.

Someone so vile shouldn't be allowed to sound charming, but the poison of his principles is laced with sweet honey. While I may taste the toxins, others lap up the words spoken into that mic, even if they're not beneficial. Maybe more than just me are developing an allergy to those twisted tongues.

Now
<u>February 6, 2050:</u>

An unseasonably balmy day allows for standing on the deck to be somewhat comfortable if bundled enough. It's damp type of chill that seeps in, instead of bitter. It sneaks up so enjoying the view of a clear day is pleasant though temporary, before my body says *enough is enough,* and the interior comforts beckon. A good view for now, to think on things.

This morning, when searching for radio signal, there was some news that stirred mixed emotions. Rumors had long since floated of the happenings within The Nation, but their validity was always questionable. The work facilities never investigated. The disappearances labeled as explainable flukes or conspiracies. Media restrictions and new ethics guidelines claimed to have been blown out of proportion. There was always an excuse or reason to dismiss any claim, or call for concern. Easy to sweep under the rug—but now there's a lump that someone just tripped over. Others around the world are no longer ignoring the rumors.

I guess it became too hard for them to ignore without looking like they're complacent, or even supportive. A few stubborn international journalists kept digging for leads, even while others claimed them to be ridiculous. Enough snooping led them down rabbit holes, sometimes delusionally, with a flimsy whiff of credibility. Some of those hunts lead to something of undeniable value.

Whether their governments took them seriously, or whether they released a story that caught fire across the globe, the word spread. Once it was out, denial became immeasurably more challenging. Then more stories corroborating one another built the scaffolding of critical suspicion and doubt of The Nation's activities by other countries. One after the other, in a cascading echo. A movement swept, and suddenly The Nation was an outsider—a pariah.

In a turn of events, other countries were demanding evidence of defense of the claims. Some now downright condemning The Nation. Slapping titles of war crimes, crimes against humanity, and crimes of aggression; all floating around. *We'll see which will stick.* Finally not alone in the state of our new world. At last, others admit to seeing the stains so many have already told them about. Finally, after all these years, they see it too.

Hearing this news from the radio announcer angrily spitting his words is a long-awaited relief, vastly overdue. A swell of gratefulness radiates, but an undeniable angst of a child forgotten at after-school pickup once everyone else has left residually remains. It's hard to not have some moments of annoyance that it took this long. When they're finally listening to what so many have been saying all along. *Believe the victims*, they champion, but only when it's convenient, or when it becomes inconvenient to do otherwise. Too long has passed, but I accept we're here as a tiny win. *What are my options, anyway?*

What's next is the unspoken, looming question. How conveniently that's not covered, though it's no surprise. It'd be incongruent for The Nation's broadcast to suggest these accusations are accurate, or that anything will come of them. It'd be blasphemous to kneel to their condemning titles. Absolutely dangerous to suggest anything else could happen. Reading between the lines, I hope for words not mentioned to provide a glimmer. A crack in the voice or perhaps a long pause would be a satisfying hint, betraying their loyalty for just a second.

Repeating what the broadcaster said over and over, trying to remember which countries said what. Searching my memories from textbooks and history from long ago. Attempting to recall what their track record in international events had previously been. Were they the ones to step in, or did they only shout support from the stands? Who were the leaders there now, or what would their position be? Many moving pieces: wishing they'd align conveniently right, for my deepest will.

A heaviness hangs in the air that's thicker than the balmy moisture point. Dew drops in the air carry the words of faraway places, waiting to descend. Standing amongst them brings a closer presence of a long-awaited reunion while waiting for their welcome. Any moment now, the weather could change. A storm could move in and alter the whole landscape if the pressure was right and atmospheric elements aligned. The crows seem to know as they fly nearby, circling overhead. Perching sporadically upon random branches to squawk their claims.

There were stories that they could traverse between worlds. Hop from the land of the living to fly with the spirits of the dead, easily floating through veils. Not of this world, yet all-knowing of the events transcending upon its lands. An omen people can't quite understand. More likely only a strange bird that makes lots of noise and looms at coincidentally inopportune times, appearing to make a statement. I prefer to think of the former, holding onto something beyond simple truths. Wishing can be harmful, or hopeful, but a gamble doesn't sound so ill-advised right now.

Watching their flights swooping in patterns, I imagine it's a show for only me. A secret message of reassurance, delivered right outside my door precisely when needed. Their feathers glisten in the spotty sunbeams, contrasted by the clouds in the distance. A predictive dance full of prophetic warnings for what hope is waiting.

Chapter Fifty
Blaze

Now
<u>February 21, 2050:</u>

I'm lying in the bed, having dozed off during a midday nap, soaking in the slumber as warm rays stream in. The cozy light and soft bed easily lured us off to sleep, and with little structure it's easy to squeeze in a few minutes of rest. In a half-sleep I can hear rustling outside and wind blowing. Janus is stirring, shifting his weight, repositioning. The longer I lie, the more he moves, and while trying to linger longer, his restlessness protests. It's still a sodden winter as chilly temps lap at our bones while sunbeams radiate warmth.

Conceding to my rest ending, Janus begins to bark. First one, then another, a few seconds apart. They don't stop as he begins to sound frantic in volume and cadence. Stirring, he is now off the bed and pushing his snout into my hand and face. Insistent I wake, persistently urging a response. Finally opening my eyes, I sit up to see he's pacing from me to the front entryway. Back and forth, demanding my attention without pause. I stand up to see what he's demanding to show. Step toward the door, then I stop. The smells of a campfire fills my nostrils.

It's sharp and burns as I breathe in, stinging down my lungs. Suddenly it's apparent the room is warmer than usual. A stuffiness surrounds me where I stand as my mind connects what doesn't seem possible. Rushing to the window—it's hot. I struggle to see out through the smoke lapping up outside. *Shit, is that fire? Why is there fire?* Straining to peer down, I see there are flames climbing the trunk. Fire crawls from the tree bark and low branches until it grabs the dangling stair remnants, rapidly consuming them. Spreading across the deck, and growing closer.

Right here, right now, seeing the fire reaches for us. As I stare it down, commands leave my mouth to Janus, as we must run. Quickly throwing on my boots and coat, I grab my pack, but there's no time to put anything else in it. Testing our time, looking to the growing danger outside, I scan the room for whatever else to possibly grab. Anything in reach would do, but everything floods my mind. As the clock ticks loudly, nothing touches my grasp under the time pressure. It's encroaching with every second hand passing. Panicked, my decisions to be proactive and logical fail.

It's inching closer when I hear voices—men speaking outside. Flight sets in and we are moving toward the door to leave, but as I move to grab the handle, it's visibly too late. The fire has reached the door and is licking, flicking underneath. Janus is hysterical in his barks and whimpers as my lungs struggle to function while our home is fills with smoke. Ducking beneath the hazy fumes, I guide him to the window by the desk still untouched, though not for long. Grabbing a pan, I ram it through the pane and rapidly clear the glass. Throwing a blanket over the sill, it musters as much protection as possible in the scurry.

Climbing out clumsily, trying to stay hidden, but exiting quickly without getting hurt are almost too many things to juggle. Almost, but not quite. Running to the back of the deck, I stretch for the rope attached to the neighboring tree. Leaning over, coercing Janus to hop inside my coat, I zip it up with the waist straps under his haunches. Lumbering with the rope as the self-made harness is haphazardly slipped on, well enough to hold our weight. A descent too quick and clunky as an erratic mix of drops and stops, but as long as we get down in one piece,—I don't care how. Just get down. Get out of the treehouse, out of the tree, away from them, and away from here. Just get down, and the rest can be dealt with when we touch soil. No time to worry about the soreness awaiting tomorrow. Just get down—*get out!*

A hard landing when my feet touch down as if the gravity was turned up, or we forgot how to stand while under temporary suspension. Scrambling to rip the harness away and release Janus from my coat, we stand and sprint to anywhere but here. Almost simultaneously with a whizzing *zing,* a shout cries out.

"Shit! There she goes!"

More rounds fly by as we run and duck down between trees until a sharp pain pierces through my left shoulder. Collapsing into the earth, writing in torment, I'm woefully aware the rounds haven't stopped and feet are coming. Lurching forward, flinging fully down the dip in the hill, we're covering ground faster than any wounded body could walk.

Rocks in the mountain jut out from a sheltered overhang, providing natural cover. We quickly crawl over to tuck away beneath the rocky ledge melting into the dirt wall. Hiding, waiting, weighing out what's next. They're talking but it's not all clear. Listening closely as they're still near. *How close?* The voices just beyond alternate between conversing and looking to the treehouse, scrutinizing the horizon.

Carefully peeking out to keep eyes on them,—I see two men dressed all in black with guns poised. The treehouse and tree are an inferno as parts crash down. Our home, enveloped and erased so that someday someone could look here and see nothing. A charred-lumber-and-fallen-ash memoriam. The safe space unable to protect itself from these men who take what they want. Taken by the flames, it's gone.

"It's toast. Let's find her."

"Why bother?"

"She's out there somewhere."

"They said deal with deplorables—dead or detained. I got the bitch."

"You sure?"

"Yea, I'm fuckin' sure! Do I ever miss a mark? Let the wolves have what's left of her. Besides, we've got other rounds to make."

They're too close. Their voices reverberate off the stones, through the valley, and curdle sour whispers in my ear. Frozen in their words, almost forgetting how to breathe, my hand precautiously covers Janus's mouth. There's no place for heroics with brutes watching near. *Please, don't come this way.*

As they stand there searching, we slink backward, down the sloping land through the slush of changing seasons, until we are below their eyesight when standing. It's slow and blindly guided by the ground, trusting we'll make it to that threshold soon. Taking far longer as each marginal movement feels monumental. Every move grasping at incremental distance. Any moment, they could approach and it would all be over. Every second, one closer to escape.

When that time finally hits, a race flag descends, and we're off. Running, fleeing as fast as our feet will carry, as far as we can possibly go. As swiftly as a sore, broken body will allow, but fear is a powerful accelerant. The land rapidly moves past in a blur. A mix of brown, green, and white, clumped together with no discernible shape to make out. Here and there I stumble, with my will further ahead than my body.

Looking back, I'm convinced they're not far behind. *Soon, they'll be here.* Surely they must be persistent, or perhaps it won't extend past the treehouse. The one seemed confident I wasn't a problem. Maybe they left, or maybe they will want their evidence of a job well done. Either way, we run.

An isolated, contained event without explanation clouds any clear thoughts. As neither man said anything regarding their presence, swirling memories of drones, or that body, or Elijah's threat—all finally catching up while the reality of the coincidental chance of being caught up in sweeps. Consuming questions with no response; not now, anyway.

All I can gather are those all-black wardrobes standing reminiscent of other oppressive figures. With no time to dwell on who they are or what they want, distance continues to be spread. As long as there's a distance between us and them, there's a chance. They saw me; I heard them. Out here in this condition, under these dynamics, there won't be a sustainable solution. *Where, though, do we go?*

Crashing down the slippery slopes, losing footing in steep sections, the trail ravenously gnaws at my limbs, marking them with dirt. Janus effortlessly cascades right behind, designed for terrain through evolution's good graces. He waits for my awkward rebound before continuing onward. Initially, how far we'd go didn't seem like a particular topic that mattered, but as we continue to run and the distance grows, my pace slows. No one visibly shares this trail. Appearances of things can be deceiving, but it became less dangerous in the sprinting sense. A light jog then a swift walk, still putting space but more controlled and quiet in nature.

The thought of navigating where to go while the sun is starting to set becomes pressing. *Hank's. We have to get to Hank's.* Time is counting down before everything will become infinitely harder. All the things that go bump in the night will begin to emerge, curious and eager. My vision not adapted for nocturnal living will weaken our defense. The Trading Post is too far to wander to in the dark; we are stranded for the impending night.

Hunkering down somewhere safe for tonight becomes necessary. As the throbbing in my shoulder grows with each heart-beat, the pressure for safety mounts. Walking and surveying for anywhere, we descend when the water gurgling becomes audible. We've made it close to the river, and as the mountain curves, I see the inlet caves. Not caves, exactly, but the rocky overhangs carved deep into the mountain's side. Erosion has provided a place to stop for now. There's a break from the wind and guard from the elements compared to everything else we've passed. Seeing the damp stones and dirt, it's far from ideal for the chilly night awaiting, but it'll have to suffice.

Sitting next to the wall, Janus curls up by my side. My head is pounding and the wound radiates as a thumping inside my chest slows. A clean shot, through and through. Couldn't ask for anything more, besides not being shot at all. Any moment, someone could come walking by. We're vulnerable, with rocks to our back if anyone looked. Hopefully protected from more than the weather; optimistically I wish anyone would not pause for a second glance. Better yet, not pass.

My gaze doesn't leave the direction we came. Eyes on the path, resisting missing anything during blinks. Tonight will be nonstop guard, unsure of what comes next. *Tonight rest, tomorrow Hank's.* Tension in waiting; even nature holds its breath, daring not to make a peep. This will be our night, and as the sun is finally fully setting, dawn can't come soon enough.

Chapter Fifty-One
A Thread

Now
<u>February 23 or 24, 2050:</u>

Yesterday it sleeted all day: a moderate, constant precipitation that made everything damp and chilled. Nothing froze solid, even at night, though the temperatures dipped cold enough to lightly encrust our surroundings. As it seeps into every crevice, staying dry is a far-fetched dream. We picked at the moss and nuts close by, but mostly we slept or dozed. Never fully drifting deeply, with senses jumping at any snapping branch, or rustling foliage.

A hazy air crowds the mountains with moisture settling in. It's gotten into my mind, clouding my thoughts, though lack of sleep and food will do that too. Minimal action and effort to conserve energy while waiting out this weather and hoping for a break. Listening to the hypnotic drops, melodically coaxing us to rest. Resisting sleep and boredom. There have been no thoughts that haven't run in circles all morning—all leading back to the final images of the treehouse falling in flames, and those men standing there watching their handiwork. All thoughts return to them half-heartedly pursuing, playing games. All worries return to their overheard conversation, sorting what to make of it.

Resting and waiting until the drops become more sparse, eventually stopping altogether. Everything is still saturated and taking its good ole time to dry out. If only the sun would peek out, and absorb some of this, but instead it continues to hide behind clouds. No blue skies in sight; the water in the air dwells down to my bones. There's still a half day ahead to hope for better weather.

Finally, a chance to check what managed to escape in tow, now that the clouds aren't actively leaking. Fingers soaked and pruney, struggling to unbuckle the clasps of hard plastic. Pushing until they finally click open, and I rummage my hands through the bag without pulling dry things to the wet ground. A woven blanket, a jar of scratch-made granola, a bottle of water, a nylon rope, a half-used book of matches, and a knife. Seeing what we have creates a longing for what we don't. My hands search the bag over and over. Reaching into every pocket, running along every nook; but they are barren, with nothing else to give. It could be worse, but I wish it was better. It could be less, but so many items didn't make it.

Staring down in the bag at the supplies, considering how to make this work, I remember the hidden caches. Our safety net, ready to catch us. There's one not far from here. I'm unsure which it is or what it may contain, but at this point I won't be picky. I walk out from where we've been tucked away, toward the trail and slowly gain my bearings. There used to be one hidden close to the ground between some of the enclaves.

Looking between rocks, I start with those directly to my side. I hoped we'd get lucky, but of course it's not that easy. There's nothing but cold, wet rock, and soil rubbing off each empty hollow. Following one nook to another, tracing the outlines of the elements eroded, I search for more. A plastic box hidden away, not belonging in the nature environment, concealing unnatural material and all the contents. Stone, roots, dirt, and water lay in plenty while what I search for what hides. Fingers ache in the cold, eluding my scouring.

Coming around the bend, the rocks and stone shelving become more intermittent, interconnected by roots clawing on and ferns blooming in the gaps. Root structures exposed, and hardened. They change into something sculptural and new, given their developing circumstances. Every spot barren. A devastating blow to hope with every vessel turning up empty. Searching quicker, shoving hands in holes, carelessly avoiding injury with guided fortune. Checking and re-checking, as if it would reappear in a place it never was.

Just as there are only a few more spots left to check, without digging up the mountainside, assuming I have the general location correct in the first place, my fingers run into something hard but cavernous. A *thud* that resonates as synthetic, polytene, acrylic—not of this earth—nestled amongst it. Hurriedly tearing away debris and dirt. Unloading it from the roots that were blocking access in between them and the rock face my hands can only move so fast. At last the plastic box, smeared with soil, is in my hands presented as the gift we've been searching for. Falling to my knees, I unclasp the lid to reveal what's inside. It's shallow and doesn't contain much. Two cans of soup, a minimalist can opener, an airtight bag of jerky, sealed bandages, and baggie of over-the-counter medication for headaches and mild pain. Its size told me there wouldn't be much, but seeing so little is somehow less than expected.

Returning to our spot that's drier than the rest in the wetness, I rearrange what we have, even if it's only a few items. Janus has gotten water from the river, and in spite of everything is rather content, or perhaps more accurately has voiced no complaints. Gathering the driest bits of small kindling, a little pile is built. A single match is lit that almost catches, but the moistures wicks it away with a *hiss*, regardless of me gently encouraging it to grow with my breath. Whipped away, as though nothing was ever attempted. Almost there, if only wind hadn't blown wrong, and maybe the last of the moisture is gone now. One more strike, whose flame fails, same as the last. This time it's practically laughing at us and this feeble do-over. Looking at the book with only eight matches left, daring not waste another. Moisture stands in the air while the effervescent scent of decomposing leaves fill my nostrils.

Opening the can carefully to not get cut on the metal, today's meal will be served up cold. Chunky soup with lumpy pieces, room temp and ambiguous in flavor. Undesirable, but with each slurp that's swallowed, calories are obtained, regardless of how much my stomach hates the cold slop that falls in. I consume every morsel. Janus devourers the jerky with vigorous joy. Dinner for for two, dining under the rock-wall overhang, watching the branches sway in the wind and hearing the sound of the river flow for another day.

Chapter Fifty-Two
Voices

Now
<u>End of February or beginning of March, 2050:</u>

Days upon days have passed, but I don't know how many. Maybe a week, more or less. They blur together, bleeding into one another, and as I fade in and out of sleep at illogical times, it turns everything more topsy-turvy than thought possible. Dozing during the day, waking during the night, sleeping for hours while the sun is up but thinking days have passed, or sleeping one night to another, not realizing it's been so long. We've been lost in twinning landscapes, and time is indecipherable in this state of being.

One night there were voices in the valley. I couldn't make out what they said, but their whispers echoed and sinisterly lapped upon my sleeping ears. Having awoken with a jolt, expecting to see faces, but I was left with nothing besides darkness and Janus. Convinced it was a dream, I drift back to slumber until it happens again, and again. A few nights later, and then multiple times in a night. Sometimes in the day, I swear I hear them too. Never close, nor any face to see. Always residing out of sight, sharing secrets as if observing a specimen, wondering what it will do next. In my ears and in my head they occupied space, having moved in without any care for how crowded or broken the place may be.

Janus doesn't react to their words, and I wonder if he doesn't hear them. *How could he not?* Bewildering indifference to their whispers. It's clear in my ears, their voices undeniable. *Does he not hear or does he not care?* Staying by my side with a watchful eye, unsure what is happening, he never looks away. Maybe he knows exactly what's going on, but I'm too broken to see. He stays close but frequents the river, or elsewhere here and there. Never gone long and rarely ever out of sight, as long as my eyes are open.

We've drifted locations, lingering at the rock overhang for a few days. Moving to a new place the day after my night was interrupted by voices. That was home only temporarily, when again voices made an appearance, and then again. It's unclear how many times, or how far apart we've moved at this point. Surely we've double-dipped back to places we've been that have looked different, approaching from new angles. There are only so many places to set up in the forest that hold some logic, but when you come at them differently, it feels as though the options have multiplied. Wandering the mountains, looking for home, when a disturbance has burnt energy and sanity with every heavy step. Circles with no plan plodding to nowhere.

Occasionally, I think I see someone in the trees. A figure flitting between trunks, but they're never there outside of the peripheral of my eyes. A feeling of accompaniment beyond Janus and I. A third keeping close, in case, though never fully present. We didn't dare to ask or pry, but we keep our eyes alert for anything. Blink once, it's gone; blink twice, I swear I see it move. Look to the left, it's gone; look to the right, and it's no longer there. A shadow that disappears when I shine my light upon it.

The packaged food has been gone for days. I savored the last bites as long as possible, spreading the granola sparingly when it could have been finished earlier. The last crumbs were far more delicious than the first, and with the final pieces lingering on my tongue, silent tears slipped out.

Foraging proved hit-or-miss as some edibles were easy to find, and others were deceiving. Never full from what was found, as the season is just now starting to bud. The gardens may offer more, but those men could still be there or near. *Where are those gardens, anyway?* There could be more men, assuming we'd return with no place to go. There could be expanding sweeps. It'd be a lie to say it wasn't more tempting with each passing day. They could be gone, but I'm sure they're there, watching, waiting. What a fool they must think I am if they truly believe I'd fall into that trap. No, we'll stay far away and scavenge what we can.

It's not always the most successful between slim pickings and false wins. Food I thought was good turned out to be bad, and brought up everything with it. Nature often creates duplicates: good plants mimicking evil twins so they survive; but then some consumers like me are duped by their trick and fall ill. Depleting both calories and energy, not to mention the overall vileness of it all. Entire stomach contents, little as they were, came up, and when there was no more to spill, my abdomen heaved more. Curled up, muscles tense, attempting to recover when there was no comfort to be had.

Moving anywhere on an already empty tank is impossibly daunting. Feet feel like miles, and everything feels as though it's made of bricks. Cumbersome and awkward maneuvers caught in quicksand, dragging me deeper. What used to be an easy accomplishment, and quick work, now requires many breaks—some of which are never agreed to. I find myself waking up from the ground, or startled by Janus licking my face, while never having consented to sleeping in the first place. It happened once, and then twice, before it began to regularly occur multiple times a day.

I crawl toward the sunbeams to thaw out from the night before as temperatures dip in the valley. The intermittent precipitation leaves little reprieve from the damp or cold that's settled in. A chill from within that cannot be warmed and demands rest. I'll lay here for a little while. Only a few minutes or perhaps, honestly, closer to an hour, or maybe a couple. Settling down in the soft leaves at the base of a tree, I succumb to the demands of my body and nature.

She is direct with her commands and whims, not to be questioned, entirely non-negotiable. I am a victim to her. Silently listening as she insists I take a nap, regardless of resistance. Nature is powerful in her presence, and lets it be known that control is not my own. As the elements surround us, I can feel my weak limbs each giving up little by little, falling to limp rest as she requested. It seems like a terrible idea. Keep moving, keep going forward, but my extremities do not move even if my mind is fleeting far away. The shadows grow and eyes become heavy as I feel Janus's warm body nestle in behind my legs. The weight of his head lies upon my calf, keeping guard, while I fall into nothing.

Chapter Fifty-Three
Smoldering

Now
<u>March 2050</u>:

One foot then the other thuds forward on solid semi-frozen muddy trails, as if I weigh that of cattle. Plodding half-heartedly is almost more than I can muster. With each step, the earth reaches up, and she grabs for my ankles, trying to hold me still. Janus is here, and then he's gone. Flitting from one spot to the other on his own adventures, or his own survival.

He smells my weakness. A rotten limb of existence; he may be okay with cutting it off to save the rest of the body from blood poisoning. When I notice his absence, a panic overcomes my soft heart, fearing what could have happened. When I notice his return, not realizing he had disappeared, I'm saddened for not having noticed his departure. Once the lead, now feeling like I'm the dangling lamprey, desperately holding onto someone whipping by faster than I can fathom.

This is how we go, one step at a time, ultimately making forward movement. This cannot continue on as it is. In my stumbles and suffering it becomes abundantly clear time is limited. Finding Hank's is more vital than ever; the disorientated landscape must be sorted. Looking around with vague bearings of the Trading Post's proximity, we must make our way. Regardless of the journey or failed wanderings since past, I don't see another viable option. Giving up these past couple weeks is a gut punch mainly to ego, but desperation rattles more than ever. No longer a pleasant choice, but a dire necessity. Ripped to my senses as death wicks my heels. *It can't end this way.* Alone, frail, weak, clinging to nothing but mud; nearly unrecognizable by the time I'd finally be found. No, this cannot be the the last sentence of my story.

Whenever the shadows crawl closer, grasping at my shoulders, I try and shake them away. Their icy fingers penetrate into stiff joints. Resisting as we move forward, pulling away, swearing today's not the day. Fighting onward until an invisible tether gives way. Flinging me forward, and my own two feet betray their purpose. Stumbling over roots and into trunks, bumping along, sometimes crashing down. Dirt and leaves and foliage mixed into my clothes and hair, each leaving their mark. Mother Nature's minions all make their bid at the inhabitant lumbering through.

Surely all the forest-dwellers are amused by the mess. What a sight to see someone falling in real time into rot. A living corpse, animated in desperate heaves, lurching forward. Maybe it's one big joke to them, one they've seen too many times before in the form of a wayward hiker, overconfident or unlucky. Maybe they equate it to their own on the decline. Maybe they place bets like at a racetrack, edging out one another on when they'll go down, and how. *Winner gets all the nuts!* Or seeds, or whatever the chips may be.

Navigating in the darkness is never clear and always hazardous. A cliff remains hidden until you're upon it, or off of it, having realized too late. Darkness mixed with fatigue; the trees spin while the ground vibrates. Drunk goggles for the nutritionally impaired. Stepping and swaying, attempting to stay stable. Avoid falling into the pit of shadows that'll swallow us whole. We could rest, but Hank's is closer if we keep moving. Janus is ahead; I see his tail disappear into the distance.

A whisper croaks out from between my lips: *"Wait."*

I stop and stand, squinting my eyes at where he went, when there's a wet nudge in my palm. With a startle I pull back and look to see Janus standing right there by my side with a confused look of concern. Meeting his eyes, I'm equally confused and concerned, unsure of what happened. No time with faulty brain function to figure out right now. Some things are better to not know.

Time drags on, but it's unknowable exactly how much has passed. It's still dark but maybe less dark. Maybe not, though, if my eyes are playing tricks. Either way, it's still dark, and we're still here. The same redundant task repetitively takes place as I slip between boredom and exhaustion. Dulling the senses already dreary. I'm so tired. Beyond tired, exhausted, empty—embers smolder, defying extinguish. It's been days of running on fumes, propelled by micro-rests when they can be caught.

We've been moving for hours as every fiber aches, crying out for reprieve. A short break won't hurt our time too much. Easily convinced by my own rationale, my body tumbles to sit clumsily where the ground meets a trunk. Nestled against the base of a large tree, the strength holding everything upright gives way. A skin sack, limp with bones removed—or rather, that's how it feels. A mass of a person sitting next to a tree attempting to compose itself, but missing the necessary components to do so. Minutes compound, and before long, the first breaks of dawn are hinting over the horizon. A tiny sliver winking at the night.

It's time to go. Rise and shine with the sun for the final stretch. *Let's go, and get a move on,* but nothing happens. I command my body to get up and move, but it refuses to listen. It lies there, ignoring me, enjoying its slumber. *"Get up!"* I shout, or thought I shouted, though no words leave my mouth. They just echo around my brain more erratically than a pinball that just got flung. Struggling to stay awake, limp legs visibly stretched out refuse to move. They're laying there lifeless; detached. They're not my legs, but really they are, and I can't engage with them. Separated from my thoughts; absent in connection.

The air is heavy against weighed-down muscles. The last of darkness holds on, pulling my back close to the trunk, wrapping its claws around my shoulders. Stalking up from behind, hunched over this form, ready to absorb entirely in its embrace. Whispering in my ears, *"Let's go."* So loud, I can hear it tangibly coaxing submission. Small groans leave my mouth, trying to form words, but they wiggle away to no success. Held closely in a space that's verging on comforting. Reassuring of the definite promises to come. Finally, to lay down the weapons, stop struggling, stop worrying, relax, and rest without concern. Let it all be washed away. All the pain can come to an end and drift to somewhere soft.

Batting heavy eyelids with each blink lasting longer and the skin getting heavier. Fighting wavering vision behind dark shutters. Closing my eyes a little longer, while the whispering won't stop. It's crowding out my thoughts. A white noise too loud that won't shut up. I wish it would be quiet and let me think. *Please be quiet. Let me think.* Voices speaking, swirling, getting closer, and surrounding as they echo throughout.

Trying to open outlets of vision; they're stuck. Trapped in a vessel that won't respond, while the world outside is actively in motion. I hear Janus barking, at first ferociously, alerted by something I do not know, and then the sounds dull. Audible footsteps and rustling of unseen sources. They're here to take me away to my end, and what choice is there at this point but to yield? Hidden in this shell, I'm swimming in a sea of ambient noise and shadows, unable to do more. Drowning down in the waters of an endless abyss, floating with no guide, fading into darkness.

I'm so sorry, Janus.

Chapter Fifty-Four
Others

Now
<u>March 7, 2050:</u>

There's ambiguous chatter circulating, but the words cannot be clearly made out. Shuffling bodies and crackling fire. Animal nails tippitey-tap across the hard floor that sounds like wood. The space feels full, occupied, thick in its warmth. Heat radiates, and the dryness of burnt logs lick my face. A closeness wraps around my body, laying here from a space of not being alone. Heavy fabric sits over my body, cocooning everything beneath it. Resting here, stiff on this furniture that I can only assume is a couch. Mentally configuring a picture of where I've found myself from any sensory detail within range, but the picture remains vaguely fuzzy. Slowly coming into existence; the sun dawning over the mountain ridge, lighting up the land.

Fluttering eyes initiate vision in small blips. Discreetly taking in all that's to be seen without being noticed as I look around, eyes moving side to side. They stretch as far as possible, searching for any details just beyond eyesight, staying in the corners. Remaining as still as possible, absorbing the living picture in view. Each moment creates more fluttering throughout my chest, as there are others here, and seeing their figures causes a crescendo of panic. Push it down and swallow those feelings in one bite, too petrified to react. Internally pleading to not give away this secretive position. *It's okay. You're okay.* A cavity of trapped butterflies swarming inside, wanting to burst out. Agitated by the view, regardless of the slow breaths coaxing them calmly.

A Rembrandt painting with Hopper subject matter acted out in full display. The room is dimly lit, filled with wooden walls and a fire blazing in the fireplace across the room. A glow from the flames creates a warmth that illuminates the space in a low light that would normally be nostalgic or comforting. Almost cozy in its dance of elements putting on a light show—if it weren't for the others.

There are chairs scattered around, and worst of all, people in them. Strangers full of potential dangers, sitting there waiting for the right moment to act. They're all chatting with one another at a contained volume with even keel conversation while looking at the hearth. Nothing particularly out of the ordinary. A gentle reminder that there's no reason to worry. No need to panic. Had they wanted me dead I would be, instead of lying here on a couch. Unless they like to play with their prey, but that sounds like an extraordinary leap fueled by all this time running. Yet the tightness in my chest holds its grip, refusing to let go as long as I look on. A push-and-pull battle of observations and cynicism. An arguably quintessential picture failing to soothe the frantic voices screaming at my brainstem.

Closing my eyes, pushing it all away, I pause to access what is known. Their voices sound louder in the darkness behind my lids, but words don't make it through. I am safe inside, and not dead in the dirt left to rot. They are people who haven't yet acted with violence toward me. How much time has passed and my location are still unknown.

Janus isn't seen from what is visible, and the worry of his whereabouts is all-consuming. Imagining the worst with nothing to contradict it. Squeezing my lids tighter, with squished crow's feet, wishing away those thoughts and wiping away a bad dream. Refusing the prospect of its truth. Contemplating the possibility of lying here indefinitely and hoping all the horrible things, the questionable moments, the hard days will pass over. Lie, and sleep away until better days come knocking—if only that was an option. Letting the world wash over never seems to pan out the way I'd hoped because here I am.

I'm slowly stretching out my legs as they break through an exoskeleton of a long extended rest when a spring toward the end creaks. The aching metal noise echoes through the room, shattering the standstill peace that was. My eyes flick open and I see a woman looking back at me, leaning over her chair's arm. Frozen, we both continue to stare as her eyes grow wide and a smile creeps across her face. It could be pure joy oozing out, but all those exposed teeth look predatory. She's ready to pounce, and there's no where to go.

"She's awake!"

Quickly I sit up, pulling the blanket closer as if it's a shield or a cloak of protection as I scurry to the furthest corner of the couch, creating distance. Reaching toward where my boots should be for my knife only to discover empty space, and socks but no shoes, and no knife neatly tucked in. Unarmed and exposed, squared away. The woman approaching with glee sends shivers from head to toe when there's a heavy footfall coming from behind.

"Oh, good! Welcome back, Jessi!"

I whip my head around to a familiar voice that fills the space. Hank is strolling across the room with a mug in his hand, and Janus right behind. As soon as our eyes connect, Janus leaps over the back of the couch and smothers my face in licks. Uncontainable energy radiating in full-body wags, squeaky barks, and kisses. Tears streaming down my face mixing with his saliva. My face is a damp mess: raw and unrestricted. Feeling his fur between my fingers as I pull him closer, holding on desperately when the thought of this moment felt unreachable. That night in the darkness, grasping to what I could as life was slipping away. My failure to him unrelenting.

I cling to him, holding all we haven't lost. Unable to express words with my face buried in his neck fluff. Looking beyond to the space behind Hank's eyes, fully understanding the culminated weight.

"I knew ya were gonna pull through, but damn, I'm so glad to see you up and awake."

"How long have I been asleep?" I ask.

"On and off the past three days. You were a little loopy when you were up." she pipes up offering a timeline of blank patches.

Examining her face, I notice vaguely familiar details trying to punch through foggy recollections.

"I don't remember being awake. I was by the tree, and it went dark, and now I'm here."

"I'm not surprised. You weren't doin' so hot when we found you," explains the elusively familiar woman.

"You were damn near dead when you were carried back," Hank adds.

Memories of that night leak in through fragmented clips of a poorly spliced film. I remember the cold air moving across my face as I floated through the air. Beneath my body, arms firmly holding my form suspended, moving forward. There was unrecognizable chatter, and an occasional whining that must have been Janus. There was a door that swung open heavily, and someone exchanged my wet clothes for dry ones. The arms became a couch, and chatter continued. The exact details are still fuzzy but at least there's something to fill the in-between. Stones to hop between, explaining a little about how we got across the river.

"Oooph" escapes in a groan as I shift my weight.

My shoulder is bandaged, but still sore. A reminiscent reminder of events I'd rather soon forget.

"Now, that's going to take some time to heal, but I made sure it's clean and bandaged."

"Right, and who are you again? I feel like I know your face."

"Lucy. I see you held on to my gift," she says while tucking a loose piece of raven colored hair behind her ear.

Pulling out the selenite from her pocket, she holds it out for me. Taking the stone in my hand, I look over its edges and milky tones, thinking back to that day months ago at the bar.

"Good thing, too. Seems like you got very lucky when your place burnt down. Even luckier than that time I dropped off the antibiotics," she muses in measured tones.

"You knew about that?"

"We saw the smoke 'cross the way. I knew ya lived somewhere up there, and when two militia men came to the Trading Post talkin' 'bout sweeps, I knew somethin' happened. Askin' if anyone saw any deplorables on the run come through … "

"They came here?" I question.

"Yea, but they didn't find shit. No one said anything. To be fair, no one had seen you or anyone else. We weren't lyin', but we didn't give 'em any reason to stay around here lookin'," Hank insists.

An unsure exhale escapes my lungs thinking of those men fading away to other places, hopefully far from here. *Is this what relief feels like?* Skeptical of this illusion of safety with the threats departed, a jittery tingle vibrates throughout my body, hyperaware of the luck and luxury of sitting here.

"Did they light your place up?"

"Yea, I think so," I respond.

"Why? I've heard of sweeps and random attacks, but setting fire —"

"Some people think it's their new method to guarantee people run," Lucy offers.

"Yea, but Jessi? How did she stand out more than them just closing in?"

"I killed one of theirs, I think."

"Well! I didn't know a little thing like you had it in you," he chuckles with a gruff expression.

"It was the wires. I guess it wasn't really me, but I did get rid of the body. Thought about leaving it to the wild, but what if they looked, and he was there—" I add in some attempt of an explanation.

"It's okay, Jessi. You made a choice to reduce variables and stay safe."

"I had to do it piece by piece because he was too heavy. He was wearing black, and had The Nation insignia. Maybe I shouldn't have. I don't know how they knew, what I missed—"

"Now, dontcha be blaming yourself. You did what you had to. They've been doin' sweeps, and it must of been bad timing when he crossed those wires," Hank consoles.

"Yea, but maybe—"

"But nothing. Eventually they woulda realized one of their boys was missin' and followed his reports. It's not like they wouldn't have hurt you, or as if they haven't hurt lots of people way worse."

He was right. Why should the guilt, the blame, the shame, rot away my conscious when a prey that sneaks in a victory when its predator stalks them feels nothing but relief, or maybe even joy? Something used to pull at my heart-strings, but with everything over the past few years escalating, there's only a dull pang where deeper feelings used to be.

"Thank you for finding me. For bringing me here," I offer.

"It was all Lucy. She was insistent. Her and Delila we—"

"Who?"

"You'll meet 'er. They went out and determined you needed help. That ya would of been seen 'round by now if ya hadn't."

"We're so glad we found you. I told Hank something wasn't right. I sensed it, and my senses never lie. We're lucky to have you in our home."

"This is your home? You're together?" I ask, attempting to mask my blatant confusion.

A chuckle can't be contained between the two, leaving me perplexed, waiting for something more.

"Our home, yes. Together, sort of. Think of it as a bit of a lavender arrangement. Keeps the nosy militia men and Blake's boys away, and we stay out of any rehabilitation centers. It's a big house, though, and there's a couple more tenants. Don't worry, you'll meet them over the next few days. And we have a room for you, of course, too!" Lucy explains.

She's beaming and he's got the biggest grin while I'm still playing catch-up, connecting all the pieces. Included into a conversation with a secret language having just been given the decoder. There's an ease about it as this conversation meanders, and smiles pleasantly spread over faces. It's almost normal given a different context.

"Let's get some food in ya, and then we can let you in on all the stuff I just know ya are gonna wanna sink ya teeth into. Fill in some gaps I think ya'll wanna know."

"You're not alone in this fight, Jessi," Lucy states.

"What do you mean?"

"Oh, sweetie, we've got people all over the place. A network. We're going to fix this place."

"What?" I ask.

I'm confused and absolutely befuddled by Lucy's casual, almost cavalier announcement. She's abundantly confident and comfortable, having securely wooed me. Her words resonate, breaking the trance the passage of time has lulled us into. Light in the darkness offering a beacon.

"Let's eat first. There's a lot to discuss. Oh, but here—this is for you."

She hands over a thick white envelope with my name on it. You can feel a stuffed density and as I carefully begin to open it, my hands shake, unsure what awaits. The pure mystery of the contents creates uncertainty.

"It's from Lilly. She's friends with your mom, and works with our network. Oh, and she's my cousin but more like a sister. Long story short, when we put two and two together. She wanted to let you know your mom is safe. You should find a letter from her in there too," Lucy says radiating a joy she's been holding in reserve.

"Oh my-"

"Sometimes a network can do more than the individual no matter how strong the person is. It got this here."

Her words fade while turning to what's written down, fully inhaling every drop. Consuming the language that traveled miles, providing a comfort I never thought possible again. The paper heavy with the weight of her voice from a far-away place, coming through clear as glass. She's there, and I'm here, but a distance has been bridged.

Chapter Fifty-Five
Community

Now
<u>March 12, 2050:</u>

Barren spaces sit empty, void of the evidence that brought them here. They sit in rot and decay, smoke, and char erasing their former vibrancy. Someone, somewhere, arrogantly thought this was a good idea. A great idea to strip all that was special. Conformity in the name of obedience. Destruction for a greater cause: their cause. Fix the problems with fiery swoops; with no regard for what was damaged in the process. They thought they were heroes—they thought wrong.

The perpetrators never cared what happened to anything here. They used the world for their gains and abandoned everyone else. False assumptions that this was the new normal. A problem dealt with and fully resolved. Always to be sunken in char and ash, because fire did its job. No need to keep an eye out, because the self-proclaimed victors won. Assumptions are dangerous, if not deadly.

Nature doesn't listen to the lies of little men. Forest growth rebounds over devastated ground. Ecological recession taking micro-steps to stabilize the soil and establish new life. Each little seed that sprouts reaches toward new light of a new day for a new tomorrow. Leaves up, arms outstretched, acting upon an idea of a promise that this could work. Slowly, green multiplies, consuming more square footage and overwhelming the space from where destruction once stood. Seeing the transition is undeniable.

Microbial entities and mycelium networks feed and flourish from within. Encouraging and spurring a whole collaboration, contributing their tiny part. Unseen and interwoven; linked arms communicating in synapses more expansively than the perpetrators could have ever dreamt. Per usual, beings with too much power dismiss what they do not understand. It's foreign and silly; a disconnection. The ecosystem laughs at their arrogance.

Before long, trees rise and flowers bloom. Birds carry the seeds, and herbaceous ground dwellers move back in. Their presence amplifies, and soon there are many. Entire herds of classically docile creatures unhappy they were ever forced to leave. Then come the predators in their packs, ready to enforce balance. Not for themselves alone, but with the entire community in mind. Protect the existence of equilibrium that is expected and demanded—needed.

Never again will they stand for such misguided abuse of their home. Every member is vital to ensure the smooth functionality of their collaborative territory. Rebuilding what should have always been for the community. Linked in cause, they will fight for their existence. A survival of a future. A thriving enjoyment of the current day and all the days yet to come. Run, perpetrators, run. The pack is here, and they are hungry.

Chapter Fifty-Six

Next

Now

<u>March 21, 2050:</u>

Weeks ago, alone, there was no particular future mapped out besides Janus and I, forever and ever, until something was to change or end. Now we're here with vastly different prospects. Options, opportunities, and possibilities abound. At the long dining room table sit myself, Hank, Lucy, Delila, and Marcus. This is the representation of the local branch of The Network.

The present attendees of The Network explain that they work like a spider who disguises itself as an ant to infiltrate the colony and consume them from within. I hold back my scoffs at the grandiose ideology, as curiosity insists we listen. They have a synergy full of cliche analogies and inspirational tidbits. How novel that a team vision board is supposed to bind us together and right all that's wrong, but the cynicism, if spoken, seems cruel. Especially when they took me in without hesitation. I suppose I owe them my attention. Not to mention they seem to have life more together than I. Maybe a mantra could be beneficial.

Neither Delila nor Marcus are originally from here, but like I, they had visited, and when their cities got bad, they left. Marcus had been charged with treason, as a smuggler of contraband to citizens who needed specific items now banned by The Nation. A personal one-man order and delivery system of things such as plan B and C, literature, seeds, luxury goods, hormones, binders, and almost anything else your heart desires. No request too lofty, though some may take more time, or money for that matter. He more or less knows everyone. Effortlessly blending to fulfill the needs.

Marcus told us he grew up in a household that was lockstep with The Nation long before it officially existed, and he fought all the time with relatives—sometimes just to get a rise. The language, the viewpoints, the mentality were all easy for him to mimic, like flipping a switch. Granting him an ease to slide in and out of trade opportunities under a ruse. He got caught in a double-cross operation when someone was desperate for money that The Nation promised, resulting in arrest. After being charged, he fled before his trial and managed to escape custody, eventually making his way to his grandfather, who Marcus described as the only sane one in his family. Keeping his secret, he stayed there until his grandfather passed of old age. Now Marcus splits his time between Hank's spare room and his grandfather's house.

Delila had been unhoused, and when The Nation started rounding up anyone without a permanent residence, she knew it was time to leave. She hopped on a bus and hitchhiked to anywhere cheaper, quieter, and calmer. Anywhere with a chance she could get an odd job to make rent, or trade for lodging. Eventually it led Delila to the Trading Post, where Lucy met her selling dried herbs, but they all had mystical names with bold claims. Hustling tonics and cures would have eventually caught up with her, as it had done in other cities. Lucy offered to be the liaison for potential employment, payment, and lodging. Of course, Hank couldn't turn away a stray, and so Delila became a pseudo employee, errand runner, and tenant.

In no time at all, they became looped into The Network via Lucy, by way of Lilly. Eagerly jumping on board, believing fully in the possibility of hope. Here we are, sitting like a family over dinner. Passing the latest news with the basket of yeast rolls from one member to the other. Warm, jovial banter about weather and seasonings that taste so good, spliced between explanations and tactical plans.

"As Lucy said, we have an extensive network. We personally may not know everyone, but we know someone, and they know someone, and so on. They're reliable, and there's back-ups just in case," Marcus informs me.

"Just in case?" I ask.

"Just in case the communication breaks down. The pathways get severed. Come on now, there can't be only one road to the destination."

"Don't let him scare you! He's always the one to analyze and overanalyze, thinking out every possibility. Not that it's a bad thing. It's kept us all safe, and the mission moving forward," Lucy interjects.

Lucy shoots Marcus a look, silently scolding him for instilling any more fear than that which already exists. With a roll of his eyes, he yields for Lucy to continue.

"So, what Marcus was getting to was the good stuff. Yes, we spread messages and news this way, but hunny, we also communicate plans and actions. We're not just waiting this thing out, hoping it goes away."

"What do you mean?" I continue to inquire.

"Pffff! What do you mean, *what does she mean?*" Delila scoffs.

Delila has a sharp tongue full of wit, and dry remarks that amuse herself if not anyone else. It's a surprise the so-called snake oil alone got her in trouble previously, though I doubt she'd admit that snark was ever a problem. She sits there with a scowl as she plays with her hair, exposing a tiny rectangular tattoo of six familiar lines that has otherwise been hidden. She's like a magician's smoke—intoxicating but pungent. Marcus seems bored by her performance even if on some level he agrees.

"I mean exactly what I said. What do you mean, Lucy? You're alluding to some plan. Something bigger than sharing information, or survival," I reiterate between tight-lipped teeth.

"Jessi, ya nailed it. It's way bigger than just intel, though that's important. Got some moves comin' up," Hank says.

"We have members in their system. In their military, in their government offices, in their news. Every place they are—we are. We're their shadows they never see," Marcus adds.

"How is that even possible?"

"How isn't it? We walk like them, talk like them, and they're none the wiser. They don't look any deeper and accept loyal minions at face value as long as there's no reason for them to suspect anything. Good disguises walking right in their midst, waiting for the right moment," Marcus elaborates.

"The right moment for what?" I ask.

"To strike! To turn this whole thing on it's head, and press reset. The right moment to cut out the cancer that's infested our country, and royally fucked everything up," he snaps.

"How? Can't we …"

"Can't we what? They can't learn if they don't listen. It's time for The Nation to touch the stove," Marcus asserts.

"Don't you want to get back to normal?!" Delila presses.

"Don'tcha worry, Jessi. You'll do great, if you want to be an active part of this." Hank reassures.

Looking toward Hank as our guiding beacon of stability, with his trust reserved for almost no one, the decision seems obvious. However, clear leaps can still be overwhelming.

"Why now, Hank?"

"What do ya mean?"

"Why didn't you tell me about all this sooner? All those times in the bar, our conversations, anytime … Why wait until now?" I implore.

"I wanted to, but I wanted ya to be safe more. Ya were, and just findin' your footing. Eventually we would of, when the time was right. When ya could make your own mind up—but ya were content alone up there."

"So, what changed?" I say, pressing further.

"The drones, the fire, the sweeps. They're closin' in, and I can't keep ya safe anymore without tellin' ya about something that's both safe and dangerous by nature."

A silent moment hangs over, accepting what was unavoidable: a judgment call of best interests. Well-intentioned protections ultimately relinquished when choice became a priority.

"And what if I say yes? That I want to be an active part?"

"Then we're already preppin your role. Figured you would," Hank says with a sly wink.

Staring from person to person, I check to make sure my mouth hasn't fallen agape. No one minds a word of the conversation, as though the unfolding play-out is a familiar scene. Taking it all in stride, each continues on focused for the future.

Everyone voraciously eating and continuing to chatter, reveling in the prospect of what that day will feel like when it finally comes. A far-flung idea to ever materialize, but their conviction says otherwise. I'm hesitant to be eager, hearing they've already thought of some role for me to slide into. Yes, I want things to change. The sparse details lacking concrete specificity creates a pause, even if the prospect aligns at first glance.

I'm sitting there eating and contributing to conversation while digesting it all. Inside, a caged animal is clawing. Scratching my innards, agitated at the tasks yet to come. A cage rattled, and it reacts in fear. *Or is it anger?* The possibility that something has awoken. Once passing as timidness, shaking that was never really shy, is an amusing thought. *What happens when the beast escapes? Who will I be if I lean into this creature fighting for survival?*

"So, then, what's next?" I inquire.

"We have false identities to go into their businesses, facilities, news, and government. Spread information to the outside world of what is happening, and stir change from those inside," Lucy explains.

"Lucy, what if they don't want to change? What if no one cares?"

"Some care. And change is coming one way or another, but those we connect with can choose whether they are the kindling to our match or debris caught in the wake," she continues.

"Okay, but what's actually next, besides theorizing?" I ask to clarify.

"Ya are right on that one. Class is ending, and we gotta get movin' 'cause Blake and his boys are closing in. Actin' bolder and rounding up. It's time for us to move out of here and start the hard work," Hank announces.

"We're leaving? When? Whe—"

"Soon. It will differ as to where. You and Marcus will pose as a couple and go to the Texas panhandle. Hank and I will go to Santa Fe. Delila will meet up with another member nearby, between. If you agree, that is," says Lucy, laying the plan they've roughed out.

"Why the panhandle?"

"There's a so-called rehabilitation facility there. A work camp dressed up under other names. They're hiring, and we have reason to believe it's where they took Anthony," Marcus offers.

Hearing his name sends my mind spinning, as my future fake

husband looks on with genuine concern. While it's been so long, the prospect of his existence rushes all the buried emotions to the forefront.

"Anthony! Is he …?"

"We don't know, but I mentioned the story ya told me to Lucy to see what we could find. Not much 'sides the place." Hank elaborates.

"But we're optimistic. And we knew you'd be motivated by this hope. I'm sorry it's not more." Lucy offers her calm condolences.

All eyes on me, waiting for the words to come next. Thoughts of a familiar face resurrected wash away the past years in an afterthought. Everything could be better. *Maybe there is a before to sink into after this is all over.*

"Okay then. I'm in," I say as the words of commitment leave my mouth without hesitation.

A gentle smile between swallows of food. Listening tentatively with encouraging eyes, I am their new sibling. Their odd, awkward sister finding footing in the pack, entrenched in the sweeping current of a hidden resistance. Wrapped up in the warm embrace of my new people dispensed by happenstance, still swarmed by conflicting inner monologue. Sure, they'd be labeled as deplorables, but in reality they're vibrant. Yes, Blake would call them terrorists, but I see them as freedom fighters. The Nation would say they're dangerous, but any cornered animal is.

United for today, and tomorrow, and every day forward. The room glows warmer and ambient conversation sounds like music. Janus is peacefully asleep, and a genuine smile creeps across my face at something biting Delila said.

Survival of the pack will not succumb to cages hunters try to put us in. We are wild and free. Taking in a simple meal feels extraordinary. This could become normal with choices made. Together, today, we'll never face the elements alone again.

Acknowledgments

Writing a book is without a doubt not possible within a vacuum. It's because of all those who have supported me along the way that In Stasis is possible.

First, I want to thank my partner, Danny Peters, for his support throughout this entire endeavor. What started as a theoretical conversation, became a New Year's resolution that grew legs and then ran away with his partner, metaphorically speaking. But in all seriousness when this idea was tossed into the ether neither of us expected the side quest to become the main road and I thank you for not only never blinking at this, but also for being my sounding board throughout.

Thank you to all the readers along the way, who read drafts that were far from refined. They were raw but you saw what nuggets they held. I am forever grateful for your feedback and support. Specifically I want to shout out Ceclilia Benvegnu whom I met through a chance encounter and led to her being an initial supporter from just an elevator pitch.

Thank you to my editor Megan Randall of Clarity Copy Co for helping me take this story to the refined place of being a book that's actually publishable. Your insight was invaluable and remarks provided encouragement that can't be summarized to their depth here.

Thank you to the writing community both in Austin TX and online. I am still floored by how supportive this creative community is and without it I would have felt lost navigating the weird world of writing.

Finally, thank you to my fur-babies: Bently, Fredrik, and Bruno. I don't know (or care) which people will be more offended by—that I thanked my dogs but not x, y, and z human or that I called them fur-babies. Regardless, they are my sanity sounding board and the thought of living a life where I get to enjoy their company every day in lieu of a 9-5 sounds pretty dreamy. Y'all don't look at me like I'm crazy when I read dialogue out loud and that is much appreciated.

Ok, TRULY finally—Thank you to all my readers. To anyone

who purchased, read, borrowed, or in whatever way supported this story: thank you! Without you the stories still may be created but they wouldn't be shared beyond my inner circle. I hope this story has provided a bit reassurance and escapism in tough days and who knows, maybe even hope. Thank you all!

This is Ashley Peters' debut novel. She resides in East Austin TX with her partner (Danny) and 3 fur-baby rescue mutts (Bently, Fredrik & Bruno). A self declared bibliophile and always a storyteller casting tales from a young age along the way.

When she's not writing you can find her out in nature far from the chaos of the world, hiking, kayaking, traveling, enjoying good, inventive food, or a matcha latte. At home her garden and library are her solitude though she deeply enjoys the artistic, quirky offerings of Austin.

"I can't predict what's next because it's always an opportunity to take part and I'd rather hop on an adventurous side quest than die a bore."

Social Media @ashley_peters_author
Website https://www.ashleypetersauthor.com